To Jamie,

MW00945207

Murder

by

Perfection

A Thorny Rose Mystery

by

Lauren Carr

My favorite Book. Stagram!

Lauren Carr

MURDER BY PERFECTION

Published by Acorn Book Services

For information, call: 304-995-1295
or e-mail: writerlaurencarr@gmail.com.

Designed by Acorn Book Services

Publication Managed by Acorn Book Services
www.acornbookservices.com
acornbookservices@gmail.com
304-995-1295

Cover designed by Todd Aune
Spokane, Washington
www.projetoonline.com

ISBN-10: 1718620233
ISBN-13: 978-1718620230

Published in the United States of America

Dedicated to the most perfect young man I know,
My Son, John Tristan

Murder
by
Perfection

A Thorny Rose Mystery

CAST OF CHARACTERS
(in order of appearance)

Tristan Faraday: Jessica's younger brother. Nigel's creator and administrator. He's an intellectual and proud of it. Works on contract for the Phantoms.

Jessica Faraday: Murphy Thornton's wife. Medical student studying forensics psychiatry at the University of Georgetown. Granddaughter of the late Robin Spencer. Daughter of Mac Faraday of the Mac Faraday Mysteries.

Robin Spencer: Jessica and Tristan Faraday's late birth grandmother and world-famous mystery author. They never met her, but received millions of dollars in inheritance.

Mac Faraday: Retired homicide detective. On the day his divorce became final, he inherited $270 million and an estate on Deep Creek Lake from his birth mother, Robin Spencer.

Gnarly: Mac Faraday's German shepherd, another part of his inheritance from Robin Spencer. Mayor of Spencer, Maryland.

Special Agent Boris Hamilton: Deputy Chief of the Naval Criminal Investigative Service, where Murphy serves as military liaison between the civilian staff and the military.

Special Agent Susan Archer: Agent with Naval Criminal Investigative Service.

Special Agent Perry Latimore: Agent with Naval Criminal Investigative Service. Susan Archer's partner.

Murphy Thornton: Jessica Faraday's husband. Lieutenant in the United States Navy. Naval academy graduate. Murphy is not your average navy officer. Hand-picked by the Joint Chiefs of Staff to serve as a member of their elite team of Phantoms. Son of Joshua Thornton from the Lovers in Crime Mystery series.

Nigel: The Faraday-Thornton home's state-of-the-art virtual butler. He's also so much more than a butler.

Commander Ross Caldwell: Doctor with the U.S. Navy Medical Service Corps. Had served as chief of the medical staff at the naval academy in Annapolis. An unidentified source informs him about something fishy going on at a private clinic.

Carol: Jessica's friend. Hosts their study group at her brownstone in Georgetown.

Brett Wagner: Medical student. Wants to be more than a friend to Jessica.

Selena Parker: Rents a room in Carol's brownstone. She's gotten close to Brett and wants to be closer.

Spencer: Jessica Faraday's Shetland sheepdog. With her blue eyes and long bluish fur, she is a blue merle. She has a long way to go in training.

Newman: Murphy's Bassett hound-mix dog. A forty-five pound couch potato, Newman won't bite—unless you try to change the channel on his television.

ICE

Reginal Baldwin: Missing investigator with the U.S. Department of Health and Human Services. Was supposed to meet Ross Caldwell at Starbucks.

Erin Caldwell: Commander Ross Caldwell's widow.

Kendall Harris: Ross and Erin Caldwell's youngest daughter. Married to Woody Harris.

Woody Harris: Kendall's roci musician husband. He doesn't work because he's an artist. His wife calls him her mistake.

Daniel Caldwell: Ross Caldwell's brother. Executor of the estate. Wants Murphy to leak inside information about his brother's murder investigation to him.

Joshua Thornton: Murphy's father. Prosecuting Attorney. Captain in the United States Navy (retired). Father of six. Married to Cameron Gates, Pennsylvania state police homicide detective.

Natalie Stepford: Caterer and owner of Natalie Stepford's Kitchen Studio. Teaches couple's cooking class. Not only does she cook, but she's hot in more ways than one.

Calvin Stepford: Natalie's husband. Wealthy lawyer. He's bought her everything she's ever needed or wanted—including a new body.

Meaghan Garland: Financial Manager. Married to Dr. Stan Garland. She's his business partner at the Garland Surgery and Laser Clinic.

Stan Garland: Noted plastic surgeon. Owns Garland Surgery and Laser Clinic. Plastic surgeon to Washington's beautiful people.

Andy: He and his new bride are students in Natalie Stepford's couple's cooking class.

Peg: She and her new husband are students in Natalie Stepford's couple's cooking class.

Izzy: Joshua Thornton's fourteen year old daughter. She takes riding lessons at J.J.'s farm from his horse trainer Poppy.

Joshua Thornton Jr. (J.J.): Murphy Thornton's identical twin brother. Criminal lawyer. Owns Russell Ridge Farm and Orchard. The farm also raises prized quarter horses, trained by Poppy Ashburn.

Poppy Ashburn: J.J.'s horse trainer. She means so much more to J.J.

Charley: J.J.'s watch rooster.

Ollie: J.J. and Poppy's newborn orphaned baby lamb.

Lee: Has been texting Natalie Stepford and traveled a long way to be with her—even though she says she's never met him.

Lieutenant Libby McAuley: Doctor with the U.S. Navy's Medical Service Corps. She interned with Commander Ross Caldwell in Annapolis. She claims their relationship was nothing but professional. If so, why is she so frightened?

Have no fear of perfection—you'll never reach it.

Salvador Dali

Prologue

Great Falls, Virginia

The artic blue Camaro convertible spun around the sharp curve leading down the wooded road. Upon seeing the emergency flares, Tristan Faraday tapped the brakes to slow down. A state police officer gestured with his flashlight for him to roll to a halt and lower his window.

In the passenger seat, Jessica Faraday's breath quickened when the black sports motorcycle parked at the bottom of the hill came into view.

"I'm Tristan Faraday. That motorcycle belongs to my brother-in-law."

The officer instructed them to park in a small gravel lot next to a fast-moving creek.

"He's okay." Tristan peered at the motorcycle as he drove past. "It's not wrecked. He wasn't in an accident. Maybe it broke down and he got a ride."

"He's only two miles from our house," Jessica said. "He could have walked home by now."

Without waiting for Tristan to turn off the engine, she rushed out of the car. She ran across the gravel lot to a barrel-chested man clad in a dark jacket with "NCIS" emblazoned across the back briefing a group of younger agents.

"Boris, what's happened? Where's Murphy?"

Special Agent Boris Hamilton took her into a hug. "We're doing everything we can. I called out my team as soon as we got the message from the police about his motorcycle being abandoned. What time did he leave the house?"

"It was around ten-thirty," Jessica said while staring at the motorcycle parked at the edge of the road. The kickstand was down, and Murphy's helmet rested on the seat. "We had a fight. He said he was going for a ride to get some fresh air."

Tristan approached the investigator examining the bike for evidence.

"Did Murphy say where he was going when he left?" Boris asked her.

"No." Jessica leveled her gaze on him. "We took a class at Natalie Stepford's cooking school tonight. He told me about her being connected to the murder of Commander Caldwell."

"Did he make contact with Stepford?" Boris asked.

Jessica nodded her head.

"Did you see anything suspicious? Did anyone seem particularly interested when Murphy spoke to her?"

"Only every man in that class," she said with a sigh. "Have you seen that woman?"

Boris chuckled.

"I hated her at first sight. Perfect hair. Perfect nose. Perfect figure. Perfect cooking skills. I'll bet she never burns anything on the stove." She allowed her voice to trail off.

"Chief!" Special Agent Susan Archer called to them. "You're going to want to see this."

Before Boris could stop her, Jessica ran to where Tristan was squatting next to an evidence marker. Instantly, Jessica recognized the reddish-brown stain in the middle of the road.

As she let out a shriek, Tristan jumped to his feet and took her into a hug. "We'll find him, Sis. Don't worry. We'll find Murphy and bring him home."

Chapter One

One Month Earlier

"Are you kidding me?" Lieutenant Murphy Thornton re-read his wife's text message that popped on the screen of his SUV's console. He had the slimmest of hope that he had misread it.

Study group running L8. Can U pick up pizza 4 dinner?

With a curse, he threw his navy cap into the passenger seat and punched the steering wheel.

"Murphy, would you like to send a reply to Jessica?" the deep voice of the Faraday-Thornton artificial intelligence network came from the SUV's speakers. Called "Nigel," the state-of-the-art artificial intelligence was a test system designed by the federal government. Nigel controlled the Faraday-Thornton household's entire technical network from communication, security, and even their calendars.

"Tell her okay, Nigel." Murphy turned on the SUV and mentally prepared to join the thousands of drivers engaged in the Friday night rush hour from the Nation's Capital. He could envision the dozens of patrons crowded in the pizza place in Great Falls.

With a wave of gratitude, he eased his black SUV in front of a blue sedan to merge into traffic leaving the Pentagon. He sped up the access ramp to take the expressway along the Potomac River.

"Jessica has replied to your text, Murphy," Nigel said as the words splashed across the console.

Can U make mine pepperoni and Italian sausage pls? Luv U!

"Yes, dear," Murphy said with a sigh.

A moment later, Nigel said, "Jessica has responded to your reply, Murphy."

Didn't make it to the store 2day. Can U pick up coffee & dog biscuits pls? Jessica ended her message with a kissy-faced emoticon.

"Murphy, how would you like me to respond to Jessica?"

"Damn it!" Murphy hit the brakes just in time to keep from rear-ending a red Jaguar cutting across two lanes of traffic to make an exit. A Mercedes barely kept from rear-ending Murphy's vehicle.

The flow of traffic had finally returned to a steady flow when Nigel announced an incoming call from Jessica. "Would you like to accept or decline?"

"Accept," Murphy said with a sigh.

"If you don't want to go to the store, just say so. You don't need to cuss at me."

"I'll go to the store like I do every day," he said, "after I pick up a pizza for dinner *again*."

"No, I'll go! After I get done with my study group, on my way home in rush hour traffic—"

"Oh, and I'm not in rush hour traffic?"

"—before I clean up the kitchen—"

"Clean up the kitchen from what?" Murphy asked. "You haven't cooked in three days."

"And we haven't had sex in ten!"

"Sorry, sweetheart, but it's kind of hard to have sex with someone who's never home!"

The console went blank.

"Did she just hang up on me?" Murphy tapped the touch screen.

"Jessica lost the signal," Nigel said.

"She did not lose the signal. Nigel, I thought lying was a *human* trait."

"My programming includes a safety feature. Your steering wheel has sensors that allow me to monitor your pulse rate. When your heart rate indicates that human emotions are reaching a dangerous threshold, then communications are shut down to allow both parties time to cool off."

"My virtual butler is giving me a time-out?"

"May I suggest you listen to some meditative instrumental music to lower your heart rate?"

A Celtic instrumental flowed from the speakers.

ᕦ ᕦ ᕦ

As Murphy had expected, the takeout restaurant was filled with patrons waiting for their pizza orders. Every one of the half dozen straight-back chairs lined up against the plate-glass window was occupied with unhappy customers. After placing his order for two pizzas, he moved to an empty corner of the crowded service area.

Along the way, Murphy spied another navy officer whose uniform bore the insignia of the medical service corps. He clutched a bouquet of fresh flowers in his arms. As Murphy's eyes rose from the insignia to the officer's face, a broad grin broke across his face.

"Thornton?" The officer stuck out his hand.

"Commander Ross Caldwell, good to see you." Murphy clasped his hand. "What are you doing here?"

"What do you think? We live on Mine Run Drive." Dr. Caldwell pointed in the direction of the national park. "Don't tell me you and your bride traded in the bright lights of the big city for the burbs."

"We're practically neighbors," Murphy said. "We moved to a place along Falls Road. Jessica traded in her socialite crown to be a med student at Georgetown."

"Which explains the pizza," Ross said with a laugh. "I don't envy you. But all the lonely nights and hard times you're going through now will be worth it when Jessica gets her MD."

"Is it that obvious?"

"Hey, I'm probably the last one that you should be seeking advice from on family relationships," Ross said with a low chuckle.

Murphy cocked his head. "I don't understand."

Ross looked at him with an arched eyebrow.

"I guess I missed something," Murphy said. "You've been married how many years. Three great kids."

"Just walked my baby girl down the aisle this past autumn," Ross said with a wide grin. "Huge wedding with even bigger bills. You didn't know?"

"Know what?"

"Your last year at the academy." Ross shrugged his shoulders. "I guess you were so busy trying to keep your spot at the top of the class that you didn't pay any attention to the dramas and scandals brewing."

"I've learned that the best way to stay on top is to block out drama," Murphy said.

"I transferred out of Annapolis after your last year. My family…" Ross's voice trailed off before he cleared his throat.

"You left Annapolis and transferred to Washington to save your marriage," Murphy said.

"I made a conscious decision to put my family first," Ross said. "Once I did that, everything else was easy." He held up the bouquet. "As hard as things are now, these hard times will only make your marriage stronger when you come out together on the other side."

"That's what my dad keeps saying," Murphy muttered.

"How is Captain Thornton?" Ross grinned.

"You heard about his promotion?"

"The military is like a family. Dysfunctional, but still family." He looked down at the ribbons on Murphy's chest. "You already got yourself a Bronze Star. But you're not a SEAL. I'd heard the SEALS wanted you really bad—"

"I got a better offer," Murphy said. "Right now, I'm military liaison for NCIS."

Ross's eyes lit up the reference to the navy's criminal investigation unit. "Are you an investigator with them?"

"I have done some criminal investigation, yes. Why? Is there something you think we should look into?"

Ross's good-natured attitude gave way to nervousness. He glanced around at the patrons crowded in the small takeout shop. "A friend of mine came to me about something suspicious happening at a private clinic. If it's what I think—I just can't believe that'd be going on here. Anyway, I called the department of health and human resources. I'm supposed to meet an investigator tomorrow." He let out a deep breath and frowned.

The clerk behind the counter called his name. "Caldwell!"

Ross stepped toward the counter, but then turned back to Murphy. "Hey, are you still running?"

"Almost every day."

"How about if we get together tomorrow morning to go running through the park? Seven o'clock? Bright and early when the park opens." Ross grabbed the pizza box and jogged outside.

Murphy took out his phone to put the running appointment on his calendar. Out of the corner of his eye, he saw a bright red Nissan convertible pull up in front of the pizza place. The driver was hard to miss with her long blond hair under a red hat secured with a scarf and dark jeweled sun glasses. As it rolled to a stop in front of him, Ross looked around before bending over to talk to the driver. His expression was serious. Then, with another quick glance to make sure no one was watching, Ross climbed into the passenger seat. The blond driver sped away before Ross had time to secure his seat belt.

Murphy cocked his head. *Mm, I wonder if that was his wife.*

CHAPTER TWO

Jessica Faraday's mind was swimming with doctors' names, symptoms, diagnoses, and psychiatric case studies. With a heavy sigh, she shoved her laptop into its case.

"We have enough coffee left for one more cup." With a broad grin, Carol, the study group's host, stood in the kitchen doorway and waved the carafe.

The medical students paused in gathering their materials scattered around the living room to make jokes.

"One more cup of coffee and I'll be swimming home," Jessica told Carol while reaching for her laptop case. When her fingers brushed across the back of a man's hand, she let out a shriek that drew the attention of her friends. She jerked around to find Brett Wagner holding out the case to her.

"I didn't mean to scare you, Jessica." The slender young man, with reddish-brown hair and a closely cropped beard and mustache flashed his bright white toothy grin at her. "Here you go."

"Thank you, Brett." She slipped her laptop into the bag and rose to her feet. "All that caffeine made me jumpy."

"Then we won't have to worry about you falling asleep while driving home." Brett fell in step with her and the rest of the students flowing through the townhome's dining room to the stairs leading down to the foyer. "Speaking of driving—"

"It's awfully late, Brett." Carol's roommate, Selena seemed to jump out from behind the dining room doorway to intercept the medical student.

A recent college graduate from the Midwest, Selena had moved to Washington to begin her career at one of the many federal agencies in the area. Barely over five feet tall and not more than a hundred pounds, she looked like she was twelve. She had usually made herself scarce during their study sessions—until Brett showed an interest in her.

"Would you like a ride home?" she asked.

Anxious to get home to her warm bed, Jessica didn't wait for Brett's response. She quickened her pace to catch up with her friends migrating toward the street.

Carol bid her goodbye at the door. "When are we going to meet your hunky navy officer husband?"

"If you haven't met him, then how do you know Murphy's hunky?"

"The way you go rushing home to him," Carol said with a grin. "You have yet to join us when we go out for dinner or drinks."

"I got all of my partying and clubbing days out of my system before I started med school."

"How long have you and Murphy been married?" Carol asked.

"A little over a year."

"You two are still newlyweds then." With a glance up the stairs to the main floor, she frowned. "Is Brett still upstairs?"

"Selena cornered him."

Carol uttered a low growl.

"Selena's new to the area, probably a little lonely—"

"And equally naïve," Carol said. "Perfect target for Brett. Ashleigh kicked him out on his ear after she found out that he'd slept with Selena—here under my roof. When I decided to take in a boarder to help pay for med school, I should never have offered the room to a girl just out of college. I thought since she was working for the FDIC that she'd be a quiet geek." She rolled her eyes. "She was until Brett got hold of her."

"Ah, there's nothing like drama to keep things exciting," Jessica said with a sigh before saying goodnight to Carol. She trotted down the front steps to make her way to her car parked on a side street.

The night breeze made her shudder. In early March, the weather was vacillating between winter or spring. That day, it had been sunny and cool. But after the sun had set, a chilly breeze had swept in to remind them that it was not quite spring yet.

The bright lights of Georgetown made it difficult for Jessica to tell if the sky was clear or not. Loud music and voices from what sounded like a college party drifted into the street from a nearby brownstone.

"Hey, Jessica! Wait up!" Zipping up his leather jacket, Brett trotted down the front stoop after her. Behind him, Carol closed the brownstone's front door. "Where's your navy guy?"

"Home." She gasped when she remembered the pizza that she had asked Murphy to pick up for dinner. She glanced at her cell phone to check the time.

Six hours ago. He's been keeping that pizza warm for six hours. I am so in trouble!

"If it's not too much of an imposition…" Brett flashed her a pleading smile.

"I thought Selena was going to give you a ride home."

"She offered, but—"

"What happened to your Beemer?" Abruptly, Jessica remembered that she had seen Brett driving a BMW convertible at other study group meetings.

"It's in the shop," Brett said. "It's been a rough month. Ashleigh kicked me out—"

"For cheating with Selena."

"Look, I made a mistake," Brett said. "My Beemer broke down and I'm sleeping on a friend's sofa until I can find time to have my new place remodeled."

"Don't tell me the details," Jessica said. "I'm tired and I want to go home to my husband—who isn't sleeping with my study group leader's adolescent roommate."

"She wasn't an adolescent."

"Goodnight, Brett." Jessica pressed the button to start her purple Ferrari.

"Okay, so I won't give you the details. But can I at least get a ride? It's late… dark, chilly… His townhouse is only a few blocks from the Rosslyn metro…" His voice trailed off.

"Hop in." She gestured at her purple Ferrari. "How long have you and Ashleigh been together?" she dared to ask once she had maneuvered the downtown Friday night traffic to cross the Potomac River.

"A couple of years. How's your sailor handling you being in med school?"

"Murphy's an officer—not a sailor." She swallowed. "We're still adjusting to our busy schedules. He gets sent out on temporary assignments overseas fairly often. Then when he is home, I'm studying. Is that what you and Ashleigh were dealing with? A clash of schedules?"

"And the stress," he said. "Med school is expensive and stressful. We thought we were committed enough to make it work. I guess we were wrong." He glanced over at her profile in the dim light of the sports car. "Guess we didn't love each other enough to make it for the long haul."

ɞ ɞ ɞ

The news of Brett's break-up weighed on Jessica's mind on her way to the Faraday-Thornton home in Great Falls. *They'd been together two years. Longer than Murphy and I have even known each other. Granted, Brett and Ashleigh weren't committed enough to get married, but still…*

Jessica tried to lift her mood by switching radio stations to find a catchy upbeat song—a dangerous process on the tight curves of the two-lane road connecting the Capital Beltway and the suburbs west of the Washington Metropolitan area.

As luck would have it, she found a bouncy tune just as she passed through the security gate to enter the Faraday-Thornton estate, which they had named Thorny Rose Manor.

She rolled the Ferrari into her slot of their seven-car detached garage and pressed the button to turn off the engine. The combination of mental exhaustion and her mood took their toll to make her utter a deep sigh and slump.

She dreaded facing Murphy. Not only did she fail to go to the store, but she'd sent him to pick up two pizzas for dinner and then stood him up.

It wasn't fear that held her back. It'd be easier if Murphy was one to lose his temper and yell at her. Then she could yell back—even though it was her fault. *How do you argue with someone who doesn't fight back? How do you fight someone who instead locks himself in the fitness room and beats up a punching bag for an hour or so? It's not fair. That's it. Murphy just plain doesn't fight fair.*

Nigel lit the pathway leading from the garage to the front door for her. Once she was inside, he turned them off. Their blue merle Shetland sheepdog, Spencer bounced up the stairs, yapping every step of the way, from the lower level to jump into Jessica's arms and lick her face.

"I love you, too." Jessica fought to ᵽ
while peeling the squirming twenty-five-pᴏ
head and shoulders.

"Nigel, where's Murphy?"

The IA's deep throaty voice projected from.   ᴜ system's speakers, which were strategically locate throughout
the house. "He is on the lower level watching a movie in the
game room."

Jessica followed the shelty down the curved stairs to the
game room.

Resembling a crusty old rock mixed in with jewels, an
old recliner rested among the chic furniture purchased for the
new home less than a year earlier. The chair was as worn as the
oversized Bassett hound occupying it. A forty-five pound canine couch potato, Newman laid in his chair—his usual spot.

This night, something was different. Instead of facing
the wide screen television, he lay with his back to the screen.
When Jessica entered the room, he regarded her with a steely
glare and let out a breath filled with contempt.

It took a full moment for her to discover the reason for
the dog's displeasure.

An old Star Wars movie was playing on the television.
Sound asleep, Murphy was stretched out on the sofa with
the remote resting on his bare chest. Such was the problem.
Murphy was in possession of the remote.

Jessica knelt in front of the sofa. Gently, she slipped the
remote out from under Murphy's limp hand and tossed it to
the recliner.

Instantly, Newman turned around to face the television.
With his nose, he positioned the remote and changed the station by slapping the remote with his paw. In a matter of minutes, Yoda the Jedi Master was replaced by Bloomberg giving
an analysis of that week's stock market.

essica studied Murphy's face. He was the most handsome man she had ever seen.

The granddaughter of the late Robin Spencer, America's answer to Agatha Christie, Jessica had spent a brief period enjoying the perks of being a rich socialite. She had many handsome men. They became history the instant Lieutenant Murphy Thornton flashed his brilliant smile with deep dimples in both cheeks and looked at her with those brilliant sapphire blue eyes.

Less than forty-eight hours later, Jessica threw in her socialite crown to become a navy officer's wife and pursue her doctorate in forensics psychiatry.

Jessica felt a warm rush through her body as Murphy wrapped his fingers around hers. She noticed that he had opened his eyes slightly to peer at her. "Hey," he whispered in a gravelly voice.

"Hey." She kissed his fingers. "Sorry, I got held—"

He cut her off by pressing his fingertips against her lips. "That's okay."

"But I sent you to get some pizza."

"I ate."

"Mine?"

"Newman and Spencer ate it during episode two of Star Wars—after it turned into cardboard in the oven." He sat up on the sofa. "I assumed you ate."

"We had ordered oriental." She rested her head on his knee. "I am so sorry, Murphy. I was getting ready to leave when I sent you that text. Then we got into that fight and you hung up on me—"

"I didn't hang up. Nigel did."

"Then someone started talking about the next chapter and we all ended up opening our books and the next thing I knew—"

She stopped when she felt Murphy's arm drape across her shoulders. He held her eyes with his gaze. "It's okay. I understand."

"Is it?"

With his finger underneath her chin, he lifted her face to his. "Yes."

"You were mad at me earlier." Her eyes narrowed with suspicion. "What happened? What did you do?"

"I've had a lot of time to think—being here alone in this house," he said. "One of the things I thought about was my first year at the naval academy. There was so much riding on me getting through the academy. I mean, my dad graduated from there. Our family's reputation was on the line. On the very first day, when we were lined up in formation, they told us to look up and down the line at our fellow midshipmen. An average of fifteen percent of us weren't going to make it to graduation."

"It's the same for medical school," she said.

"They make it hard on purpose. If you can't cut it, they want you out," he said. "If it hadn't been for the support of my family—doing everything they could to help me, I would never have made it." He ran his fingers through her raven hair. As he gazed into her teary violet eyes, his voice deepened. "I promised to stand by you for better or worse. Between the stress and busy schedules, medical school is that worse and I am going to be here for you. If it means getting petrified pizza during Friday rush hour—" He grinned. "I'm a Phantom. I can handle that."

"I love you, Murphy Thornton," she blubbered as he took her into his arms.

Their mouths crashed together while he pulled her up onto the sofa with him. She wrapped her arms around his bare shoulders and straddled him. "You know what we should do?"

He pulled her shirt up over her head to reveal a lilac lace bra. "I have some definite ideas."

She tossed the shirt aside. "We need to have a date night once a week. Our marriage is a priority and we need to treat it that way. One night a week, we go out to dinner or watch a movie together or—" She took in a deep breath. "—'what not'."

He brushed his fingers across her shoulders and down to her bosom. "Oh, I vote for 'what not'."

She brought her lips to his. "We haven't done 'what not' in ten days."

"So I heard." He grasped her hips. "What do you want to do about that?"

"What not."

ↄ ↄ ↄ

The next morning, Jessica woke when Murphy got up and dressed before the sun rose. She tried to will herself back to sleep until at least when he returned from his run.

Upon seeing Murphy take his running shoes out of the closet, Spencer scampered across the bed and launched herself in his direction to beg him to take her along.

"Don't worry," he said in a whisper, "you can come, too."

After dressing, he stood to the foot of the bed and took in the beauty that was his wife. Once again, he thanked God for bringing Jessica Faraday crashing into his life.

"You're staring at me again," she murmured without opening her eyes.

He knelt next to the bed and brushed a dark lock of hair from her cheek. "I love looking at you. You're like one of those paintings in an art gallery. The more I stare at you, the more intrigued I become."

"Intrigued or aroused?"

"That too." He kissed her cheek and rose to his feet. "I'm meeting a friend to go running at the park. I should be back by nine."

Anxious to embark on the run, Spencer stood up on her hind legs and clawed at him. He picked her up.

"I'll cook breakfast then." Instead of climbing out of bed, she pulled the comforter over her head and burrowed deeper among the covers.

Great Falls Park was only a short jog along the Potomac River behind the Faraday-Thornton home. Murphy and Jessica had worn a path to the treacherous trail that ran dangerously close to a steep rocky drop-off along a rapid portion of the river. The path led to Great Falls Park, at which point the national park service provided barricades and railings to protect runners from tumbling into the falls.

As soon as they reached the river, Murphy checked the time on his tracker to discover that he was running late. It was seven o'clock on the nose. Even at a run, he was going to be a few minutes late. Murphy and Spencer picked up their pace.

They reached the top of a hill leading down to the park entrance when Murphy heard a gunshot in the distance.

With a yelp, Spencer turned around and looked imploringly up at him.

Murphy recognized the sound. It was a gunshot from a semi-automatic handgun. He gathered up Spencer's leash to keep her close and stepped up his pace to a sprint—practically dragging the dog behind him.

The edge of the park's parking lot was in sight. There was one sedan in the lot since the park had opened only minutes earlier. As Murphy raced down the hillside, a figure dressed in a blue running suit entered the trail heading in his direction. Upon seeing him, the runner spun around and sprinted in the opposite direction.

"Wait! Stop!" Dropping Spencer's leash, Murphy slid on his rump to the bottom of the hill and jumped to his feet to pursue the figure who turned onto another trail leading to the main road.

As he ran past the sedan, Murphy saw that the driver's side window was shattered, and the front windshield was covered with blood. He heard the shooter fleeing down an alternate dirt path several feet away. Murphy raced after the assailant only to come to a halt when the trail broke into a fork. One branch headed toward the river while the other led deeper into the woods.

In silence, he strained to listen for any sound to tell him which way to go. Hearing none, he ran back to the parking lot where he found Spencer whining and pacing with her leash dragging behind her at the end of the path. Not wanting her to walk through the broken glass, Murphy picked her up and tucked her under his arm before stepping up to the car.

Ross Caldwell was slumped across the middle console into the passenger seat.

"Ross? Ross, are you okay?" Murphy said, even though he knew that his friend could not answer. The inside of the sedan was drenched in blood, bone, and human tissue.

"Ross?" a feminine filtered voice called out breathlessly from inside the SUV. "Are you still there? What was that noise?"

Careful not to touch anything, Murphy peered through the broken window to locate the source of the voice. It sounded like it was coming from a cell phone.

"Ross, you're scaring me," she said in a loud filtered voice. "Why aren't you saying anything?"

Finally, Murphy located the cell phone lying on the floor on the passenger side of the car. He jogged around to the other side of the SUV, pulled his sleeve down to cover his hand, and carefully opened the passenger side door.

"Ross baby, speak to me!" She was hysterical when Murphy picked up the phone and put it to his ear.

"Hello?"

"Who is this and what have you done to my husband?"

"I apologize, Ma'am," he replied in an official tone. "I'm Lieutenant Murphy Thornton, United States Navy, assigned to the Naval Criminal Investigative Service."

"What's happened to Ross? I had called him to tell him to stop at the store to pick up bird seed on his way home. Then I heard a loud bang. What's going on?"

"I'm sorry, Ma'am—"

"Oh, Ross! My Ross! No!" She broke down.

CHAPTER THREE

Murphy was helping the state police set up the perimeter with yellow crime scene tape when the deputy chief for the Naval Criminal Investigative Service (NCIS), dressed in jeans and a plaid flannel shirt, arrived.

Murphy had secured Spencer to a fence post with her leash to prevent her from contaminating any potential evidence. The shelty voiced her displeasure about being ignored by the investigators in high-pitched cries that steadily grew in volume.

Boris Hamilton had spent his whole career serving his country as a marine officer. With his broad chest and military bearing, he quickly took control of the investigation since the victim was a naval officer. It wasn't like he was going to get much argument from the park rangers who had their hands full with detouring visitors to the other lots while Boris's team examined the scene for physical evidence. After sending the park rangers on their way, Boris gestured for Murphy to join him while he examined the scene inside the car.

Sensing that the shelty's protests were getting on the forensics investigators' nerves, Murphy untied Spencer and tucked her under his arm.

"Friend of yours?" Boris asked while slipping evidence gloves on.

"Yes," Murphy said. "Commander Ross Caldwell. He was chief of the medical service corps in Annapolis when I was there. Last night, I ran into him at the pizza shop. First time I've seen him since I'd graduated."

Boris was bringing up Ross's records on his tablet. "Assigned to Bethesda."

"He bought a place here in Great Falls." Murphy extracted the evidence bag containing the cell phone from the inside of his jacket. "He was talking to his wife when he was killed. Her name is Erin."

"How's their marriage?"

Murphy shrugged his shoulders. "I couldn't tell you. He came from money. His family has a lot of connections. They have three daughters. All grown and married."

"Reason I asked," Boris said while studying the phone in his hand, "is that if you two were going running first thing in the morning, then we can assume he left his home, where his wife is. Why did she call him just a few minutes after he'd left the house?"

"You wouldn't believe how often Jessie calls me just minutes after I leave the house to send me to the store."

"Good point." Boris laughed. "My wife doesn't trust me to go to the store for her."

"You're a lucky man."

"There's advantages to not being trusted."

"Well," Murphy said, "Erin was still on the phone when I found the body. She's hysterical. I told her that you'd be stopping by."

"She heard the shot? Why didn't she call the police?"

"Denial?"

"You said you saw the shooter."

Murphy led Boris along the parking lot, being careful not to step in the dirt where the shooter had run through the grass to take the alternate path. "Yes, but I didn't get close enough to even be able to tell you if it was a man or woman. Could have been a woman or teenager." He pointed down the path where he had seen the shooter disappear. "This path comes to a Y. Go to the right and you come out at the river. The left takes you deeper into the woods and eventually you come out at one of Great Falls' older housing developments. That's about where Caldwell lives."

"Did you see a gun in his or her hand?"

"No but based on the sound of the shot and the appearance of the wound, I'd say it was a large caliber semi-automatic," Murphy said. "He could have stuffed it into a pocket in his running suit." He tapped Boris on the shoulder. "It was a blue running suit. Medium blue. Not dark or light."

"I'm willing to bet the gun is in the river now," Boris said.

"Me, too. In this part of the river, with the falls, we'll never find it." Murphy turned around in time to see Special Agents Susan Archer and Perry Latimore climb out of their vehicles.

An exceptional investigator, Susan Archer was a friend. Murphy noticed that she was dressed in the same suit she had worn the day before. The last he had seen her, she was on her way to meet a friend for happy hour in Crystal City. He concluded he was a very good friend.

"Medical examiner is on the way," Susan told them while peering through the shot-out window. "What happened?"

"Murphy reconnected with an old friend last night and this morning he's dead." Boris handed the cell phone to her. "His wife heard the shooting go down. Susan, you come with me to talk to her."

"Just how I wanted to spend my Saturday, questioning a widow who heard her husband get murdered."

"Hamilton," Murphy said, "Ross did reveal a possible motive last night."

"What's that?"

"He got very interested when I told him that I had been assigned to NCIS. He told me that a few days ago a friend had told him about something weird going on at a private clinic." Murphy shook his head. "He gave me no specifics. But he did say that he had contacted the department of health and human services and he was meeting with an investigator this morning. Caldwell said that if it ended up being what he suspected that it would be big."

Boris directed Susan, who was thumbing through the phone, to find out who Ross had talked to at the department of health and human services. "Perry, you process the scene."

"Caldwell was going to meet Reg with HHS at Starbucks in Reston at eight-thirty this morning," Susan said.

Murphy checked the time on his fitness monitor. "Five minutes from now."

"Looks like we're going to Starbucks," Boris said.

"But which one?" Susan asked. "His calendar only says Reston. There's three in Reston. One in Reston Towne Center. Another at Plaza America."

"There's also one in South Lakes Village," Murphy said.

"Split up," Boris said. "Each one of us take one. We need to connect with this guy to find out what information Caldwell had."

"Wait a minute." Perry held up his hand. "With all due respect, sir, Thornton is only the military liaison, not an investigator. In this case, he's a witness. For all we know, he's a suspect. You can't be sending him out to hunt down witnesses."

Boris narrowed his eyes to slits. "Okay, then, Latimore. Do you know where this Starbucks is in South Lakes Village?"

Perry hesitated.

The medical examiner's van pulled up to the scene.

"I'll drive." Murphy handed Spencer to Perry and jogged to the agent's SUV. "When Caldwell's contact gets there, and no one's there to meet him, he's going to leave. Latimore, you come with me to South Lakes Village—unless you're afraid I'm going to off you along the way."

☙ ☙ ☙

"Why does she have to sit in my lap?" Perry turned his head and held his breath to evade Spencer's tongue as she licked the tip of his nose with the enthusiasm of a child attacking a lollipop.Her tail wagged so hard that it looked like it was going to fly off her butt.

"She likes you." Murphy plunged his foot on the accelerator and spun the steering wheel to race around a mini cooper threatening to stop at the yellow light of a busy intersection. "You should be flattered."

The clock on the console read eight-thirty-six. Late for Ross's scheduled appointment, they could only hope the investigator would wait a few minutes before leaving.

Perry grabbed the edge of his seat when the SUV raced across six lanes of traffic. "If you aren't careful, you're going to wreck my car and your wife is going to be mad at you."

"If I wreck your SUV, I'm going to be mad," Murphy said. "What does Jessie have to do with it?"

"She'd have to buy me a new car."

Murphy felt his jaws clench to refrain from responding to Perry's insinuation about him being a kept man living off his rich wife.

Perry's cell phone buzzed. He struggled to reach under the dog to unclip it from his utility belt. The caller was Susan. He put her on speaker phone.

"Did you find the guy?"

"No," Susan said. "No one here. I called HHS to see if I could reach anyone. The office is closed but there was someone there. She checked the calendars and thinks the investigator Caldwell was meeting was a Reginald Baldwin. He lives in Reston—near Lake Village."

"That's the one they're meeting at." Murphy spun the steering wheel to make a left turn through an intersection.

"I've got his phone number," Susan said. "I'll call him to tell him to wait for you."

As expected, the coffeehouse was packed. Murphy noticed a couple who looked barely out of their teens at one of the dinette tables in the courtyard. In the large shopping plaza, with the chilly March morning breeze, the majority of the customers chose to dine inside. Most likely, the young lovers wanted to be alone, even if it was in a busy parking lot.

Murphy and Perry left Spencer in the car and split up to make their way through the restaurant in search of the investigator. Every patron appeared to be with friends or using the place to work on their laptop or tablet.

Unsuccessful in their search, they returned to the front door.

"We missed him," Perry told Murphy who had called Susan back.

"Did you reach him?"

"My call went straight to voice mail," she explained.

"Is Ross's phone on?" Murphy asked her. "Most likely he'd call—"

"I thought of that, too," she said. "No call. HHS says he's driving a dark blue SUV with government tags."

Murphy returned outside to the young couple. They were so busy whispering into each other's ears and giggling that they did not notice him until he said, "Excuse me."

They jumped in their seats and released each other's hands.

"I didn't mean to scare you," Murphy said with a grin. "We were supposed to meet someone here. We were late and wondered if you may have seen him."

"What did he look like?" the girl asked.

Murphy was embarrassed to admit he didn't know.

"He was driving a blue SUV with federal government tags."

"Yeah, we saw him," the boy said. "But I doubt if he was the guy you were looking for. I mean, whoever he was meeting met him already. They left like almost a half hour ago."

"What do you mean whoever he was meeting with met him?" Perry asked.

"The guy didn't even make it in the door," the boy said. "I noticed his license plate. The guy parked over there." He pointed to the first row of parking spaces. "He was walking up to the door, and another guy met him on the sidewalk."

"He called him by his name," the girl said. "It was weird because you don't see that many people come here and leave without getting something. The fed got back into his SUV and the guy got in the passenger side and they drove off."

After thanking them, Perry got the couple's names and information to contact them with questions later.

Meanwhile, Murphy called Susan and Boris with the news. Commander Ross Caldwell's killer had intercepted Reginald Baldwin. "Someone's cleaning up."

"We need to find Caldwell's friend," Boris said, "and find out what's going on."

CHAPTER FOUR

"I hate funerals." Murphy's statement came out of the blue while driving to Saint Catherine of Siena Catholic Church in Great Falls for Dr. Ross Caldwell's funeral.

"I don't think anyone loves funerals." Jessica adjusted the angle of her black hat, an accessory for her black Chanel suit, which featured a pencil skirt. "My mother used to have one black dress that she always wore to police funerals with Dad. She called it her funeral dress. That was one of the first things she threw out when they split up."

One full week after his murder, Commander Ross Caldwell was being buried with full military honors. The NCIS team was working on the assumption that the same person who had kidnapped Reginald Baldwin, the HHS investigator, had killed Commander Caldwell.

As a witness, Murphy was kept in the dark with what the NCIS team had managed to uncover during their investigation. They were focusing on tracking down his source for the lead he had acquired about something illegal happening at a private clinic.

It was an unseasonably warm sunny day—hinting that spring was on its way. The parking lot was almost filled. A group of navy officers and their spouses huddled together at the end of the pathway leading to the church's main entrance. They took note as Murphy rolled by in his SUV. Like him, the officers were all clad in dress black uniforms.

"Hey, it's Blue Eyes!" one of the men called out. They all waved and shouted greetings.

"Blue Eyes?" Jessica asked.

"I have blue eyes." Murphy pulled the vehicle into a space and turned off the engine. "It could be worse."

"How much worse?" she asked with a grin.

Murphy unbuckled his seat belt. "Much."

They waited while Murphy put on his cap and opened Jessica's door. "I guess we finally get to meet *Ms.* Blue Eyes," one of the officers said. The women made no pretense of not being anxious to catch a glimpse of Robin Spencer's granddaughter.

"Eat your hearts out." Murphy told them while taking Jessica's hand to assist her out of the SUV.

"I haven't seen most of these guys since the academy." He brushed his fingers across the back of her hand where she had slipped it through his arm.

The collection of military officers consisted of three male navy officers, two female, and one army captain. A West Point graduate, the captain was married to one of the navy lieutenants. Two of the officers had married each other the day after they had graduated from the academy. The remaining navy officer was a dashing Italian-American with dark eyes and wavy hair. Tony had brought the only other civilian in the group—his pregnant wife, Abril, a Mexican immigrant with a thick accent.

After exchanging introductions, the army officer, Captain Fuller said, "They say you were the one who found him, Thornton."

"We were going to go running in Great Falls Park," Murphy said. "I had bumped into him the night before—first time since the academy. It turned out we lived like five minutes from each other."

"Was it a mugging?" Abril asked as the group moved in a double line toward the stairs leading up to the main entrance.

"In Great Falls? Isn't their crime rate zero?" Tony laughed.

"Not anymore," said Captain Fuller who was directly behind them.

They came to a halt on the threshold for the main doors. Jessica and Murphy held hands and waited while many raised up onto their toes and craned their necks to determine the cause for the delay. Others leaned sideways to peer around the mob.

Inside the sanctuary, a woman was chattering and laughing in a loud voice, "Oh, thank you so much for coming! Ross would be so glad you came!" A moment later, she shrieked, "Michelle! You look mar-ve-lous, darling!"

"I thought this was a funeral," Jessica whispered to Murphy.

"That's Erin Caldwell," Kimberly turned around to whisper to them. "There's no mistaking that voice."

"Caldwell?" Murphy replied.

"The widow?" Abril whispered with wide eyes.

Erin's loud laughter turned into a cackle.

"Merry widow." Jessica whispered to Murphy, "Don't expect me to be that happy at your funeral."

"Why do you just assume I'm going to die first?"

There was a flurry of activity up ahead.

"Mother!" a feminine voice said in a chastising tone before the pathway was cleared.

The mourners spilled into the sanctuary.

A slightly built young man handed programs to each guest. His appearance was one of contradiction. His tight suit, white shirt and tie, projected middle-class family values while his pitch black dyed hair, goatee, earplugs, tattoos, and body piercings represented a hard living lifestyle.

"Thank you for coming," he repeated to each guest while shoving a program into their hand—not unlike a robot. His eyes conveyed a deep desire to be elsewhere.

"Are you one of Ross's sons-in-law?" Kimberly asked.

"I'm Woody. Kendall and I got married last fall."

"Kendall is Ross's youngest daughter?"

With a nod of his head, Woody pointed to where Ross's three daughters were attempting to corral their mother. "Mine is the hot redhead." His description made it easy to pick his mate out of the group. There was only one redhead among the Caldwell women. Her hair was trimmed in a becoming short pixie style. The widow and her daughters were having an intense exchange while making their way to the front row.

Ross's widow, Erin was a slender woman with a pointy nose and bony features. Her hair was an ashy blond that she wore in a neat, easy style.

Traumatized by their father's sudden death, Ross's grown daughters struggled to usher their mother to the front pew of the church—an endeavor hampered by Erin stopping to greet each mourner. One would have thought they were attending a wedding instead of a funeral.

"I've never seen anything—" Murphy started to say after Erin Caldwell was finally herded into her seat in front of the flag-draped coffin.

"She's in shock," Jessica said as she and Murphy moved into a pew to sit next to Abril and Tony. "It hasn't hit her yet. When it does—" She grasped his arm. "Don't ever die and put me through that."

"I'll try not to." From his seat on the aisle, Murphy looked over his shoulder.

In a suit and tie, Boris Hamilton was watching the entire scene from the last pew. He acknowledged Murphy with a slight nod of his head.

A woman with long blond hair under a wide-brimmed black hat took a seat at the far end of the same pew where Boris was sitting.

Where had I—the convertible!

Murphy remembered the woman whose car Ross Caldwell had climbed into after leaving the pizza place. He had dismissed the incident because at the time he thought she was his wife. Murphy turned around to look at the front of the church. *But she's Ross's wife. Then who is —* Murphy glanced back over his shoulder.

She was still there. Her dark glasses covered her eyes and most of her face. They weren't the same sunglasses as those he had seen that night. Those had been adorned with rhinestones.

It has to be the same woman.

Ross had mentioned leaving Annapolis because of a scandal. Bad habits do die hard. Could he have chosen to take up cheating again? But what about all that talk about putting his marriage first? That could have been guilt talking.

Murphy took his cell phone out of his pocket and tapped out a text to Boris:

Check out blonde in hat & big sunglasses at 9 o'clock. Saw her w Caldwell night before the murder. Source or mistress?

Murphy turned his head and watched Boris out of the corner of his eye. Boris read the message, then slipped the phone back into his pocket. Ever so casually, he cast a glance in the direction of the blonde.

It was getting close to the scheduled time for the funeral service to begin. Woody and Ross's other sons-in-law joined their wives in the front pew.

Silence fell over the sanctuary.

The church bells rang to mark ten o'clock—time for the funeral to begin.

As the last tones of the bells faded the last mourners made their appearance.

At first glance, Murphy thought the man was Ross Caldwell. He had the same height and build. As he drew closer while hurrying down the aisle, it became apparent that his hair was dyed to cover the gray, contrasting with his wrinkled face. His black tailored suit was accented with gold cuff links and tie clip.

The middle-aged woman on his arm was a bottled brunette in a black pantsuit and high heels. She sashayed down the aisle with her hand looped through the man's arm. Her head held high, she looked down her nose at the mourners.

"Ross's older brother, Daniel," Kimberly whispered to Jessica and Abril. "Harvard law school. Runs the family business."

Upon reaching the front of the church, the couple made a show of working their way down the pew, greeting each sobbing daughter with a hug and kiss. He would then greet her husband with a firm handshake and pat on the shoulder. Meanwhile, Erin remained motionless in her seat.

When Daniel bent over his brother's widow to offer his condolences, she reached up to slap him.

The sound of her hand connecting with his cheek echoed throughout the silent sanctuary—as did the gasps that followed.

"You bastard!" Erin bound out of the pew to continue the assault but two of her daughters' husbands held her back. In tears, her daughters hugged each other. "Ross isn't even buried yet, and he's already turning over in his grave!"

"I've never!" Daniel's wife said with a huff and hurried to the pew across from them.

"Watch it, Joy!" Erin said. "It's not polite to lie in God's house!"

"Mother! Please!" the eldest daughter screamed. "This is Daddy's funeral!"

The priest had hurried out from behind the altar to demand Ross's family calm down and asked if Erin needed a tranquilizer.

Murphy turned around in his seat. Boris caught the scene as well. As the two exchanged glances, Murphy saw a movement directly behind the investigator.

The blonde in the dark glasses was leaving as fast as her shapely legs could carry her.

CHAPTER FIVE

Instantly, the two civilian spouses, Jessica and Abril had struck up a friendship. After the service, Jessica invited the other couple to ride with them to the graveside service at Mount Olivet, one of the oldest Catholic cemeteries in the Washington, DC area. It was where Ross Caldwell's parents and grandparents had been buried.

Abril seemed to have a permanent broad smile across her face that made people just naturally grin back at her. In the back seat of the SUV, the two women exchanged stories about their experiences as navy wives.

As Jessica had guessed by Abril's thick accent, she had immigrated to America with her family, which included uncles, aunts, and cousins, as a small child. Each family member worked multiple jobs to save enough money to start their own restaurant and lounge in Annapolis, near the academy.

Against all odds, the dive with fabulous authentic Mexican food became a favorite of the academy's midshipmen—especially one in particular.

"Tony became our unofficial PR man," Abril said with a grin. "Every time he came in, he had a half a dozen friends with him. They would bring their friends." She added with a whisper, "That's why my family approves of him—even though he is a gringo."

"He was more interested in showing off his girlfriend than the food," Murphy said.

"What's not to show off?" Tony asked. "I got myself the prettiest girl in Annapolis. Of course, I was going to show her off."

"And here I didn't have any idea," Abril told Jessica. "I thought he was coming in because he liked the food. One day, my cousin Anita says to me, 'No, Abril, Momma's cooking is good, but it's not *that* good. Tony's coming here for *you*.'"

The two women giggled.

"How did you and Blue Eyes meet?" Abril asked Jessica.

"Oh," Jessica said, "one day a gang of international terrorists tried to kidnap me and Murphy saved me." She smiled at his reflection in the rearview mirror. "We got married the next day."

Abril's eyes grew wide. Her mouth dropped open.

"Dude, couldn't you have just used a wing man like everyone else?" Tony asked.

"You haven't changed one bit, Blue Eyes." With a laugh, Abril reached up to tap Murphy on the head in the driver's seat. "And I like Ms. Blue Eyes, too."

"Good to see you and Tony, too, Abril."

"Sick about why we're getting together again," Tony said. "I heard you're the liaison at NCIS. Any word? Do they know who did it? Why would anyone want to hurt a nice guy like Commander Caldwell?"

"I don't know," Murphy said. "I found the body. That makes me a witness. So I can't really comment. But if you know anything—"

"I haven't seen him since graduation," Tony said. "He requested a transfer out of Annapolis during our last year."

"Because his wife was sick," Abril said.

"Sick with what?" Jessica asked.

"I don't know for sure," Abril said. "Cancer? Someone told me that she needed treatment and the best place to get it was up here in Washington."

"I heard Caldwell was forced to transfer out of Annapolis because he was caught having an affair with his intern," Tony said.

"Which is it?" Murphy asked. "Is it because his wife was ill and needed to be up here in Washington for treatment or because Commander Caldwell was having an affair and was forced out?"

Both Abril and Tony shrugged their shoulders.

The Caldwell family was already seated graveside by the time they had parked and made their way across the grass to where the coffin had been carried out to rest. A chilly breeze blew across the old hillside and darted among the tombstones.

Unlike at the church, Erin Caldwell sat still and silent in the folding chairs provided for the immediate family. She ignored her daughters who surrounded her on all sides not so much to offer comfort, but to control her behavior.

Spotting Boris standing under a tree far away, Murphy broke away from his friends to join him.

"That was quite a display by the widow at the church," Boris said while keeping his eyes on the priest standing next to the coffin. "Did anyone tell you what it was about?"

"Nothing," Murphy said with a shake of his head.

"What about that blonde you pointed out to me? Notice anything about her—besides her legs? Which were exceptional by the way."

"I think I recognize her," Murphy said. "The night before his murder, Caldwell told me that he had to leave Annapolis because of a scandal. He had to adjust his priorities and put his wife first."

"Sounds to me like he was caught with his pants down. Do you think the blonde was his mistress?"

"That night, I saw him get into a red convertible—it was a late model Nissan—with a beautiful blonde. She was wearing a hat and big dark glasses."

"Not unlike the woman in the church."

Murphy grimaced. "With the hat and the glasses, it's hard to say for certain they're the same woman. She was definitely a blonde with long hair."

"There are a lot of beautiful blondes with long hair in this town, Murphy."

"How many would feel compelled to come to Dr. Caldwell's funeral?"

"And his burial." Boris jerked his chin in the direction across the way.

They both recognized the wide brimmed black hat and the blond hair falling to her shoulders as she closed the door to a silver SUV.

"That's not the car, though," Murphy whispered.

"She could have more than one vehicle."

As they watched, she lingered at the edge of the section of the cemetery like a prey animal fearful of a trap. The long stemmed red rose stood out against her black suit.

Once the graveside service was over, Murphy rejoined his friends.

Ross Caldwell's daughters ushered their mother up to the coffin where they each placed a rose on it. Before anyone had a chance to offer one last word of condolence, they scurried Erin away.

Daniel Caldwell repeatedly told everyone that his sister-in-law was not feeling well. "It just hit her during the church service that Ross is not coming home." He and his wife hurried away as if they didn't want to field any more questions.

"That happens more often than you'd think," Jessica told Murphy. "It isn't real until you're sitting there in front of the coffin containing the body of the man you love. That's when you realize he's not coming back." She tugged on his arm to escort him to the coffin to place their roses on top.

When he turned toward Jessica, he discovered that the blonde in the black hat was ahead of her. He cut in in line to get closer. As he approached, the blonde moved in close to Ross Caldwell's coffin and reach out with the rose clutched in her hand. She placed her hand on top and pressed against the cold coffin—as if to take in his touch one last time.

Murphy's eyes took in her long slender white hand— blemished with an ugly red scar down the length of its back. Never had he seen a scar like that on a hand.

Determined to speak to her, though he was uncertain what he would say, he tore his attention from the hand and scar to say, "Excuse me, but have we met?"

She turned to him. Her face concealed by the dark glasses. The top of her head covered by the black hat. Without a word, she spun around and hurried into the crowd of mourners.

"I thought you gave up picking up other women when we got married," Jessica said as Murphy watched the woman in the black hat drive away.

⁂ ⁂ ⁂

"I would be very surprised if she showed up here," Murphy said to Boris while they talked in low voices in an out-of-the-way spot in the dining room. Jessica was being entertained by Murphy's friends with stories about his days at the naval academy.

Many of the mourners had returned to the Caldwell mansion for a catered reception. Less than two miles from where Ross Caldwell had been murdered, the older colonial style home was nestled among tall thick trees and beautifully land-scaped gardens.

"Of course she's not going to come here," Boris told Murphy in a displeased tone. "You spooked her. Need I remind you, Thornton, you're not an investigator. You're the navy liaison at NCIS, plus you're a witness. We can't have you taking an active role in the investigation. Our killer's defense attorney will have us for lunch."

They paused as a strikingly beautiful woman, wearing a bib apron with "Natalie Stepford's Kitchen Studio," strode into the dining room. She carried an enormous silver platter filled with an assortment of appetizers.

It wasn't the food that had captured the attention of every man in the room. Caterer Natalie Stepford's flawless figure, face, and features made every head turn.

"Did you at least get her license plate number?" Murphy asked after recapturing Boris's attention when Natalie returned to the kitchen.

"No, too many cars between me and her vehicle." Boris gestured toward the kitchen. "That woman——"

"She's the caterer and you're married."

"Her name is Natalie. At least, that's what's on the apron. Caldwell was getting and receiving phone calls on his cell from someone named Natalie. And she's a gorgeous blonde—not unlike the woman at the funeral."

"Could be the same woman," Murphy said. "With that hat and sunglasses—both the night before the murder and today. The woman at the funeral had a nasty scar on the back of her hand."

"Possibly a burn while cooking in the kitchen," Boris said. "I'll go check her out."

Boris hurried toward the kitchen as one of Ross Caldwell's daughters, a glass of wine in her hand, blocked Murphy's path. With her short red hair, Murphy recognized her as the one who had recently married Woody. In contrast to her husband, she had a clean appearance. Possibly, it was the demure black dress she was wearing, but she did not look like the type of girl who would have married Woody, a rock star wannabe. Her frosty minty scent reminded him of toothpaste.

"Lieutenant Thornton." She shifted the glass to her other hand to shake his. "I'm Kendall Harris, the baby of the family." She had her mother's sharp, bony features.

"Lieutenant Murphy Thornton." He shook her hand. "I'm sorry for your loss. I'd met your father at the academy."

"Most of the navy officers here did." She held up the wine glass. "Would you like a drink?"

After he declined her offer, she freshened her own drink by pouring more wine from the bottle into her goblet. "I grew up in Annapolis. Miss it a lot. Great Falls is so—" He waited for her to say, "Boring," Instead she lowered her voice to a whisper and said, "I was told that you found his body."

His eyes dropped to the floor. "Yes, I wish I could have done more. I chased the shooter, but I lost him. I'm sorry."

"Was Dad…" her voice trailed off. Her eyes moistened. "I mean, did he say anything?"

Murphy laid his hand on her shoulder. "He didn't suffer."

The two of them stood together in silence. She wet her lips. "I was at work that day." She let out a deep breath. "Mom called and told me."

"Where do you work?"

"A call center out by Dulles. I had to drop out of school this past fall. Between the wedding and everything—I got burnt out." She brightened. "But I'm planning to go back to school next year. Dad insisted that I couldn't take time off to recharge my batteries. The work ethic was a big thing to him. I work first shift—six in the morning to four in the afternoon."

"Do you have any idea who would want to do this to your father?" Murphy asked.

Kendall picked up a toothpick from the buffet table and stuck it between her teeth. After a moment, she said, "There was one crazy lady. She worked with Dad in Annapolis. Was obsessed with him. As a matter of fact, she even stalked him for a while. I think her name was Libby."

"Annapolis was four years ago," Murphy said.

"I thought I saw her at the hospital where my dad worked," Kendall said. "I hoped I was imagining it. It would have been right up her alley to kill Dad because she couldn't have him."

"Hey, Kendall, you'll never guess who's here?" With an excited bounce in his step, Woody swooped in from the living room to drape his arm around her shoulders. He clutched a handful of compact discs in his hand. "Jessica Faraday."

Murphy put on his best poker face.

Kendall was unimpressed. "Jessica…"

"Her old man is Mac Faraday," Woody said. "Her family *owns* the Spencer Inn in Deep Creek Lake. That's the resort where everybody who's anybody goes to. Five-star restaurant and lounge." Annoyed by her lack of response, he flapped his arms. "They book some big-named bands there—especially every Saturday night on the plaza during the summer. All of the biggest DC groups play there. If I can get her to put in a good word for me with her old man, we'll be on our way." He waved the CDs around. "I'm going to give her my discs now." He hurried away.

"You do that." Kendall raised her eyes to meet Murphy's. "Woody is an artist."

"So I gathered."

"He's my big mistake." She let out a deep breath. "Dad didn't approve of Woody. When I first met him, I was so impressed to be dating a rock musician." She rolled her eyes. "A better description would be babysitting."

"Kendall, darling! My favorite daughter."

Murphy recognized Erin Caldwell's voice. Kendall appeared equally surprised when her mother practically tackled her in a tight embrace. "Mom, I thought you were tired and wanted to take a nap," she said while unwrapping her mother's arms from around her shoulders.

"I can't, dear," Erin said while waving a hand to indicate the many guests. "We have company." She grinned at Murphy. "Who is this young man, dear?"

"This is Lieutenant Thornton."

Erin extended her hand to Murphy as if she expected him to kiss it. Surprised by the act, Murphy gently gave the back of her hand a peck.

"Oh, you are a good-looking buck," Erin said with a salacious grin.

Kendall shushed her.

"I see you've met our baby, Kendall," Erin said.

"And her husband," Murphy said.

"For now. It's incredibly easy to get a divorce nowadays."

"Mom," Kendall said with a roll of her eyes, "you've already talked to Murphy on the phone. He's Dad's friend. He was running with his dog when he ran into the killer on the trail along the river."

"Ms. Caldwell, I am so sorry for your loss." Erin's eyes were glazed over—making him wonder if she had been sedated since the funeral service.

"Ross was the most gifted human being," Erin said. "I used to say that I wished I could bottle him and sell him to other women as the perfect husband."

"He was a brilliant doctor, too." Murphy noticed Kendall hurrying in the direction of one of her sisters. "He was never too busy to listen to any of the midshipmen—"

"That's what he was doing when he died," Erin said.

"Excuse me, Ma'am."

"I was ranting and raving to him about Woody, our son-in-law. I had asked him to do one thing for me." She held up her finger to show him. "One thing and one thing only. Clean up the mess he had made in the garage. Ever since he's moved in, he's left his junk stacked up all over the place. We have a seven-car garage and half of it is taken up with Heather's stuff—winter clothes and garbage from their tour in Pearl Harbor. It's also packed with Woody's trash. Now I can't do anything about Heather's stuff, but Woody—he promised he was going to get rid of it that day. He goes out to the garage—" She flapped her arm. "I go out to feed the birds, walk into the garage, and no Woody! He'd taken off." She moved in closely to whisper in his ear. "Keep your hand on your wallet. Not only is he a bum, he's a thief."

Kendall returned with one of her sisters in tow.

"Mom, Dr. Stevens suggested that you lay down," the older daughter said.

"No family is as perfect as it seems," Erin said to Murphy in a low voice as she was ushered back upstairs.

"Mom has been having a very hard time since Dad's death," Kendall said. "Her doctor has had to medicate her." She trotted up the stairs after her mother.

"Lieutenant Thornton." Abruptly a hand was thrust in front of him from behind. Murphy turned to find himself face to face with Ross Caldwell's brother Daniel. "We finally meet. I was told that you found my brother."

"Yes. Unfortunately, I didn't get a clear look at the killer. I couldn't even tell you if it was a man or a woman. I'm sorry."

"Don't be," Daniel said with a grin. "Spoken like a defense attorney."

"I have two criminal lawyers in the family," Murphy said.

"Young or old?"

"Excuse me?"

"The killer. Was he or she young or old?"

"Too far away for me to tell," Murphy said. "Very slender. Slightly built." He kept the information about the killer wearing a blue running suit to himself.

"Slight build," Daniel said.

"Do you know of anyone with a slight build who would want to hurt your brother?" Murphy asked. "Someone told me that Commander Caldwell had a potential stalker when he was assigned to Annapolis."

Daniel's eyebrows rose high on his forehead. "Stalker? Oh, no. Who told you that?"

"Kendall. Maybe it wasn't a stalker but just a woman who was extremely interested in him."

"Ah, that explains it," Daniel said.

"Explains what?"

"Kendall's a good kid, but she has an active imagination. Ross was a devoted father and faithful husband. He never even looked at another woman."

"Kendall didn't say this woman caught him."

"He had women interested in him, but he never said anything to me to indicate an obsession that could lead to murder." Daniel jerked his chin in the direction of the stairs up which Erin and her daughters had left. "I must apologize for Erin. This has all been very hard on her. Ross was her whole world, and she was very dependent on him. When he last updated his will, he impressed on me his utmost wish that Erin be well taken care of."

"I understand. Is anyone staying with her?"

"Kendall and Woody live here."

"Woody the rock musician," Murphy said.

"Kendall loves musicians." Daniel chuckled. "She spends every weekend downtown hanging out with the various rock bands. She's gotten quite a reputation for being an amateur promoter. One weekend, she made the mistake of bringing Woody home. Next thing Ross knew, she married the bum."

"From what I understand, they're still newlyweds."

"The honeymoon was over before it began," Daniel said. "I doubt very much if that marriage is going to make it to the one-year mark."

"Does Woody work?"

"Woody can't work," he said in a mocking tone. "He's an artist."

"Jessica has a friend whose husband has the same mentality. He's a writer." Murphy joined in the laughter. "Erin said something about Woody being a thief."

"Did she really?" Daniel seemed amused by this news.

"If he's stealing, maybe that's a sign of something worse than laziness," Murphy said. "Like a drug problem. Drugs are big in the rock music scene."

"Well, if Woody is a thief, then that would be ironic."

"Because…"

"Erin is a kleptomaniac."

Murphy cocked his head at him.

"Erin has a lot of problems," Daniel said, "as you probably noticed. One of them is a tendency to pick up pretty little things that don't belong to her. Ross spent a lot of time and money covering up for her. So," he chuckled, "if what you say is true, and Woody is a thief and Erin is a kleptomaniac, and here is Kendall living with both of them." His chuckle grew louder. "No wonder she's never home."

Murphy stepped into the living room doorway. He watched Woody pitching his rock band to Jessica. A grin came to his lips while he watched Jessica's violet eyes darting around the room—searching for him to save her. He stepped behind Daniel. "Could Woody be into drugs?"

Watching the scene as well, Daniel shrugged. "I think he's more into living the rock star lifestyle and not getting a job."

"Could he have—"

"Killed my brother so Kendall could receive her inheritance?" Daniel mulled over the idea. "That would have taken initiative, which Woody doesn't have."

Murphy turned to him. "If the alternative was going out to get a job, Woody may have been motivated to do it. You'd be surprised at how much energy some people will put into avoiding work."

"Personally, I think my brother's killer is further away from home." Daniel thrust a business card into Murphy's hand. "As a personal favor, for Ross, could you personally keep me informed of the status on NCIS's investigation into my brother's death?"

"I'm not on the investigative team."

"But you are the naval liaison. And my brother was a navy commander. Think of it as liaising between—"

"With all due respect, sir, that would be leaking." Murphy placed the card back into his hand. "I don't leak." Before Daniel had a chance to argue, he crossed the room to rescue his wife from Woody, who was threatening her with an impromptu audition on the spot.

Chapter Six

One Month Later

"Don't take this the wrong way, Thornton, but I hate eating lunch with you." Boris cast a guilty glance at the salad sprinkled with chopped salmon set in front of Murphy,

"You don't hate it enough to pass on that double cheeseburger." Murphy grinned at the server who had paused to flash him a warm smile while setting a fresh glass of water next to his plate. She barely glanced in Boris's direction when giving him a second soda.

"You don't even miss a big juicy burger?" Boris took a bite from the sandwich and uttered a pleasure-filled groan.

"I don't miss what it does to my body." Murphy stirred the wild salmon sprinkled across the salad into the greens. "I've gone so long without it that I become physically ill when I eat meat. Your body adapts when you go a long time eating a certain way. I have a lot of trouble digesting junk." He ate a forkful of lettuce. "To tell you the truth, I'm not the dietary saint you think I am."

"You're a closet carnivore."

"No," Murphy laughed. "I did not wake up one day and decide to become a pescatarian. It happened gradually—like over a year. At the academy, I was competing against the best of the best. I needed to have my body in the best shape possible. To do that, I had to treat it right—feed it good stuff. After a while, my body was craving more of the good stuff and not liking the bad stuff."

"Well, you're a better man than me." Boris dipped a fried potato into the catsup.

"But I'm not one hundred percent. When I go back home, I can never say no to my sister's homemade cheesecake, which is crammed full of dairy." Murphy sat back and wiped his mouth. "It took me a long time to figure out that no one and nothing is perfect. We can strive to be perfect, but we'll never make it. Somewhere, somehow, we will mess up. The thing is not to beat yourself up over your screw-ups or imperfections—"

"Or to throw in the towel," Boris interjected with a nod of his head.

"Accept your imperfections and keep on going. Once I realized that, I was much happier. Plus, it gave me a license to say yes to Tracy's cheesecake."

"Speaking of culinary delights…" Boris glanced around to see who was seated nearby before leaning across the table in Murphy's direction. "How much do you and Jessica enjoy doing stuff together in the kitchen?"

"Depends on what you mean by 'doing stuff together.'"

Boris frown. "We're getting nowhere on the Dr. Caldwell murder. He was killed with a nine-millimeter bullet. There's no match for the bullet in the federal database."

"So the weapon was never used in another crime."

"Commander Caldwell had two nine millimeters registered to him—both military issued. They were locked in the gun safe and the bullet didn't come from either of them."

"Does forensics have any idea what kind of gun was used?" Murphy asked.

"We're looking for a Colt semi-automatic."

"And you've got nothing from the BOLO for Reginald Baldwin, the HHS investigator Ross was going to meet that morning?"

"No sign of his car." Boris shook his head. "No activity on his finances or cell phone. It's like he disappeared off the face of the earth." He took another bite from his burger.

"What about Natalie Stepford, the caterer who Caldwell had been exchanging phone calls with?"

"She claims she was giving him cooking lessons to surprise his wife," Boris said with doubt in his tone. "They'd met last fall when she catered Caldwell's daughter's wedding. That's why they hired her to cater his funeral."

"Sounds like you're not buying it," Murphy said. "What connection would a caterer have to a private clinic?"

"Maybe Caldwell's murder has nothing to do with the stuff happening at a private clinic. You said Caldwell's brother asked you to feed him information about what we were turning up in our investigation."

"I think he knows more than he's telling," Murphy said.

"So do I. Didn't you say Caldwell requested a transfer out of the academy because of some scandal? He had a plum position there. Chief of the academy's medical corps. That's not something that people leave voluntarily."

"I'm getting two stories from my navy buddies. Half say he was having an affair with an intern and his wife found out and threatened to leave him. He requested the transfer so they could start over again with a clean slate. The other half say Erin Caldwell became very sick, presumably cancer, and they wanted to move up to Washington for treatment."

"She strikes me as being somewhat needy. That could be because she's been ill." Boris shrugged his shoulders. "Everyone that we've interviewed claim they had a picture-perfect marriage. Caldwell was devoted to his wife."

"What about her behavior at the funeral?"

"We did check into that," Boris said. "Her daughters claim it did not hit Erin Caldwell that her husband was dead until the funeral itself."

"I overheard mention of Ms. Caldwell being on meds."

"Mild tranquilizers," Boris said. "Her doctor issued one prescription to get her through the funeral. Everyone assured me that usually she is quite normal, and their marriage was solid. Besides, she couldn't have done it."

"You've ruled her out?"

"She was at home—on the phone with him when he was shot," Boris said. "You said so yourself in your statement. She was calling to him from the phone when you found the body. She heard the shot. His blood was on the phone and forensics confirms that he was talking on it. That confirms both of your statements."

"Did Ross's daughters say anything about an affair with this caterer?" Murphy asked.

Boris tossed a fry into his mouth and shook his head.

"Does the caterer have a nasty scar on her right hand?"

"No scar," Boris said. "Her skin is flawless."

"Then she wasn't the woman at the funeral or gravesite," Murphy said.

"That woman most likely has nothing to do with the murder," Boris said. "There were a lot of people at Caldwell's funeral. You yourself said a half dozen of your friends from the academy who hadn't seen Caldwell in years came out of respect for the man. None of them have anything to do with the case."

Murphy took a bite of his salad. "My gut tells me that this woman was different. She wanted to be there, but she didn't want to be noticed." He tapped his fork on the plate.

"Caldwell's youngest daughter told me that he had a stalker in Annapolis—a woman who was obsessed with him."

"Which is it? Was Caldwell having an affair with an intern or was he being stalked?" Boris arched an eyebrow in Murphy's direction while wiping a smudge of catsup from the corner of his plate with a fry.

"Could it be both?" Murphy said. "He had a brief affair with an intern who didn't take it well when he ended it."

"I saw that in a movie once."

"Yet," Murphy said, "the commander's brother claimed none of that ever happened."

"No stalker has shown up on our radar—neither here nor there," Boris said. "My money is on Natalie Stepford, the caterer, and I don't think he was having an affair with Stepford."

"Because she's out of his league?" Murphy smirked.

"She's out of everyone's league." Boris shrugged his shoulders. "The call pattern between them doesn't indicate an affair. Since his daughter's wedding, there was no contact between Caldwell and Stepford until six weeks ago. Stepford called him. There were a few phone calls between them—and always before or after he talked to Baldwin at HHS."

"What did Stepford say when you questioned her?"

"Stepford's swearing up and down that her contact with Caldwell was for private cooking lessons," Boris said. "We're not buying it and she's spooked. She's cut off all communication with our team. Her husband is a big lawyer with a lot of connections. No one can get near her. I don't want to do this, because you are a witness, but we need your help."

"Sure. Anything. What do you need?"

"Stepford teaches cooking classes," Boris said with a grin, "in Great Falls."

"My neck of the woods," Murphy said.

"She's got a six-week course coming up for couples—it's supposed to promote intimacy between couples by cooking together. It starts tonight."

Murphy shook his head. "Tonight isn't good. It's our date night."

"Perfect. It's a couple's class. If you don't take Jessica, you'll blow your cover."

"Boris—"

Boris's tone was firm. "Murphy, it's very important that you do this. We think Natalie Stepford could be in danger. We got a warrant to tap her electronics and our forensics people found that someone else is already doing that. We need to get word to her. Warning her could help make her trust us enough to tell us what's going on. You and Jessica are the only ones able to mix in with the type of people who take her classes."

"Okay then," Murphy said. "I'll do it."

"I knew I could count on you." Boris checked a message on his phone. "As for your date night, Natalie Stepford advertises that these classes are guaranteed to bring you closer together. The chief is calling me back for a briefing. You go ahead and finish your lunch." He wolfed down the last of his burger. "Let's get together this afternoon and I'll fill you in with the case details before tonight." With that, he slapped cash down in the middle of the table and hurried away.

Murphy took out his phone and studied Jessica's image on the home screen. A soft smile came to his lips as he fingered it. In silence, he worded and reworded how to text her the message that date night was off—or rather there was a change of plans for their activity. He had been looking forward to a long evening of 'what not.'

"Lieutenant Thornton?"

Murphy looked up to discover Erin, Dr. Ross Caldwell's widow, standing next to his table.

"Ms. Caldwell." Murphy hurried to his feet and offered to shake her hand. "It's good to see you. How are you doing?"

The answer was in her face. It was pale and drawn—a contrast from weeks earlier when he had seen her at the funeral. The reality of her husband's death had hit her like a ton of bricks.

"I had an appointment with my lawyer," Erin said.

"Daniel, your husband's brother?"

"No." She practically spat out her response. "He's a snake in the grass. Kendall told me that he's been talking to her sisters behind my back." She glanced around. "I thought I'd have a little lunch before heading back home. I noticed you sitting over here and—"

"Would you like to join me?" Murphy offered her the seat across to him.

As soon as she sat down, the server arrived to take Boris's empty plate and hand a menu to Erin, who quickly set it aside without reading it. "I'll have what you're having. I'm not hungry anyways. I just didn't feel like fighting the lunch hour traffic."

"That's why I eat close to the office," Murphy said returned to his salad. "This is only one metro stop from the Pentagon."

"That's right," she said. "You mentioned that before. You're assigned to the Pentagon." Her eyes seemed to glaze over.

"How are you doing, Ms. Caldwell?" Murphy took a sip of his water.

"Ross's brother is the executor of his will." She looked up at him. "He's turned my daughters against me. If it wasn't for Kendall…" She dabbed her eyes with a tissue.

"How is that?" he asked.

"He's a manipulative son of a bitch. Nothing like Ross. He never did approve of me. I was never good enough for their family." Her eyes teared up. "They want me to see a psychiatrist." She patted her chest. "Me? Woody's a grown man, and he has the attention span of an inch worm. He still hasn't finished cleaning out the garage which he started a month ago. If anything, he's made it worse. That day he said he was going out to clean it, I went to get the bird seed to feed my birds and found that he had dumped over a bin of Heather's clothes. She hasn't worn any of them since college. I told her to give them to Goodwill." She shook her head. "Woody never did clean that mess up."

"What'd he do after dumping over the bin?" Murphy asked.

His question sidetracked her vent. "Huh?"

"You said he knocked over the bin of Heather's clothes," Murphy reminded her. "Where did he go after doing that?"

Erin gazed at him for a long moment.

"Ms. —"

She snapped her fingers as the memory returned. "He went to the river."

"The river?" Murphy asked. "Do you mean the same river where your husband was killed?"

"Do you think he killed Ross?" she asked. "Kendall told me just the other day that he has three guns. She hated to suggest it because he is her husband—"

"What kind of guns does he have?"

"I don't know," she said. "I never saw them. Kendall told me about them. They aren't registered. No one knows where Woody was when Ross was killed. That's what I was telling Ross—" Her voice broke. "I went out to fill the feeders with bird seeds when I saw the mess and called Ross to tell him to pick up bird seed. I was so mad, that I went off and was telling him about the mess when—" Her voice broke.

"When did Woody come back home?"

"After the police came," she said. "He came driving up in that old car of his with Ross's kayak tied to the roof."

"He'd gone kayaking?"

"That good-for-nothing bum even helped himself to Ross's wetsuit without asking. He said he'd found it in the garage and wanted to check it out before deciding whether or not to toss it out."

"He was driving?" Murphy asked.

"And he'd put on Ross's wetsuit." She curled her lips in disgust. "If Ross was alive, he'd have a fit. I told Kendall to clean it up since he's her husband. She just blows me off and goes out with her friends. If it's going to get done, I guess I'll just have to do it myself. And they think I should go see a shrink! If Ross knew what they were trying to do, he'd come back and haunt them all." She uttered a heavy sigh. "Ross was such a good man."

"Yes, he was. I imagine a lot of women envied you having him for a husband."

"My Ross was quite a catch," she said with a proud grin.

"Was there any woman who crossed the line?" Murphy asked. "I guess I would say—"

"Yes," Erin said. "At the academy. She actually stalked my husband." She covered her mouth with a gasp. "The week before—I went to the hospital to meet him for lunch and I swore I saw her walking down the hallway." Her voice grew louder. "Ross insisted it wasn't her, but Kendall told me that she thinks she saw her, too. You don't think—" Agitated, her voice trailed off. Her eyes filled with tears.

Murphy reached across the table and grabbed both of her hands. "What was her name?"

Erin worked her mouth, but no words came out. Finally, she stammered, "I can't remember."

"It will come to you. Let's talk about something else." After calming her down, Murphy sat back in his seat.

Erin's salad arrived. She picked up her fork and poked at the lettuce. "Any other father would've thrown Woody out on his ear the night Kendall brought him home. But Ross insisted that we allow Kendall to figure it out on her own. Ross even walked her down the aisle when she married that bum."

"Ms. Caldwell," Murphy said, "at the reception after the funeral, you warned me that Woody was a thief."

"He is," she said in a matter-of-fact tone. "Thirty-five hundred dollars was stolen out of the safe yesterday."

"Thirty-five hundred dollars? Did you report it?"

Erin nodded her head. "I went to complete a police report this morning. Kendall had a fit. I told them Woody took it. He had to. She says Woody doesn't have the safe combination." With a laugh, she arched an eyebrow in his direction. "Like I'd believe she didn't give it to him. This isn't the first time money has disappeared in that house." She shook a finger at Murphy. "And it only started happening after Kendall brought him home." Her eyes teared up. "Woody says it's me."

"Because?"

"I have a problem with pretty shiny things." She raised her voice. "*Cash* is not *pretty* or *shiny*."

Aware of heads turning in their direction, Murphy gestured for her to lower her voice.

"I've been hearing a lot of arguing coming from their bedroom." She took in a deep breath. "I hope Kendall realizes what a mistake she's made. She could really use her father right now. We both could."

"I am so sorry, Ms. Caldwell."

"No one could have had a better husband." Her voice took on a dream-like tone. "He adored me. He called me his delicate little flower." She dabbed her moist eyes with the napkin. "That was how he treated me. So gentle. Loving."

"You've suffered a tremendous loss, Ms. Caldwell. Grief counseling couldn't hurt."

She swallowed. "Ross used to bring me flowers every Friday."

Murphy remembered the bouquet Ross was holding in his arms when he had met him at the pizza shop, the night before the murder. *So those flowers were for his wife. What man would buy a bouquet of flowers for his wife and then take them for a hook up with his mistress? She must have been his source for information about the private clinic.*

"He bought me that house because of the gardens. I love gardening. He said that I deserved a palace because all princesses need a castle to live in." Erin's eyes were filling up with more tears. "He never forgot a birthday or our anniversary or—"

"I can only imagine how hard all of this is."

"He was all I had. What kind of evil would take him away from me?" Tears rolled down her face as she looked pleadingly at him. "I can't stop thinking about that moment—the sound of the gunshot. It was so loud." She covered her ears. "I never imagined. In an instant—" Her hands shook when she placed them back on the table.

Murphy patted her hand.

The touch of his hand on hers made her jump. "I didn't know what to think—what to do. I kept telling myself that it couldn't have been a gun shot. It was only a car backfiring or something. I kept calling to him." She lifted her eyes to his. "But then, you picked up the phone and said those words— they're branded in my memory."

"I'm sorry, Ma'am," Murphy said to her in a soft voice.

"Yes, that's what you said. 'I'm sorry, Ma'am.'"

"Ms. Caldwell, I assure you, we're going to do everything we can to find out who took your husband away from you."

She squeezed his fingers.

After paying the bill for both of their lunches, Murphy called Boris while making his way to the metro stop. "Hey,

Boris, I think I got a possible break for you. Guess who has three unregistered guns and was living under Commander Ross Caldwell's roof at the time of his murder."

CHAPTER SEVEN

With a sensuous grin at her reflection in the mirror, Jessica applied an extra dab of cologne behind her ears—all the better for Murphy to nibble on. She rose from her seat and stepped back to study her reflection.

Her new silk hand-painted robe. Naked underneath. Wait!

She snatched the scissors from the dressing table and clipped off the price tag. After tossing it into the waste basket under the vanity, she resumed the inspection.

High heels? All the better to show off long legs. Spray on tan? No missed spots? Check. Hair? Not one strand out of place. At least until Murphy runs his fingers through it. Champagne chilling for me. Organic grape juice for Murphy. Raw oysters and Caesar salad in the fridge. Spa ready to go. Strawberries dipped in chocolate for afterwards. Everything is ready for date night. What could possibly go wrong?

Her cell phone erupted into song to signal a call from one of her medical school friends. She checked the caller ID. It read Brett. With a sigh, she connected the call.

"Hey, Jessica. What cha doin'?"

"Cooking dinner and waiting for my husband to come home." She made a point of referring to Murphy's imminent arrival. Ever since his relationship with his live-in girlfriend had ended, Brett seemed to be too close to her for comfort. She wasn't sure if it was her imagination or not. In either case, she decided to insert a reminder of her marital status whenever possible.

"Playing the happy homemaker, huh?"

"That's right. What's up, Brett?"

"Well, a group of us are going to blow off steam by going to that new Marvel movie that's releasing tonight. Wanna come?"

"Thanks, but I intend to blow off some steam myself with my husband." She let out a wicked laugh. "If you know what I mean."

Brett responded with his own chuckle. "Aw, sounds like you're going to have a more exciting evening than I am."

"I'm sure I will."

"I don't suppose you would care to take any pictures to show me what I'm missing?"

Jessica was struck speechless. When she found her voice, she said, "Excuse me?"

"You heard me."

"Murphy has arrived," Nigel's voice came through the speaker.

"Who was that?" Brett asked.

"Our butler. Goodbye, Brett." She disconnected the call. Her heartbeat quickening with anger at Brett, Jessica ran the brush through her hair one last time.

Determined not to allow him to ruin date night, she shoved his inappropriate comment out of her mind and focused on Murphy before hurrying down the stairs. She landed in the middle of the two-story foyer as he stepped through the door.

"Welcome home, darling!" She dropped her robe to the floor.

Murphy's eyes grew wide. His mouth dropped open.

"It's date night." She winked at him.

In her fantasy, she expected him to grab her up into his arms and ravage her—hopefully right there on the floor in the foyer. At the very least, she expected him to give her a hug and a kiss.

Instead, he stood before her with his hat in his hand—looking horribly guilty.

"Your CO called you," she said. "You have to go on a mission."

"Not exactly," he said while looking her up and down. "Kind of. Sort of."

Her hands landed on her bare hips. "What do you mean 'kind of, sort of'?"

He picked up the robe from the floor. "I'm not going out of town."

"Great." She grasped his belt and pulled him to her.

He wrapped the robe around her shoulders. "The good news is that we're going to have our date night."

She gazed up into his eyes. "And the bad news?" she asked in a breathy voice.

He looked her naked body up and down. "We're going to have to spend it fully dressed."

Her bottom lip stuck out in a pout.

"But we can still do 'what not' afterwards." He set his hat on the foyer table. "As a matter of fact, to make it up to you," he proceeded to unbutton his shirt "—I'd be willing to squeeze some 'what not' in beforehand if that's what it takes to put a smile to your face."

☙ ☙ ☙

Natalie Stepford's Kitchen Studio was easy to miss. The caterer's storefront was tucked in the back corner of a chic upscale business complex filled with woodsy boutique shops in the heart of Great Falls. In the year that Jessica and Murphy had lived in the area, neither of them had been aware of the caterer and cooking school only a few miles from their front door.

One could assume Jessica's lack of knowledge about the cooking school was due to her disinterest in learning how to cook beyond the basic skills. While she was a good cook, and even dabbled in some complex techniques, she had never been moved to take actual classes.

In silence, they observed the array of vehicles parked in front of the Kitchen Studio. They ranged from mid-sized economy cars to SUVs to expensive sports cars that rivaled Jessica's purple Ferrari. Murphy parked next to a Porsche SUV with a placard stuck on the side panel that read "Natalie Stepford's Kitchen Studio."

Jessica turned to Murphy. "You owe me an explanation."

"It'll be fun." Murphy focused his attention on a couple who appeared to be in their early twenties making their way up the walkway to the door. They held each other's hands tightly. He opened the door for her, and she kissed him before stepping inside.

"You're lying, Murphy."

He turned to her. "Jess—"

"I can always tell when you lie, Murphy," she said. "You do it rarely, but when you do, I can tell."

"I have never lied to you."

"Bull," she said with a scoff.

"When have I lied to you?"

"When you told me that you love my vegetarian lasagna."

Murphy looked straight ahead. "I do love—"

"You hate my lasagna."

"How did you know?"

"You can't look at me when you lie." She pointed out the front window. "You look out there. You look over my shoulder at the wall behind me. You look up at the sky." She pointed at her own eyes. "You don't look at me when you lie."

"This case is important, Jessie. I wouldn't do this if I didn't have to."

"Our marriage is supposed to be a top priority. That's why we have date night."

"Yes, our marriage is a top priority, but so is my military career. So is my loyalty to serving my—*our* country. You knew that going in."

"I'm as loyal to our country as you are," she said. "But I can't help you if I'm going in blind. If you need to give up our date night—which means *I* have to give up our date night because it takes two to make a date night—then I need to know what I'm giving it up for."

In silence, they watched a dark red Porsche convertible pull into a parking spot next to them. Dressed in a stylish business suit, a middle-aged woman slid out of the passenger seat and observed the purple Ferrari while stepping up onto the sidewalk. Upon noticing Murphy behind the wheel, a slow grin came to her lips. Her companion, a middle-aged man in a button-down shirt, hurried ahead of her to go inside.

"This has to do with Commander Caldwell's murder," Murphy told her in a low voice. "Shortly before he was killed, a friend had given him information about something going on at a private clinic. That's all he told me. He said that if it was what he suspected, it was something big. But we don't know who his friend was or what clinic they were talking about. It's been a month, and the case has gone cold." He pointed at the front door of the cooking school.

"What does a caterer have to do with a navy doctor's murder?"

"They'd been exchanging phone calls shortly before his murder," he said while climbing out of the car. After opening the passenger side door, he took her hand to help her out. "My job is to get close to her."

Jessica took note of his jeans and light sweater. "You changed out of your uniform to put her at ease. Good move." She stepped ahead of him to lead the way to the school entrance.

"Actually, I changed because I wanted to be comfortable."

He slowed his pace when he noticed a fire engine red sports car parked in the last space at the corner of the building. "That's the car."

"What car?"

Murphy ran to the other side of the parking lot to examine a shiny red Nissan 370Z sporting personalized Arizona license plates that read "SXKITTY."

"Sex kitty?" Jessica said. "It doesn't take a doctorate to tell you what this car owner is all about."

Murphy peered through the windows. "Ross Caldwell got into this car the night before he was killed. A blonde wearing a hat and dark sunglasses was driving it."

"Ross and Natalie were calling each other. He got into *this* car, which is now parked only a few feet from Natalie's boutique." With a flourish, Jessica gestured toward the sign for Natalie Stepford's Kitchen Studio. "One guess who that car belongs to."

He took her hand and led her to the door. "For Natalie's sake, I hope she lets me help her because someone is already watching her. Our cyber team picked up a tap on her cell phone and laptop and email."

"The killer?"

"Who else could it be?"

CHAPTER EIGHT

Six couples made up the class, which was set up in a spacious classroom behind Natalie Stepford's gourmet shop. The classroom consisted of six separate kitchen stations plus a main one at the front of the classroom. Each L-shaped station consisted of a sink, stovetop and wall oven and microwave. The small counter, which doubled as a desk, had two stools for the couple to sit at.

Like Murphy and Jessica, two of the other couples were professionals in their mid-twenties. A middle-aged couple took the station closest to the front of the classroom, directly across from Murphy and Jessica. While the rest of the students mingled, the husband of the middle-aged couple sat on his stool. His arms crossed, he stared straight ahead at the main kitchen as if he were waiting for the instructor to magically appear.

The instructor's kitchen included a camera and smart board set up on which she could record and project close-ups of her techniques for the students. With cameras, speakers, lights, and monitors, it resembled a small television studio.

"Pretty fancy," Jessica told Murphy. "This isn't what I was expecting at all."

"Natalie Stepford actually has her own online cooking show," Murphy said in a low voice. "She has a lot of followers."

The wife of the older couple scurried over to them and stuck out her hand to Jessica. "Hello, I'm Meaghan Garland." She thrust her card out to Murphy while pointing in the direction of her spouse. "That's my lesser half, Dr. Stan Garland. Do you live here in Great Falls?"

Murphy showed the business card, identifying Meaghan was a financial manager, to Jessica. It was apparent where their conversation would be heading.

"Yes," Jessica said. "We moved here a little less than a year ago—the Thorny Rose Manor."

"*You* own the Thorny Rose Manor." Meaghan's eyes grew wide. "You must be—"

"Jessica Faraday. This is my husband Murphy."

"Is your father—"

"Mac Faraday."

"Your dog, Gnarly, is the mayor of Spencer, Maryland!" the wife at the station next to Murphy and Jessica said with a squeal in her voice. "I love Gnarly! I'm his biggest fan!" She patted her husband's arm. "You remember Gnarly, dear. He saved the mother cat and her two hundred kittens from a burning building. They awarded him a fancy medal, and the town elected him mayor." She turned back to Jessica. "Can you get me an autographed picture of Gnarly? Please?"

Meaghan was more interested in who was managing Jessica's money than her father's German shepherd. "One of my clients is the real estate agent who handled the contract on your house. He told me that you were planning to convert it into a fully functioning smart house."

"My brother likes to try new things and has been using our house as a beta project," Jessica said.

"There's a big market for smart homes," Meaghan said. "If he needs help managing–"

"Our family has an attorney to manage our money," Jessica said.

"That's what they all say." Meaghan tapped the business card in Murphy's hand. "Doesn't hurt to keep your eyes open for new opportunities." She peered into his face. "Who did your dimples?"

Murphy shot a glance in Jessica's direction. Judging by the shake of her head, she was equally confused by the question.

"Excuse me?" he asked Meaghan.

"Your dimples. They are outstanding. Who did them?"

"Best cosmetic surgeon in the business." Murphy chuckled. "God."

"You were *born* with those?"

Jessica placed her hand on his. "My husband has been very blessed."

"Next thing you're going to tell me is that those aren't implants either," Meaghan said while looking directly at Jessica's abundant bosom.

"Darn tootin' they're real," Jessica said.

With a scoff, Meaghan returned to her husband's side.

The woman who had declared herself Gnarly's biggest fan hurried over to introduce herself as Peg and her husband Andy. "We just got married on Valentine's Day."

"We're taking this class because neither of us can cook," Andy said with a wide grin. "Natalie Stepford is the best." He winked at Murphy. "Have you seen her show online?"

"I haven't," Jessica said. "I think Murphy has. He signed us up for these classes."

"I've been a big fan for quite a while." Andy smiled like a child waiting to open the big present at his birthday party. "Learned a lot from her."

"Andy has learned some *fabulous* techniques," Peg told them with a giggle.

Natalie Stepford breezed in and strode down the center of the room. Long golden blond locks bounced past her shoulders.

Andy and Peg hurried back to their stations. Andy was practically drooling while watching her long legs swish by in her four-inch high heels.

"I have a feeling he's not watching her show to learn how to *cook*," Jessica whispered.

Murphy flicked his eyes in the direction of Dr. Stan Garland, who was equally transfixed on their instructor.

"Good evening. Welcome to the Kitchen Studio. I'm Natalie Stepford and I'll be teaching you how to grow together as a couple through the love of cooking." She took out her laptop and opened a three-ring binder. "I have five couples signed up for this class. We must have a late registration."

It took massive self-control for Jessica to not grab Murphy's arm to keep him by her side. He extracted an envelope from his breast pocket and stood up from his stool. "That would be my wife and me."

Natalie's attention was focused on a message she was reading on her phone when Murphy stepped up to the counter. He was careful to keep his back to the rest of the class. Her eyes narrowed to sapphire slits. "Excuse me." She picked up the phone. "Can you believe it? Some idiot has been texting and refuses to believe me when I tell him he's got the wrong number." Her plump lips pursed together as she stabbed out a message. "What part of 'I don't know you' are you having trouble understanding?" With a deep sigh, she turned off her phone, dropped it into her bag, and turned her attention to Murphy.

His eyes met hers as he held out the envelope to her.

Could she? Murphy stared into her face. He searched his memory of the blonde with whom Ross Caldwell had driven away the night before he died. *Could she, Natalie Stepford, be that blonde? She certainly looked like her. What information could she possibly have that would be so valuable that it would get Commander Caldwell killed?*

She extracted the check and registration form from the envelope. There was a note clipped to the top of the registration form.

My name is LT. Murphy Thornton with NCIS. Our investigation has uncovered that your phone, laptop, and email are being monitored by an unknown party. You are in danger. Do not tell anyone this information. I will hand you a secure phone. Call the number listed in contacts when you are alone to talk about keeping you safe.

Motionless, she read the note over and over again. The secure phone hidden in the palm of his hand, Murphy waited for her response. Finally, she ripped the note off the registration form and shoved it into her dress pocket. She then folded up the registration form and check and tucked them into a pocket in the three-ring binder.

"Well," she said in a sultry voice, "welcome to the class, Murphy." She stuck out her hand. He grasped it in both of his.

He could feel her hand trembling. He flashed her a reassuring grin and squeezed it to comfort her. "My wife and I are looking forward to it."

She quickly slipped the phone into the pocket with the note.

"Looks like your husband made a new friend," Peg whispered to Jessica.

"I'm so sorry I'm late, darling!" A silver-haired man breezed into the classroom and up to the desk like a star making a grand entrance. He paused to kiss Meaghan Garland on the cheek and slap her husband on the back on his way to the main cooking station. He swept behind the counter to kiss Natalie. "Hello, everyone. I'm Calvin, Natalie's husband. I'm her assistant for the couple's class."

Murphy mouthed to Jessica. "He's also her attorney."

Taking note of Calvin's arm around Natalie's waist, holding her close, Jessica whispered, "Good luck getting her alone to question her."

Murphy was too busy noting Andy's and Stan's fixated gazes on their teacher. He suspected they weren't taking the class to learn how to bake a cake.

CHAPTER NINE

"I really liked that vegan lasagna tonight," Jessica called out to Murphy from her dressing room while changing out of her clothes into an oversized navy t-shirt.

"So did I," Murphy replied from the bedroom.

"I'll download the recipe from Natalie's website and try it for you next week." She tossed her worn clothes down the laundry chute and turned around to pick out her clothes for the next morning. Searching through her dresses, she asked, "Did you pick up my red dress at the dry cleaners?"

"Was I supposed to?"

Giving up in her search, she stepped into the bedroom. Exhausted after the long day, Murphy had undressed and climbed into bed as soon as they had returned home.

With Spencer stretched out next to him, he was checking his phone for messages when she went up to the bed with her hands on her hips. "I told you to pick it up yesterday."

He stopped reading. Slowly, he turned his head and lifted his eyes to look at her. "When did I become your errand boy?"

"You drive right past there."

"So do you."

"I was planning to wear that dress to the special workshop tomorrow. Dr. Foster is partial to red and I'm hoping for a recommendation from him for a fellowship. You said you were going to help me."

"What about you helping me?"

"What do you think I spent all night doing? I gave up our date night to go watch Natalie, the Happy Stepford Wife, cook up edible foreplay in front of a bunch of horny men and their not too sharp wives. Did you even find out anything?"

"No. Her husband slash lawyer was sticking to Natalie like glue. I wouldn't be surprised if he was the one tapping her electronics. We just have to give her time. She'll cooperate."

"What makes you so sure?"

"Because she didn't know her electronics were being tracked."

"She could have thought you were lying to scare her into cooperating."

Murphy shook his head. "I saw the look in her eyes. Not only did she believe me, but she knew instantly who was doing it."

"It's her husband." Jessica climbed into bed and urged Spencer to move to the foot of it. "He's at least twenty years older than she is and insecure. He was sticking close to her to make sure every man in that class knew she was his property. To him, she's not his wife or partner. She's a possession."

"He also wanted to make sure she wasn't talking to the police about whatever it is she knows."

"Meaghan Garland introduced her husband as a doctor," Jessica said. "But she didn't specify what type of doctor."

Murphy chuckled. "Yes, she did, didn't she?"

"I thought maybe you were too busy checking out Natalie's boob job to notice."

Murphy sat up. "Will you stop it?"

Spencer jumped off the bed.

"Stop what?" Jessica asked.

"Do you really think I'm like Andy or Stan? Some horny guy who only sees women as sexual vessels made solely to please men? Maybe, if the guy's really lucky, he'll hook a woman like you, who's not only good in bed, but foolish enough to support him in the lifestyle he wants to become accustomed."

"That is not what I think of you."

"When you make comments like that, I wonder."

"So I'm supposed to monitor what I say in front of you so that I don't hurt your little feelings?"

Murphy threw back the blankets and climbed out of bed. Naked, he went into his closet and slammed the door.

"Where are you going?" she asked when he emerged fully dressed in his jeans, leather jacket, and boots.

"I'm going out for a ride on my bike." He grabbed his phone from the end table and went out the door.

Jessica checked the time on the clock. "It's half past ten at night."

"I know how to read time," he yelled on his way down the stairs.

જી જી જી

As angry as he was, Murphy couldn't push Jessica's notice that Stan Garland was a doctor out of his mind. Of what, Meaghan Garland had not mentioned, but it did appear to be a step in the right direction. Based on how Calvin Stepford had greeted the couple when he'd arrived at the class, the Stepfords knew them beforehand. That meant Dr. Garland may have been connected to the information Natalie offered to Commander Caldwell.

Mulling over the few details they had of the case, Murphy sat on his motorcycle in their garage. He stared at the screen of his phone—willing Natalie to call him. Their class had ended over an hour and a half earlier. Calvin and the Garlands were lingering behind to help Natalie clean up, which made it impossible for him to talk to her without raising suspicions.

"Nigel," he said into the phone, "I'd like a background check on a Dr. Stan Garland of Great Falls, Virginia."

"I have found a match for a Dr. Stan Garland in McLean, Virginia."

"Married to Meaghan Garland, financial manager?"

"That is correct," Nigel said. "He is the owner and chief of staff at the Garland Surgery and Laser Clinic." The home page for the private clinic splashed across the screen of Murphy's phone.

"Clinic," Murphy muttered to himself while studying the website.

"That's what I said," Nigel replied. "Surgery and laser clinic. He's a cosmetic surgeon."

"And Jessica claims Natalie had to have had work done," Murphy said to himself. "That would have given her access—"

"Do you need me to check our records for this Natalie lady? If so, I'll need a last name. There are several million people in my wide variety of databases with the name 'Natalie.'"

"No, Nigel." Murphy put on his helmet and pressed the button on the remote to open the garage door. "Plug the address for Dr. Garland's clinic into my bike's GPS." He stuck the phone's Bluetooth into his ear and tucked the phone into his jacket pocket.

ↄ ↄ ↄ

In silence, Jessica allowed her temper to simmer in anticipation of Murphy's return. Upon hearing the roar of his motorcycle racing out of the driveway, she cursed and turned off the light.

Be that way!

Curling up in the fetal position, she tried to make herself comfortable in the king-sized bed, which always seemed much too big when Murphy wasn't there.

She grew angrier with each toss and turn. By the time she heard the click of the back door shut downstairs and footsteps across the kitchen floor she was more than ready for round two. Throwing back the comforter and flailing into her bathrobe, she raced Spencer down the stairs and through the dining room to the kitchen.

"Where the hell have you been?" She turned on the light. "I've been worried sick!"

Her younger brother Tristan spit out the milk he was drinking from the carton and rushed to put the cap back on before putting it back in the fridge.

Jessica's sigh was filled with disappointment. "Tristan, what are you doing here?"

"What I'm always doing here?" He took a carton of ice cream out of the freezer. "Mooching."

Jessica often wondered where Tristan, with his tall lanky frame, put all the junk food that he seemed to eat unceasingly.

Tristan jerked his head in the general direction of the driveway and main road outside. "I guess Murphy got called out on a case. I passed him out in McLean. He was heading out while I was coming home." He took a bottle of chocolate syrup from the cupboard. He didn't notice her sad expression until he turned around. "Are you two kids having a fight?"

"Yeah," she mumbled.

"Do you need a hug?"

Her bottom lip stuck out. She nodded her head. Tristan pondered what to do with the food items he had gathered in his arms. Deciding to keep them in his grasp, he took her into an awkward embrace and patted her back with the chocolate syrup. "What did you do to him?"

Her eyes blazing, she shoved him away. "Why do you assume I did something to him?"

"Well, you aren't exactly the easiest person to live with."

She grabbed the carton of ice cream and chocolate syrup from him. "For that, you can buy your own ice cream."

"It's the truth." He grabbed them back. "If you can't trust me to tell you the truth, who can you trust?" He set the ice cream and syrup on the table. "What are you fighting about now?" He took two bowls out of the cupboard.

"He forgot to pick up my red dress from the dry cleaners." She plopped down at the table.

Tristan froze. His eyes grew wide behind his dark frame glasses. He dropped the bowls onto the table and covered his mouth with both hands. "No!" He staggered as if he had become weak in his knees. "He didn't? Not that?" He grasped her shoulders. "You poor, poor girl!" He snatched his cell phone from his pocket. "I'm calling Dad right now. We'll call the lawyer and get this marriage *annulled*." He waved toward the back staircase. "Better yet, we'll drag Murphy's stuff out into the front yard and set it all on fire in front of him when he gets home."

With a heavy sigh, Jessica rolled her eyes. "You think you're so funny." She grabbed the lid off the ice cream. "It wasn't about the dry cleaning."

"Obviously, the dry cleaning was a symptom of something else." He handed a spoon to her and proceeded to scoop the ice cream into the bowls.

"We're both under a lot of stress. Lately, it's like we're not communicating. We used to be so in sync. He'd zig, and I'd zag. Now he zigs and I zig and totally miss him when he zags in the opposite direction." With a sigh, she took the bowl Tristan offered to her.

"It's just a phase your marriage is going through. Every relationship goes through that. You're done with the Oh,-isn't-it-cool-that-you-love-ice-cream-as-much-as-I-do-phase. Now you're in the If-I-have-to-eat-one-more-takeout-pizza-for-dinner-I'm-gonna-throw-up-in-your-shoes-phase."

"As a doctorate student studying psychiatry, I feel like I shouldn't be having these issues," Jessica said. "I should be able to anticipate the problem and remedy it before it happens."

"You mean you don't think you and Murphy should be fighting?" Tristan peered at her out of the corner of his eye.

"Well…" Her voice trailed off.

"Mom and Dad didn't fight."

"Yes, they did," she said. "What did you call it when Mom got a new man and tossed Dad out on his ear?"

"Their marriage was dead and buried by the time Mom decided to trade up from Dad and they got divorced. Think back to when we were kids. Mom and Dad *never* fought."

"Or maybe they did fight, but not around us."

Tristan shook his head. "Dad would bend over backwards to give Mom whatever she wanted." He tapped the table with his spoon. "Studies have proven that couples who fight are closer. What it comes down to is that they care enough about each other and their relationship to fight. I think Dad didn't fight with Mom because deep down he didn't care about their marriage enough to fight for it. He cared more about being a brilliant detective."

Jessica lifted her eyes from the ice cream in her bowl and cocked her head at him. "Dad did love Mom."

"Not the way he loves Archie." Tristan told her between spoonfuls of ice cream. "His relationship with her is totally different. He loves Archie enough to fight with her. The last time I was home, they got into a huge argument because she booked that month-long river cruise through Europe. She says he cleared it first. He forgot about it because he was busy at the time with Gnarly stealing their neighbors' packages off their porches and hiding them in the garage."

"But Dad did agree to go on the cruise and when I talked to Archie this morning she said he was having a great time."

"Only because one of the passengers got poisoned in Paris and they're chasing the killer through Bordeaux." Tristan licked the spoon clean. "I hate to break the news to you, Sis, but our family is dysfunctional."

Sick with worry, Jessica shoved her bowl of ice cream aside. She had only eaten a few bites. "You don't think Murphy and I are in trouble, do you?"

"How should I know?" Tristan asked with a shrug of his shoulders. He slid his empty bowl aside and proceeded to finish hers.

"Has Murphy said anything to—"

"Guys don't talk about that stuff—especially to their wives' brothers."

"You said I wasn't easy to live with."

"Because I used to live with you. I know from personal experience—and that was before—" Tristan uttered a deep sigh.

A wave of panic washed over her. "Before I went back to school."

"This has nothing to do with school."

"Then what?"

Tristan turned serious. "I've been out to the pub with Murphy a few times."

Jessica swallowed. "And?"

"Murphy has a lot of pride. He has reason to be proud. It's not easy getting selected for the naval academy and he graduated at the top of his class. He was hand-picked to be a Phantom, part of this ultra-secret special ops by the Joint Chiefs of Staff. He's the best of the best of the best and he can't tell anybody."

"I know all that, Tristan. What are you trying to say?"

"Guys, not just guys, look at Murphy and they see one of thousands of military officers making a middle-class income doing their day-to-day job, serving their country. Only, unlike his peers, Murphy's an extremely good-looking guy married to a rich beautiful woman and living in her mansion in an upscale neighborhood."

Jessica sat up with a sense of realization.

"Half the guys envy Murphy for being able to pull it off," Tristan said. "The other half diss him for living off a beautiful woman. Because he's married to you, he has to work twice as hard to prove he's worthy of being your hus—"

"Anyone who knows Murphy knows he's not a gold-digger," Jessica said.

"In his head, he knows that," Tristan said. "But it's still hard when you're getting that attitude from your peers."

"Maybe that's what it looks like. But any grown up knows that when you look underneath the covers, things are never what they seem."

ભ ભ ભ

Garland Surgery and Laser Clinic was located in a four-story office building tucked away in a park-like setting just inside the Capital Beltway.

Late at night, Murphy expected to find the clinic closed for business. As he pulled into the lot, he noticed the motion detection security light was on, which illuminated a car parked along the side of the building.

Probably the security guard.

Murphy turned off the lights on his bike and rolled up along the side of the building—careful to avoid getting close enough to trip any motion sensors. As he drew closer, he saw a truck parked next to the car. Then, a car parked on the other side of the truck. Next to that was an SUV. The lot behind the building contained almost a dozen vehicles.

Even though the window blinds were pulled and shut, Murphy could see lights on inside many of the first-floor offices.

Looks like Garland Surgery and Laser is open for business.

Murphy sped the bike up to continue around the corner of the building and out of the parking lot. He then made a right turn and another right. Jumping the curb, he rode across the grass to a small picnic area provided for employees to enjoy their lunches on nice days. He found a spot behind a bush to hide the bike, took off his helmet, and placed it on the seat.

Avoiding the motion detectors, Murphy made his way back to the rear of the building. As he approached the edge of the lot, a car pulled in and raced around to the rear lot.

Murphy moved in closer. On his hands and knees, he crept in close to watch as a woman dressed in surgical scrubs ran out the supply entrance to meet the driver of the car.

"You're two hours late!" she shouted.

"They had to change course and land in Hagerstown. The feds were watching the airport in Leesburg."

Murphy saw the man in the car hand the woman a cooler.

"The donation is viable for only so long. Another few hours and you might as well have not bothered making the trip."

"Hey, don't bitch at me about it," the man said. "I already told Garland that Leesburg, and Hagerstown for that matter, are getting too hot with feds watching for drug shipments. We need to find a private airstrip close by to slip in and out without getting unwanted attention."

With a "humph," the woman ran inside with the cooler. With a shake of his head, the driver climbed back into the car and drove off.

Mulling over the conversation he'd overheard, Murphy backed up behind the SUV. His phone vibrated on his hip. Grabbing the phone from the case, he read the caller ID.

The caller ID read, "Natalie."

ᑳ ᑳ ᑳ

In a French country style farmhouse in Chester, West Virginia, Joshua Thornton Jr. tossed and turned in his bed.

In the foggy world of his subconscious mind, he was riding a motorcycle down a dark winding road. The roar of an engine caught his attention as another bike and rider pulled up next to him. They were identical to him and his motorcycle. Rearing his bike up on its back wheel, his twin raced ahead of him.

Far ahead, the fog cleared enough for J.J. to see the back of a white van. Afraid that his twin was going to crash, he screeched his bike to a halt.

"Murphy! No!" he shouted as his identical twin raced through the van.

They both disappeared.

Gunning the engine on the bike, J.J. went after him only to fall into a deep hole—falling—falling—falling—all the while screaming out his twin brother's name—

"Murphy!"

With a scream, J.J. Thornton sprang up in his bed.

Chapter Ten

Tristan Faraday's artic blue Camaro convertible spun around the sharp curve leading down the wooded road. Upon seeing the emergency flares, he tapped the brakes and rolled to a halt. He lowered his window and the state police officer shone a flashlight into the car's front compartment.

In the passenger seat, Jessica Faraday's breath quickened when she saw the black sports motorcycle parked off to the side of the road.

"I'm Tristan Faraday. That motorcycle belongs to my brother-in-law."

The officer instructed them to park in a small gravel lot next to a fast-moving creek.

"He's okay." Tristan peered at the motorcycle as he drove past. "It's not wrecked. He wasn't in an accident. Maybe it broke down and he got a ride."

"He's only two miles from our house," Jessica said. "He could have walked home by now."

Without waiting for Tristan to turn off the engine, Jessica scrambled from the car and ran to where Boris Hamilton was briefing a group of younger agents.

"Boris! What's happened? Where's Murphy?"

Boris took her into a hug. "We're doing everything we can. I called out my team as soon as we got the message from the police about his motorcycle being abandoned. What time did he leave the house?"

"It was around ten-thirty," Jessica said while staring at the motorcycle parked at the edge of the road. The kickstand was down, and Murphy's helmet rested on the seat. "We had a fight. He said he was going for a ride to get some fresh air."

Tristan approached the investigator examining the bike for evidence.

"Did Murphy say where he was going when he left?" Boris asked her.

"No." Jessica leveled her gaze on him. "We took a class at Natalie Stepford's cooking school tonight. He told me about her being connected to the murder of Commander Caldwell."

"Did he make contact with Stepford?" Boris asked.

Jessica nodded her head.

"Did you see anything suspicious? Did anyone seem particularly interested when Murphy spoke to her?"

"Only every man in that class," she said with a sigh. "Have you seen that woman?"

Boris chuckled.

"I hated her at first sight. Perfect hair. Perfect nose. Perfect figure. Perfect cooking skills. I'll bet she never burns anything on the stove." Realizing she was grumbling, she allowed her voice to trail off.

"Chief!" Special Agent Susan Archer called to them. "You're going to want to see this."

Before Boris could stop her, Jessica ran to where Tristan was squatting next to an evidence marker. Instantly, Jessica recognized the reddish-brown stain in the middle of the road.

As she let out a shriek, Tristan jumped to his feet and took her into a hug. "We'll find him, Sis. Don't worry. We'll find Murphy and bring him home."

Another investigator handed a cell phone encased in an evidence bag to Boris. "It's Thornton's phone, sir. We found it in the shrubs on the other side of the road."

"No!" Jessica let out a gut-wrenching cry. "Murphy!"

"We're going to find him, Jessie," Tristan whispered into her hair. "Come see this, Hamilton. I think we found something."

Before Boris could stop her, Jessica followed Tristan to where he had been squatting next to the motorcycle. He had unhooked a wire and plugged it into his own phone.

On the opposite side of the bike, Special Agent Perry Latimore was shaking his head. "Hamilton, I told him not to touch the bike, but he just went ahead—"

"I've plugged my phone into Murphy's GPS to find out where he went after leaving the house. You want to find him ASAP, don't you? I set up a sophisticated program specifically for him." Tristan winked at Jessica—sending a silent message that he was disabling Nigel's program on the bike. The last thing they wanted was for NCIS's forensics team to inadvertently discover the classified Phantom program.

"Chief, he's tampering with evidence," Perry said.

"I'll take responsibility for it, Latimore."

"He went to a medical office park on Chain Bridge Road in McLean." Tristan read the specific address to Boris off the phone. "That was shortly after eleven o'clock last evening. He left there at seventeen minutes after eleven and came back to Great Falls."

"He must have been coming home," Jessica said.

Tristan shook his head. "The bike then stopped at Walker Road."

"There's a pub there." With a wink and a smirk, Perry said, "Maybe he was meeting a friend."

"Natalie Stepford's Kitchen Studio is in the same plaza," Jessica said. "Murphy gave her a secure phone this evening to contact him."

"He must have gone to meet her," Boris said.

"Twenty-five minutes after he arrived there, he left, heading this way," Tristan reported. "Then the bike was powered off—and so was the GPS."

"He pulled over and turned off the bike two miles from our house," Jessica said.

Boris looked at the dark trees and road around them. There were no homes in sight. "Why?"

❧ ❧ ❧

Jessica insisted on her and Tristan following Boris and his team to the last place that Murphy had been before disappearing. Possibly, they would discover some clues that would tell them what had happened to him.

"There's something we need to keep in mind," Tristan told Jessica while they followed Boris's SUV to the other side of Great Falls.

"That Murphy's a Phantom. Therefore, he can take care of himself."

"True," Tristan said. "Also, that GPS is attached to Murphy's motorcycle. That tells us where his *bike* has been. For all we know, he disappeared in McLean and his bike was dumped here in Great Falls."

"What was he doing in McLean?"

Tristan turned the Camaro into the business complex. "That location is a medical office park."

"Murphy is investigating the murder of a navy doctor. We met a doctor at the cooking class this evening. His last name was Garland."

In the middle of the night, the business park's lot was practically empty, which made the red sports car with the

99

Arizona license plate reading "SXKITTY" stand out. Natalie's Porsche SUV was still parked in front of her studio.

Jessica was out of the car as soon as Tristan brought it to a halt. Boris held out both hands to stop her from following him into the Kitchen Studio. The lights in the back offices of the business glowed from inside.

"You need to stay out here, Jessica," Boris said while waving for Perry Latimore and Susan Archer to go around to the rear door to check inside.

"I forgot to tell you that Murphy and I met a Dr. Garland last night at Natalie Stepford's cooking class

"There's a Garland Surgery and Laser Clinic at the address that Murphy went to in McLean," Tristan called out from behind the wheel of his car. He had checked the address on his phone.

"Okay, we'll check that out, but first we need to see if we can find out what Murphy was doing here, which was the last place he'd been before going missing." With his hand firmly holding her by the elbow, Boris ushered Jessica back toward Tristan's car.

"Sir!" Susan Archer ran around the corner of the building. "You're going to want to see this."

"Is it Murphy?" Ignoring Boris's order, Jessica ran past Susan to find the rear door that she had left open. Perry caught her in his arms but was only able to hold her for an instant before she elbowed him in the ribs and sprinted into the kitchen classroom.

As soon as she saw the blood that splattered on the walls, she stopped and covered her mouth to control the scream spilling from her lips. Terror made her want to turn away. Hope that it was not Murphy's blood forced her to look again.

Abruptly, she was aware of Tristan lifting her up off her feet and carrying her outside. "It's not Murphy, Jessie. It's okay. It's not Murphy," he said over and over again while holding her tightly.

"It's Natalie Stepford," Susan Archer told Boris. "Whoever killed her made mincemeat out of her face."

CHAPTER ELEVEN

The Russell Ridge Farm and Orchard

Along a rugged country road tucked between the rolling hills in West Virginia, a simple "Welcome to Pennsylvania" sign was nailed to the top of a fence post. Two miles before that sign, travelers might notice a long-paved driveway and a white four-rail fencing that seemed out of place on the worn country road. A white sign with black block letters informed visitors that they'd arrived at the Russell Ridge Farm and Orchard. The driveway ended at a long white equestrian barn with black trim. The main house was a matching two-story French country-style home with floral gardens and an indoor swimming pool behind it.

The sun had just started to peep over the hilltops to shine on the horse pastures when Joshua Thornton turned his SUV onto the lane. "Your mom is going to pick you up after work tonight."

In the passenger seat, Izzy, his fourteen-year-old daughter, nodded her head—causing her ash blond curls to bounce.

"You'll call to tell us as soon as you hear anything about Murphy, right?"

"Of course." Joshua flashed her a reassuring grin even if he didn't quite feel it. "Your brother is fine." Seeing J.J. sitting on the front porch of his house, he quickly added. "Don't say anything to J.J. Let me tell him."

Izzy was too focused on the creature at J.J.'s feet to hear him. It was a small white fluffy animal with hooves. "It's a lamb!"

Joshua had barely brought the SUV to a complete halt before Izzy was out the door. She ran to the porch where J.J. was feeding the little lamb between his knees. A blanket draped over his back, the little creature was hungrily sucking on a baby bottle that J.J. held for him.

"What's his name?" Izzy took the bottle from J.J. to take over feeding the baby.

"Ollie," J.J. said. "Short for Oliver, as in Charles Dickens's *Oliver Twist*. His mom died while giving birth to him last night. The farmer was going to kill him because he couldn't care for him, but his wife called Poppy and asked her to save him."

"Of course, Poppy said yes," Joshua said while petting a number of dogs who had gathered around him to be greeted.

The farm had a half dozen mixed breed dogs who helped to protect and herd the horses and cattle. It also had several chickens ruled by a huge white rooster named Charley, who was more territorial than all the dogs put together.

While J.J. and Izzy tended to the newcomer, Charley watched from the porch swing—blinking his beady eyes and cocking his head back and forth. The rooster had yet to decide whether to welcome the addition or not.

"He's less than a day old?" Izzy took a second bottle from J.J. to resume feeding. The lamb was so anxious to continue feeding that he stepped on the corner of the blanket and pulled it off.

"Less than twelve hours old." J.J. draped the baby blanket over Ollie. "He has to be fed every two hours and kept warm."

"Does that mean your farm is now taking on sheep?" Joshua asked.

"Ask Poppy." J.J. looked beyond his father to the barn where Poppy Ashburn, the horse trainer, was leading an appaloosa gelding into the barn.

Joshua took note of the soft longing look in his son's eyes as he admired the redhead clad in jeans and riding boots. "It's your farm, son."

"They couldn't let Ollie die, Dad," Izzy said.

Seeing that Ollie had finished feeding, Joshua suggested that Izzy carry the lamb back to Poppy at the barn. Once she was out of earshot, Joshua took her seat on the top step next to his son.

"Something's happened to Murphy," J.J. said.

"Have you talked to Jessie?"

J.J. shook his head. "I feel it. I had a horrible nightmare last night. Woke up around twelve-thirty and haven't been able to go back to sleep." He turned to him. "He's in trouble, Dad."

"Tell me he's alive."

J.J. nodded his head. "But he needs our help."

"I'm going to Washington to help look for him. Do—"

J.J. leaned back on the step, reached behind the railing, and extracted a suitcase that he placed there hours before. "I'm all packed and ready to go. Poppy'll take care of the farm until I get back."

☙ ☙ ☙

"Nice looking place."

In Great Falls, Boris Hamilton stepped back to the edge of the front stoop of the upper-class home and peered up at the blue trim on the stone sided home. The mansion was on a corner lot of an upscale development located near the border of Sterling.

Calvin Stepford's blue BMW was parked in the driveway. They had found Natalie's Porsche SUV parked in front of her store.

"He's home," Boris said.

Susan Archer pressed the doorbell a third time.

"No sign of him in the back. They have a nice pool and spa." Perry Latimore rounded the corner from where he had gone around the house in search of Natalie's husband.

"Maybe—" Susan stopped when she heard a thump from inside the house. She peered through the window to see Calvin Stepford stumble down the stairs in the foyer and crash into the window that she was peering through. "Looks like someone had a rough night."

After fumbling with the lock, Calvin Stepford, wearing only his underwear, yanked open the door. "What's going on? What are you people doing here?" He turned around to yell into the house. "Natalie! Why didn't you answer the door?"

"Mr. Stepford," Boris interrupted him, "I'm sorry to disturb you."

Calvin squinted at them. "Not as sorry as you will be." He staggered into the house. "Natalie! Where the hell are you? Can you turn on the coffee? I have a blazing headache."

Boris and his team followed him into the kitchen where Calvin stopped in the middle of the floor and pressed both hands against the side of his head. "Damn! Have you ever gotten a migraine? My head is pounding."

"Mr. Stepford," Boris said gently, "I'm sorry to disturb you, but when was the last time you saw your wife?"

"Why are you asking? What's going on?"

"Just answer my question," Boris said. "When was the last time you saw your wife?"

"Last night, when we went to bed," Calvin said. "She…" He looked at each one of them. "She must have gotten up early to go to—Natalie! Sweetie! Baby doll!" He ran for the staircase to take him up to the bedroom, but Boris blocked him.

Calvin grabbed the special agent. "Where's my wife?"

"How did your wife seem when you saw her last? Was she anxious? Did anything strange or out of the ordinary happen? Did she say anything to you?"

"No. Nothing. Natalie had a cooking class at her studio last night. It was a couple's class. I assisted. After the class was over, I helped her clean up. We came home. Had a glass of wine and went to bed. Slept all night until you woke me up just now." He checked the time on a clock on the wall. It was six thirty. "Where is she? What's happened to her?"

"She was found at her studio a little while ago." Boris held him by the arms. "I'm sorry, Mr. Stepford, but your wife is dead."

With a wail, Calvin Stepford dropped to his knees and clutched his chest.

"Mr. Stepford, are you okay?"

With a shake of his head, Calvin Stepford grasped Boris's arm. "I think – heart —" he gasped out before losing consciousness.

❧ ❧ ❧

"Dad just talked to Josh," Tristan reported to Jessica while grabbing both sides of his car seat as she made a sharp right into the gravel parking lot. After she screeched her Ferrari to a stop, he resumed reading the text. "Josh and J.J. are on their way out and Josh says the Phantoms will be helping to find Murphy. Would you like Dad to come home?"

"Nah." Jessica jumped out of the car and trotted to the road, which had been reopened to traffic after NCIS had finished collecting all the evidence they could find. "Between Josh, J.J., and the Phantoms, and us, we'll bring him home."

Tristan scratched Spencer's snout. The shelty had been riding in his lap during the harrowing ride. "I'm not supposed to tell you this, Spencer, but Gnarly has been having a spring-time fling with a French poodle during their trip in Paris."

Spencer whined upon hearing the news that her favorite German shepherd was involved with a pampered Parisian canine.

"I agree. Gnarly can be such a hound sometimes."

"Tristan, stop playing with Spencer and come here!"

"Coming, Sis." Tristan sighed. "I guess being bossy isn't something big sisters outgrow." As he climbed out of the car, he told Spencer, "Keep my seat warm, will you?"

Standing at the edge of the busy curved two-lane road, Jessica was staring at the spot where they had found a pool of Murphy's blood as if she could telepathically learn how it got there.

"What do you need, Sis?" Tristan squeezed her shoulder.

"You're Murphy."

Unsure of where she was leading, he nodded his head. "Okay. I'm Murphy."

"And you love your souped-up motorcycle—his manly toy that he bought himself as a present after graduating from the naval academy."

"I love my bike," Tristan said with a nod of his head.

"Why would you park that bike you love so much there—" She pointed to the edge of the busy road. "—on a hairpin curve instead of parking in the lot out of traffic?"

Tristan looked from the spot along the road where Murphy's bike had been found to the gravel parking lot. NCIS had taken the motorcycle in to examine for evidence. "Only because I can't."

"Exactly." Jessica pointed to the ground at her feet.

Tristan squatted to study the gravel in which there was a deep rut made by what appeared to be a vehicle that had backed off the road or possibly making a U-turn—blocking traffic. "This tire mark could have happened any time, Jessica. It could even have been left by one of Hamilton's team."

"Maybe," Jessica said. "I don't think Murphy disappeared by accident."

"Could his CO have sent him off on a mission and he—"

Jessica shook her head. "They don't operate that way. Yes, he could have been sent away on short notice. Happens all the time. Once he had to leave with less than an hour's notice, but he still let me know. They're sensitive about putting the family through unnecessary heartache."

Tristan rose to his feet. "Suppose someone blocked the road to force Murphy to stop his bike—" He shook his head. "I can't see Murphy stopping his bike. If he saw a threat, he can turn that bike around on a dime and head in the other direction."

"He'd only stop if he came upon a scene that he didn't see as a threat."

"Like a car broken down or an accident—blocking the road."

"Murphy would stop to help," she said. "They got the jump on him."

"Disarmed him and tossed his phone so that he couldn't be tracked."

"But who?" Envisioning the scene in her mind, Jessica blinked the tears from her eyes.

"Jessie," he said gently, "there's something we do need to consider."

"Someone from one of his missions—"

"You're a rich woman."

Gasping, Jessica backed away from him. "You mean this is all my fault?"

"No!" He grabbed her by the arms. "No matter what happens, it's not your fault."

"If someone grabbed Murphy and is holding him for ransom to get money from me—"

"It was their evil decision to do it. Not yours." He wrapped his arms around her. "We're going to find him, Sis." He rocked her in his arms. "The best thing we can do for Murphy right now is go home and wait for his dad to get here."

Chapter Twelve

It took all of Joshua Thornton's willpower to wait until he was racing down the Pennsylvania Turnpike before calling Boris Hamilton to ask for the status in their search for Murphy.

"Will all due respect, Captain Thornton," Boris said, "I cannot comment on an open investigation."

"I'm not the media," Joshua said. "I was told that a witness who Murphy had been trying to make contact with has been murdered and you have reason to believe Murphy had been there."

"We don't know if he was there at the time of the murder. According to his motorcycle's GPS, that was the last place it had been before it was abandoned."

"Have you found any indication that the bike had been driven by anybody other than Murphy?" J.J. asked.

"Who's that?" Hamilton asked.

"That's J.J.," Joshua said. "Murphy's brother. He's coming out to help us look for him."

"He sounds just like Murphy," Boris said with a chuckle. "Spooked me there for a minute. I didn't know what was going on."

Joshua looked across the front of his SUV at J.J. Being their father, he would often forget how much Murphy and J.J. were truly mirrors of each other. J.J.'s heart, liver, and spleen were on the opposite side of his body to mirror Murphy's organs—an even rarer trait of identical twins. As their father, Joshua had practically no problem telling them apart even when they had been babies. The birthmark on opposing hips had been a big help.

As they had grown up into men, they had stepped out of each other's shadows to forge their own separate identities. While in college, J.J. had adopted the casual manner of a student, pre-law professor, and now a gentleman farmer. He had allowed his hair to grow into layers down to his collar. The military officer, Murphy's hair was short, and he had the regal posture and bearing that comes with a military lifestyle.

"Do you have any suspects in this witness's murder?" Joshua asked Boris.

"Not yet. Natalie Stepford's husband is in the hospital. He had a heart attack when I gave him the news."

"Does anyone know about Murphy being missing? I'm talking about your suspects in the Stepford case."

Boris paused. "So far, only our team and law enforcement know. I ordered Jessica to stay home and wait in case there's a ransom demand. I don't know if she's doing it though. She's as bull-headed as your son."

"Then your suspects in Natalie's murder wouldn't know about his disappearance unless he or she had something to do with it. Right?"

"What are you thinking, Captain?"

Joshua looked over at J.J., who was looking questioningly back at him. "You're going to need a haircut."

ও ও ও

"Jessica, a watched cell phone doesn't ring." Tristan tried to lighten the mood in the living room back at the Thorny Rose Manor.

Several hours had passed and still no one had seen or heard from Murphy. His commanding officer had called to assure Jessica that his Phantom team mates were out searching for him. Even Nigel was searching the Internet for some email or social media chatter to indicate that some foreign enemy had snatched Murphy.

All was silent.

Jessica felt like a toy top that was wound up so tight that her spring was about to break. When her cell phone did ring, she felt her feet leave the ground. A shriek escaped her lips while she fumbled with the phone to read the caller ID.

Carol.

"Ugh!"

"Who is it?" Tristan asked.

"A friend." Jessica put the phone to her ear. "Hi, Carol, I can't really talk—"

"Are you on your way?"

"On my way where?"

"Dr. Foster's workshop," Carol said. "We're all waiting at my place to carpool to Baltimore."

Burying her face in her hand, Jessica collapsed onto the sofa. "I forgot."

"How could you forget? You've got a fellowship riding on this workshop. Otherwise, you'll be nothing more to Dr. Foster than another name on a list of applicants."

Jessica felt a sob escape from her lips. "I'm sorry, Carol. We've got a family emergency here."

"What's happened?"

"Murphy's missing."

Tristan jumped out of his seat. "Jessica, have you lost your mind? We don't want to spread that around."

At the same time, Carol replied, "Missing? What do you mean Murphy is missing?"

"We think he's been abducted—maybe for ransom," Jessica blurted out. In the background, she heard members of her study group pelting Carol with questions.

"Has anyone made any ransom demands?" Carol asked.

"No," Jessica said miserably before Tristan grabbed the phone out of her hand.

"Carol? This is Jessica's brother. Listen, the police are investigating Murphy's disappearance, but it's really very, very important that you not tell anyone about this. Murphy's life may depend on it."

"Oh, I understand." Carol's voice shook. "Mum's the word then." With a wish for their and Murphy's well-being, she disconnected the call.

"I'm sorry." Jessica rubbed her face and tired eyes with both hands. "I know better than that. I don't know what I was thinking."

Rubbing her back, Tristan sat next to her. Spencer jumped up to press against her on the other side. Jessica pulled the dog close and buried her face in her blue fur.

Chapter Thirteen

Upon reaching the stream crossing Georgetown Pike in Great Falls, Joshua Thornton turned his SUV into the gravel lot and parked.

"Shouldn't we check to see what evidence they've collected before we go over the scene again?" J.J. asked.

"The most critical time in a missing person's case is the first twelve to twenty-four hours." Joshua unbuckled his seat belt. "Murphy's been missing ten." He slid out of the driver's seat. "I'm most interested in finding one particular item."

Referring to the cell phone pictures that Tristan had sent to him from the crime scene that morning, he made his way to the side of the road. "This is where they found Murphy's bike. It was parked off the side of the road."

Being careful of the steady flow of traffic racing along the twisting main road, J.J. stepped over to the bridge that crossed the fast-moving stream. "The road must have been blocked so that he couldn't make it into the lot."

"That's the general consensus." Joshua took note of the taped outline in the middle of the road that marked a dark brownish stain—Murphy's blood. It was a large stain. *He'd lost a lot of blood. But not enough to kill him. Still. My son is hurt. Badly. I have to find him. Soon.*

"What are you looking for, Dad?"

Joshua was startled. He looked up. Seeing Murphy's face looking back at him—hearing what sounded so much like his voice—he stared until he realized that it was J.J., his hair freshly cut in a military style to make him truly identical to his twin.

"You said you were looking for something in particular," J.J. said. "What is it?"

Joshua swallowed. "That's right." He reached into the inside pocket of his jacket and removed a black cell phone. "This is a heavily encrypted cell phone given out only to Phantoms. It is specially configured so that if it's turned off, it can be remotely turned on via satellite and then the agent can be tracked via GPS."

"Great," J.J. said.

"But Nigel hasn't been able to turn it on."

J.J.'s heart sank. "Which means he's out there without a lifeline."

"It must have been damaged when they took Murphy, or got destroyed when they tossed it." Joshua picked up a rock from the ground.

"But what's the point if Nigel hasn't been able to turn the phone on?"

"Even if it's damaged, we have to find it," Joshua said. "It's got extremely sensitive information on it. Phantom contacts. Maps. GPS data for missions that Murphy's been on. The data's still on it and someone who is not friendly to us and who knows how to—"

J.J. held up his hands. "I get the picture."

"Let's say they found the phone, but didn't know what it was and tossed it." Joshua tossed the rock as far and as hard as he could. It bounced on the opposing hillside and rolled down into the stream.

"If it landed in the water, it would have been washed downstream and gotten water damaged." J.J. jogged across the parking lot and down to the water's edge. "That would explain why it can't be turned on."

While his son searched for the phone in the stream, Joshua went to the SUV and reached into his valise in the back to extract a plastic bag. He had closed the door just as J.J. called out, "Found it!"

After climbing back up to the lot, J.J. shook the water off the phone and dropped it into the open bag. "Even if they can repair it, it's not going to do Murphy any good."

"Murphy keeps this phone tucked away in the inside pocket of his jacket," Joshua said. "The fact that they found it means they searched him."

"That doesn't necessarily mean they're enemies of the state," J.J. said. "Murphy dresses nice, drives an expensive bike, lives in an uptown area. They could have been common thugs looking to rob him."

"If they were common thugs, they wouldn't have gotten the better of Murphy. He's got an umpteenth degree in mixed martial arts and carries two weapons on him at any given time. There could have been six of them and they wouldn't have been able to take him down."

"With all due respect to Murphy, you, and the Phantoms," J.J. said, "didn't one of America's top snipers get gunned down by a basic nobody?"

"Son, I don't even want to go there," Joshua said.

"I know, Dad. But, given the choice, I would prefer that Murphy be in the hands of a nobody who just got a lucky leg up in snatching him than a highly trained foreign assassin intent on torturing him for government secrets."

ℰℐ ℰℐ ℰℐ

"Captain Thornton is entering through the front gate," Nigel announced.

"There's going to be hell to pay when Josh catches up with whoever took Murphy," Tristan said with a chuckle.

"It'll be worse if I catch up to him first." Jessica hurried through the foyer to meet her father- and brother-in-law as they pulled up in front of the house. As soon as she opened the door, Spencer launched herself outside like a rocket taking off and leapt from the top step to land in Joshua's arms.

With Spencer squirming between them, Joshua took Jessica into a warm hug and held her while she sobbed briefly into Spencer's fur.

"Have you heard anything?" J.J. asked Tristan, who shook his head in response.

Pulling away, Jessica turned around and stopped upon seeing J.J. with his freshly cut hair. "Murph—" She swallowed.

"Sorry to scare you." J.J. gave her a hug. "Dad has a plan."

"Oh, you got your hair cut," Tristan said.

"Really sharp, Tristan." Joshua slapped him on the back before opening the SUV's rear door to unload their bags.

"Now I won't be able to tell them apart when Murphy comes home," Tristan said in a low voice.

"I don't know why," J.J. said with a grin. "I've never had trouble telling the two of us apart."

Tristan's phone buzzed to indicate a message. "Boris Hamilton and Susan Archer are here." He pressed the phone's remote button to open the gate and helped J.J. to carry their luggage inside.

Before J.J. could step inside, Joshua grabbed his arm and whispered to him. With a nod of his head, J.J. glanced up the driveway before slinging his duffle bag across his shoulders and stepping inside.

Jessica was waiting on the porch's bottom step when Boris Hamilton pulled up behind Joshua's SUV.

Susan climbed out and took her into a hug. "Jessica, how are you holding up?"

In an upbeat tone, Joshua replied before Jessica could answer. "Much better than she was doing."

Abruptly, the door flew open and J.J. rushed down the step. "Hey, gang! It is so good to see you! I am so sorry for all the trouble I caused—especially for my buttercup." He grabbed Jessica and gave her a quick kiss on the lips.

Susan's mouth dropped open. "Murphy? Where have you been?"

"Bike broke down," J.J. said while hugging Jessica. "I hitched a ride."

"And you didn't go home?" Susan asked.

"I was still mad at Jessie. So I hitched a ride to a pub. Just got home a bit ago. It never occurred to me that Buttercup would be calling out the cavalry. When I saw how upset I made my buttercup—" He grinned. "I'll be making it up to her later." He winked at them.

Susan glanced at Boris whose lips curled upward. He arched an eyebrow. "Pretty good."

"Needs some work," Joshua said.

"Over the top?" J.J. released Jessica.

"Just a little."

"Wait a minute You mean you're not..." Susan glanced back at Boris. "He's Murphy's brother? That's right. Murphy told me he had a twin. I didn't know you were identical. Boris, you knew right away?"

"As soon as he kissed Jessica," Boris said with a laugh.

Joshua was nodding his head.

"Murphy would have kissed her," J.J. said.

"Yes, he would have," Joshua said. "It was *how* you kissed her that was wrong. You kissed her like she was your sister." He went inside.

"But she is my sister."

"I hate to say it, J.J.," Jessica said in a low voice, "but Murphy is a much better kisser than you are."

"And you kiss like a dead fish."

"I'm not going to ask when and why you've been kissing dead fish."

"It's a long story, and you had to be there."

⁀⁄ ⁀⁄ ⁀⁄

"Did you uncover any evidence from Murphy's bike?" Joshua asked Boris for an update as soon as they had gathered together in the living room.

"Nothing," Boris said. "We found only his fingerprints. Nothing mechanically wrong with it. No signs of collision or tampering. He had to have pulled over for some reason and turned the bike off."

"And set his helmet on the seat," Tristan pointed out. "It wasn't tossed or dropped, which indicates a lack of urgency when he stopped."

"Even so, that gravel lot was only a few yards away," Jessica said, "but Murphy parked along the side of the road. He wouldn't have parked there unless the lot was inaccessible."

"Sounds like a set up all right." Joshua turned to Boris. "Have you looked at any of Murphy's cases with NCIS?"

Boris shook his head. "Still looking, but I doubt if there's a connection. Murphy's only the military liaison. He hasn't been on the front lines in any cases. If he was snatched by someone with a grudge against him, then it's got to be connected to a military operation his commanding officer had sent him out on."

"Tell me about this case that Murphy was working on yesterday—the one involving a cook," Joshua asked.

Boris corrected him. "Caterer."

"Cooking instructor," Jessica said. "We went to her couple's class last night."

"What time was the murder?" Joshua asked.

"Between one and two o'clock in the morning," Boris said. "She died of head trauma. She was beaten about the head and face with an aluminum meat mallet."

"Weapon of opportunity," Jessica said.

"It was clearly a crime of passion," Susan said. "Every bone in her face was broken."

"We found the weapon at the scene," Boris said. "The killer sterilized it by running it through the dishwasher."

"The dishwasher was still warm when we found the body," Susan said. "We determined it was the murder weapon because of the clear checkered pattern left on the victim's skull."

"And the GPS on Murphy's bike indicates he had been at the crime scene," Joshua said. "Was he there before or after the murder?"

"Before," Tristan said. "According to the bike's GPS system, he left the Kitchen Studio at twelve minutes after midnight."

"That's over forty-five minutes before the window of time when the murder was committed," Boris said. "Plus, we found no evidence to indicate that Murphy had been at the crime scene during or after the murder."

"If he had been, he would have secured it and contacted us," Susan said. "That's what he did when he found Commander Caldwell's body."

"Unless he went after the killer," J.J. said, "and didn't get a chance to notify anyone."

"But the GPS says he left the Kitchen Studio way before the murder happened," Jessica said.

"Assuming he saw Natalie Stepford," Boris said, "she could have given Murphy information that would have been damaging to the killer."

"In which case," Joshua said, "if the murderer was hanging around, he could have been the one chasing Murphy instead of the other way around."

"Were you able to uncover anything from Murphy's cell phone?" Tristan asked.

"Just a call from the encrypted phone he passed on to Natalie Stepford," Boris said.

"We suspect Natalie had information about something happening at a private clinic," Susan said. "Caldwell had contacted an investigator at the department of health and human services. According to his phone records, he talked to Natalie both before and after he talked to the investigator."

"The day that Caldwell was supposed to meet with the investigator, he ended up dead and the investigator is still missing," Boris said.

"How is a cooking instructor or caterer connected to dirty dealings at some private clinic?" Tristan asked.

"What kind of private clinic are you talking about?" J.J. asked. "Drug dealings at a rehab clinic?"

"I'm thinking a plastic surgery clinic," Jessica said. "There was a plastic surgeon in our cooking class. Dr. Stan Garland. According to the GPS on Murphy's bike, he went there last night before he went to Natalie's studio."

"Dr. Garland could have been Natalie's doctor," Susan said. "The medical examiner's report indicates that Natalie Stepford was half plastic. She had practically every type of cosmetic surgery known to man. Breast implants. Liposuction. Nose job. Lip and cheek implants. Face lift."

"Plastic and implants weren't the only thing the medical examiner found in Natalie Stepford's body," Boris said. "He also found a GPS chip in her forearm."

Joshua shook his head as if to determine if he heard Boris correctly. "A GPS chip? Do you mean a chip to track the victim's location by satellite?"

"That's how GPS chips work," Boris said. "This was medical grade. There are medical laboratories making chips for implanting in humans so they can be located. Some parents are implanting them in their children for safety in case they get snatched."

"I don't think I'd want Dad to be able to track me down anytime or anywhere with a simple phone app," J.J. said.

"Some governments are considering chipping their military in order to locate soldiers if they're captured or go MIA," Tristan said.

"I don't like that idea," Joshua said. "If our government had a system to track our soldiers' locations, then it'd only be a matter of time before our enemies hacked into it to track our people."

"Yes, but if Murphy had a chip like that in him, we wouldn't be sitting here wondering where he is," Jessica said in a soft voice.

Joshua let out a low groan. He glanced over at J.J., who squeezed Jessica's hand.

"Can you trace this GPS chip to find out who inserted it?" J.J. asked Boris.

"Had to be surgically implanted by a doctor," Boris said. "Our people are tracking down who it had been sold to by the serial number."

"Dr. Stan Garland is a good place to start," Jessica said. "Now that Natalie Stepford has been murdered, I guess that means you can take her electronics into evidence to find out who had put a tap on them."

"Already working on it," Boris said with a nod of his head. "Her husband is the logical suspect. He had the most access to them and Dr. Garland most likely implanted the chip on his orders."

"Sounds like Calvin Stepford had some heavy-duty trust issues," J.J. said.

"Maybe Murphy found out whatever it was Natalie told Dr. Caldwell about. They followed him back to Natalie's studio, killed her, and then snatched him to keep him quiet," Susan said.

"Why kill her and snatch him?" Joshua asked. "Why not just kill them both?"

"It's very possible that her murder had nothing to do with Caldwell's investigation," Boris said. "We found some really funky things at the Kitchen Studio."

"What do you mean by funky?" Tristan asked.

"Her phone showed several long text threads from some person, I'm assuming to be a guy, named Lee," Susan said.

"On the surface, the texts looked like he'd sent the messages to a wrong number," Boris said. "Except when you send a text to a wrong number and the respondent says she doesn't know you, the normal reaction is to stop texting her."

"This guy refused to stop," Susan said. "He kept insisting her name was Kitty and that he had traveled a long way to see her."

"Kitty!" Jessica sat up straight in her seat. "Sex Kitty?"

"What are you talking about?" Joshua asked.

"Sex Kitty," Jessica said. "Yesterday, there was a red sports-car parked at the end of the parking lot with Arizona vanity plates that read Sex Kitty."

Susan referred to her notes. "We've tracked down the registration on that car because it appears to have been there all night. We hoped that the owner saw or knew something."

"Who is the car registered to?" Joshua asked.

Checking her messages, Susan uttered a low gasp. "*Kitty* Katt. Her address is in Scottsdale, Arizona."

"And what does this Kitty Katt have to do with Commander Caldwell's murder?" Jessica asked. "Murphy swore that he saw Caldwell get in that same car with a blonde the night before he was murdered."

"Are you sure about that?" Boris asked.

"Positive," Jessica said. "We assumed the car belonged to Natalie Stepford since you'd already determined that she was connected to his murder in some way."

"But the car isn't registered to Natalie Stepford," Susan said. "It's registered to some sex kitten in Arizona."

"Something really fishy is going on here," Joshua said.

"Why would this Lee dude be sending Kitty's texts to Natalie?" Tristan asked. "And if her address is Arizona, why is this guy traveling a long way to northern Virginia?"

"Where'd he travel from?"

"The texts came from a phone registered to Samuel Payne," Susan said. "His home address is Louisiana. Latimore is following up that end of the investigation to find out if there is any connection between the texts and Natalie's murder."

"And Murphy's disappearance," Joshua said.

"So this Lee traveled a long way to meet Kitty." Jessica stood up. "Have you interviewed the students who were in our class last night?"

"We're still trying to get a list," Boris said. "Have you got any suggestions of who we might want to talk to?"

"Start with a newlywed couple. The husband's name is Andy. He is one of Natalie's biggest fans and I don't think it's her cooking that turns him on."

CHAPTER FOURTEEN

J.J. changed into one of Murphy's navy uniforms and rode with Susan Archer to Andy and Peg Albert's home in Sterling, Virginia. Jessica had filled them in with as many details as she could recall from the night before. Joshua opted to accompany Boris Hamilton to the Garland Surgery and Laser Clinic while Jessica remained home to await any contact from Murphy.

With Susan at the steering wheel, they pulled up in front of the older split-level home in a lower middle-class neighborhood. Two sedans filled the driveway under a weathered car port.

"How do you want to do this?" Susan asked him while they both eyed the seemingly quiet home.

"You take the lead," J.J. said. "The less I say, the better. If I talk too much, there's too much of a chance of my slipping up and them realizing I'm not Murphy."

"I would have thought—"

"That Murphy and I made a habit of changing places?" He shook his head with a laugh. "That's only done in bad sitcoms."

"So you've never done this before—pretend to be your identical twin?"

Saying nothing, J.J. opened the door and slid out.

Getting out of the driver's side, Susan joined him to walk up the driveway to the front door. "I take that as a yes you did."

"Once." His expression was serious when he pressed the doorbell.

She sensed that the incident did not end in the same way it usually did in family-style situation comedies.

There was a crash from inside the house.

Susan and J.J. exchanged questioning expressions.

"NCIS," Susan called out. "Mr. and Ms. Albert, can you please open up?"

There was a sound of running feet from the other side of the door followed by another crash.

J.J. punched the doorbell again. "Andy, this is Murphy Thornton. We have questions regarding Natalie Stepford."

Abruptly, the door was yanked open.

Tying the belt to a robe wrapped around her, Peg Albert stood before them. Her face was flushed and her hair askew. "Excuse me? You said you were from N-C—?" She looked J.J. up and down. "Weren't you at the cooking class last night?"

J.J. stuck out his hand. "Lieutenant Murphy Thornton. I was with my wife Jessica."

"Gnarly's sister." With a wide grin, she opened the door and invited them inside.

J.J. was caught off guard because Jessica had forgotten to mention Peg Albert's adoration for her father's German shepherd.

Luckily, Peg's focus was on a cooking apron, the bottom of which was hanging below the hem of her shorty bath-robe. "What was that you said about having questions about

Natalie?" She tugged on the lower half of the apron and pulled it out from under her bathrobe.

For a split second, J.J. caught sight of her upper thigh and hip through the opening of her robe. She was naked underneath. Obviously, at the time of their arrival, she had been wearing the apron and nothing else.

Tucking the tail of his shirt into his jeans, Andy galloped down the stairs. "Murphy, how nice of you to stop by?" He stuck out his hand to shake. When he spotted Susan, he paused. Then, a salacious grin crossed his face. "What do you need? Some cooking lessons?" He slapped Peg on the behind. "Well, we have quite a few recipes we'd be glad to share." He winked at Susan. "Even some for parties of three... or more."

"This is my *colleague* Special Agent Susan Archer," J.J. said. "She's with NCIS, the Naval Criminal Investigative Service."

"NC-I-S," Peg said with a grin as she pieced together the acronym.

A look of worry crossed Andy's face. "What does that have to do with us or Natalie's cooking class?"

"Natalie Stepford was murdered after the cooking class." Susan said.

"Oh, dear!" Peg covered her mouth with her hand. "We only just saw her last night. She taught us how to cook lasagna with a special red wine sauce. Why would anyone want to kill her? Do you know who did it?"

"That's what we're trying to find out," Susan said.

"You certainly don't think it was us, do you?" Peg wrapped her arms around her husband, who took her into a comforting embrace.

"Last night was the first time we'd met her in person."

"But you did know Natalie before the class," J.J. said.

"Most everyone did," Andy said. "She was an Internet celebrity."

"I didn't realize her cooking show was that popular," Susan said.

Andy's eyes grew wide.

"She's an excellent teacher," Peg said. "Andy's learned a lot about cooking watching her videos. Haven't you, dear?"

"Yes. She's taught me a lot."

"For example?" Susan asked.

Andy looked to J.J. for help. Seeing no sign of a rescue, he uttered a deep laugh. The corners of his lips curled up in a wicked grin. "No one knows how to cook like Natalie."

"And Kitty?" Susan asked. "How good of a cook is she?"

Andy's eyes flicked in the direction of his wife.

"Who's Kitty?" Peg asked.

Susan and J.J. looked in Andy's direction. Andy, however, was looking at J.J. like a trusted friend who had broken a sacred confidence.

Abruptly, Susan broke into a coughing fit. Grabbing her throat, she asked with a hoarse voice, "Can I have a glass of water please?" She coughed again. "I seem to have swallowed down the wrong pipe."

"Oh you poor thing. I know just how you feel." Leading Susan through the dining room to the kitchen, Peg recounted an episode during their wedding. A bridesmaid had been rude enough to break into a coughing fit during their ceremony.

As soon as they were out of earshot, J.J. spun Andy around. "Spill it. Tell me about Kitty."

"I don't have to tell you anything. Besides, what does the military have to do with Natalie's murder, anyway? She was a cook."

"She was also a witness in the murder of a naval officer," J.J. said. "She may have been killed to keep her quiet."

Andy scoffed. "Which has nothing to do with me. I'm not in the military and all I know about Natalie is what I've seen on her website."

"What have you seen on her website?"

"Are you for real?" Seeing J.J.'s blank expression, Andy laughed. "You really did go to Natalie's class thinking that she was just a cooking instructor." He continued to chortle. "You were probably the only guy there last night—except her husband, of course, who didn't know who Natalie really is."

"Was. Past tense. Someone killed her."

"Maybe her husband found out why she's so popular in the kitchen."

Sensing that their time was ending quickly, J.J. urged him to elaborate. "Who is Natalie Stepford?"

"Kitty Katt, the sex kitten."

CHAPTER FIFTEEN

"What kind of stuff can be happening at a clinic for plastic surgery that would warrant killing someone over?" Boris asked as he turned into the parking lot next to Stan Garland's Surgery and Laser Clinic.

Since it was Saturday afternoon, there were only a few cars in the lot—most of them parked close to the building's main entrance.

"Hopefully, we'll find out." Joshua slid out of the passenger seat and approached the front of the building. He gazed up at the dark tinted glass panes that covered the four-story building from the ground up to the rooftop.

Murphy could be in there. Wherever he is, he has to be okay. J.J.'s right. If his twin brother was dead—he'd feel it. Joshua shuddered. *Don't even go there.*

"Murphy's okay." Boris's voice shattered through his thoughts. "He's one of the toughest guys I know. I don't mean tough as in a brute. I mean tough as in strong willed. He'll make his way back—no matter what."

"Have you got any kids, Boris?"

"My wife Claire and I have been blessed with four. Two boys and two girls. The boys are in college. The girls are in high school. Each one is my reason for living." Boris patted him on the shoulder on his way to the front door. "I can only imagine what you're going through." He yanked the door open to enter the lobby as a man, pulling a large cooler on wheels, hurried in their direction.

"Hold the door, please." A woman dressed in a suit and high heels hurrying behind the man with the cooler asked them to clear the way for him.

"Excuse me," Boris asked as the man rushed by, "we've come to see you, Dr. Stan Garland."

Stan Garland froze. "Oh, I'm sorry. The clinic is closed on the weekends. You'll have to make an appointment when we're open again on Monday."

"I may look like I need a tummy tuck, but that's not what I'm here to see you about." Boris presented his investigator's shield. "NCIS. We have some questions about Natalie Stepford."

Joshua was observing the hazardous waste warning labels on the cooler. "You'd think an upscale private clinic like this one would contract with a medical waste disposal service to pick up their hazardous waste, wouldn't you, Boris?"

"Yes, they would. What's in the cooler, Dr. Garland?"

"No habla inglés," the woman said.

"Seriously?" Joshua asked. "You can show us what's in the cooler now, or later after Special Agent Hamilton returns with a warrant to make you remove the lid."

Stan and Meaghan regarded each other for a moment.

"It's your decision," Boris said.

"Run, Stan!" Meaghan sprung at Boris.

Stan shoved his cooler in Joshua's direction, turned on his heels, and sprinted across the parking lot.

"Ah, damn." Muttering, Joshua darted around the cooler and gave chase.

Meaghan jumped onto Boris's back. She held onto him with her legs wrapped around his waist.

Getting beaten about his head and shoulders, Boris twirled around like a horse trying to buck a wildcat off his back. He collided with the cooler. With a thud, it overturned, and the plastic lid popped off.

Stan was wheezing by the time he reached the end of the parking lot and the hillside leading up to the picnic area.

"What a moron." Joshua slowed down to a trot and leaned against the side of Boris's SUV. "Where does he think he's going to go?" With an air of disgust, he yelled at the top of his lungs, "Bang!"

Instantly, Stan stopped and threw both of his hands up into the air. "I give up!"

"What do you know," Joshua said. "It worked."

Losing patience, Boris reached around to peel the woman off his back and hurl her onto the pavement. He pinned her to the ground while cuffing her hands behind her back.

Joshua escorted Stan, his hands cuffed behind him, back from the other side of the parking lot. Her previously flawless appearance had dissolved under smeared makeup, disheveled hair, and a scuffed business suit. Meaghan sat on the curb with her hands also cuffed behind her back.

Boris jerked his chin at Stan. "Did he tell you anything?"

"No. Her?"

"Nothing. And we have a lot of questions that need answering." Boris crooked his finger at Joshua to follow him to the overturned cooler. He pointed at the spilled contents.

Joshua squinted at what appeared to be raw meat. He instantly recognized one organ as a human heart. The other was a liver.

Fear gripped Joshua—followed by fury.

"Now, Josh—" was all Boris uttered before Joshua grabbed his weapon out of its holster on his hip, whirled around, and aimed it at both Stan and Meaghan. "Who is that and what had you done to him?"

With a shriek, Stan ducked behind his wife for cover.

℧ ℧ ℧

"It can't be a real name," Jessica told Tristan. "What kind of parent would name their daughter Kitty Katt?"

Tristan didn't bother looking up from the keyboard. "What kind of parents would name their kid North West?"

"Point taken."

Jessica and Tristan were in the control room on the ground floor of the Faraday-Thornton home. When the mansion had originally been constructed in the 1990s, the corner efficiency apartment had been used for a housekeeper's quarters. Since the apartment had a separate entrance, Murphy realized that it could easily be converted into a panic room—useful in his line of work as a Phantom.

The two outside windows were replaced with specialized bulletproof glass. The sunlight could shine in, but no one could see through the glass to the interior. The door had been reinforced with secure fingerprint- and retina-scanning locks. Only Murphy, Jessica, Tristan, and other family and friends who had been cleared by Nigel could open the door.

The pantry off of the kitchenette was stocked with enough food to feed four people and two dogs for a week. There was a queen-sized pullout sofa bed and a full bath.

The space was also home to Nigel's brain—the communications command center in which Nigel's server was based. Murphy and Jessica's home was able to send and receive data instantly through control panels on computer tablets stationed throughout the house, guesthouse, and garage.

Inside the command center, a bank of security monitors provided a view of every room and the grounds. They were able to turn on and off lights and adjust the temperature from a control panel. They could even turn on water faucets, electric fireplaces, and various appliances, including televisions and sound systems.

When away from home, they could contact Nigel via an application on their cell phones. For example, if a visitor arrived at their house before they did, they could instruct Nigel to open the front gate and turn on the lights. Nigel could even pop open the front door and tell their guest to make himself at home—not unlike a human butler.

It irked Jessica that Tristan, who had offered his technical expertise to set up Nigel, had more security clearances than she did. Thus, as soon as everyone left, he was able to gain access to Natalie's cell phone records to examine the text threads between her and the mysterious Lee.

"Nigel, do you have a last name for the Lee who'd sent those text messages to Natalie?" Tristan asked while Jessica studied the text thread on one of the monitors.

"Evidence indicates that it could be Douglas," Nigel said. "The phone number that the texts originated from is registered to Samuel Payne, who resides in New Orleans, Louisiana. He has been married for the last twelve years to Gladys Payne. She has a twenty-year-old son from a previous marriage named Lee Douglas."

"What do we know about Lee Douglas?" Tristan asked.

"Graduated from high school in New Orleans two years ago," Nigel said. "Went to community college one semester. Got academic probation. Has been listed as a dependent on Samuel Payne's income tax every year for the last twelve years."

"But Lee Douglas is not in New Orleans now," Jessica said.

"The signals for Lee's text messages to Natalie bounced off the tower in Reston. He was in the immediate area when he sent those texts."

"Which makes sense since he says he traveled a long way to see her," Jessica said.

"To see Kitty," Tristan corrected her.

"Is this a case of mistaken identity or are Natalie and Kitty Katt one and the same?" Jessica jumped when her cell phone rang. They had been so busy trying to find Murphy that they had forgotten that they were waiting for a possible ransom call.

Holding up his finger in a silent order to Jessica to wait, Tristan said, "Nigel—"

"I am on an automatic trace and record for all incoming calls to every family member of Lieutenant Murphy Thornton," Nigel said.

Jessica read the caller ID.

Brett.

Disappointed, she let out a groan and pressed the button to connect the call.

"Hello, Brett."

"Jessica, are you okay?"

"I'm okay," she said with a sigh. "I really can't talk right now."

"Carol told us about Murphy."

"What?" Panic gripped her by the heart. "Brett, listen to me. It is very important that you and everyone Carol told about Murphy's disappearance not tell anyone about it. If he was kidnapped and his abductors find out that the police know about it, then they'll kill him. Please, Brett. I'm begging. Please don't tell anyone."

"Of course, Jessica," Brett said. "We only know because we were with Carol when she called to find out where you were this morning. I'll make sure everyone knows to keep hush-hush. You're my friend, Jessica. I'm here for you. If there's anything that I can do in any way to help—all you have to do is ask. I know how much you love Murphy."

Jessica's eyes teared up.

"And I know that you'll do anything for him. Have the kidnappers contacted you with a ransom demand?"

"No," she said. "We're beginning to think that whoever took him isn't after money. I mean, if they were, they'd have contacted us by now. Wouldn't they have?"

With a hiss, Tristan ran his finger across his throat in a signal for her to end their conversation.

"I guess so. Well, like I said, Jessica, you know my number. Call me if you need anything—even just a shoulder to cry on."

"Thank you, Brett. Goodbye."

Tristan shook his head while she disconnected the call.

"What?" she asked.

"You have such a big mouth," Tristan said.

"Give me a break. I'm distraught."

"Susan Archer and Murphy have passed through the front gate," Nigel announced.

Jessica spun around in her seat only to see Tristan point at the monitor showing the SUV. With a shake of his head, he said, "No, Nigel. That's J.J."

Jessica's heart sank.

"I apologize for my error," Nigel said. "It is difficult for my system to distinguish between Murphy and J.J. because they share both visual and biological characteristics. It was easier before J.J. changed his hair style to match his identical sibling."

"I know what you mean." Tristan gathered his notes and tablet on which he had downloaded traffic cam surveillance videos from around the area. He urged Jessica out of her chair. "Come on, Sis. We need to secure the control center before Susan comes into the house." He picked up her cell phone and stuck it into her hands.

"Tristan," she sucked in a shuddering breath, "tell me that Murphy's going to be okay."

He clasped her shoulders in both hands and looked into her violet eyes, moist with tears. "Sis, Murphy loves you so much, that nothing—no kidnapper, terrorist, or psychopath is going to keep him away from you. He will move heaven and earth to come home to you."

"I just wish I hadn't fought with him last thing before he left," she said with a sob in her voice.

Aware of J.J. and Susan entering the house—and the control center door being wide open for anyone to discover, Tristan scoffed. "Those are words, Sis."

"Words have meaning, Tristan."

"Actions speak louder than words." With that, Tristan yanked her out of the room and pressed the button concealed behind a print on the wall to close the door.

The thick door which contained a book case, slid along the threshold, to conceal the entrance into the control room.

In the front foyer, Spencer was yapping a greeting to the visitors. She leapt into J.J.'s arms and licked his face.

"Where's Jessica and Tristan?" Susan asked while glancing up and down the stairs. "I expected them to be waiting to find out what we've uncovered."

"Tristan probably dragged Jessica out for a walk." Raising his voice for them to hear, J.J. glanced down the stairs. "It's nerve wracking just sitting and waiting. I'm sure some fresh air would have done her some good. Want some lemonade?" He ushered Susan into the kitchen and away from the stairs leading down to the control room.

"Lemonade sounds great." Susan asked, "Do you put sugar in your lemonade?"

J.J. paused with the refrigerator door open. "Lemonade without sugar is just lemon water."

"Murphy doesn't put sugar in his lemonade," Jessica said with a frown on her way into the kitchen. "You'll need to spoon some sugar into the glass for her."

Taking the jug of lemonade out of the fridge, J.J. shot Jessica a reassuring grin. "One of those quirky differences between the two of us."

"I'm assuming no ransom call," Susan said.

Shaking her head, Jessica accepted J.J.'s offer of a glass of lemonade. "Did you find out anything from Andy and Peg?"

"Andy ended up being a wealth of information." While handing out the glass and a bowl of sugar to Susan, J.J. jerked his head in Tristan's direction. "Open up the browser on your tablet."

After doing as he'd requested, Tristan handed the tablet to J.J. to tap in a website address. They followed him into the living room. Tristan and Jessica sat on either side of him to watch the website open to reveal Natalie Stepford's Kitchen Studio. The website contained a listing of gourmet food and cooking items, photographs of elegant dishes, as well as a page promoting her catering business. There was also a page devoted to videos of the chef illustrating how to prepare gourmet recipes.

"So she's an Internet cooking star," Jessica said, noting that all the videos had hundreds of thousands of hits. "These videos were shot at her cooking school. That kitchen is the same one she uses to conduct her class."

With a sly grin, J.J. tapped in another website address to take them to another website—a restricted paid site that required a credit card to enter. J.J. was about to input his credit card when Tristan took the tablet.

"Allow me," Tristan said with a sly grin. He closed the browser and then reentered through an application located on Nigel's server.

"Did you just hack into that website?" Susan asked with an arched eyebrow.

"No," Tristan said while handing the tablet back to J.J.

Despite her high security clearances, Susan Archer and the rest of the NCIS staff were not authorized to know about Murphy's position as a Phantom or Nigel's real role in their home.

A sensual melody floated from the speakers of the tablet. The screen opened with a splash of red followed by big blue eyes framed in ultra-lush eyelashes. The camera pulled up to reveal Natalie Stepford, gazing up at the camera with her red lips pouting. The camera angle provided a clear shot down the plunging neckline of her red negligee to show off her abundant bosom.

"Hello, there, boys," she purred. "Kitty Katt here to share in your fantasies." The camera pulled back. She picked up a strawberry dipped in chocolate and wrapped her plump lips around it. Slowly, she took a bite out of it and chewed. Her sultry eyes never left the camera. "What are you hungry for tonight?"

"During her live performances—" J.J. said.

"Which aren't anymore because she's now dead," Susan interjected.

"We're watching a recorded video," J.J. explained, "which costs forty-five dollars for fifteen minutes. But, before she was killed, she had scheduled live performances and men—or even women—would pay to enter the live chat and *direct* her performance."

"Direct?" Jessica asked.

J.J. and Tristan exchange uncomfortable glances.

"She'd take off certain articles of clothing. Blow kisses." J.J.'s cheeks turned pink. "Touch herself in certain places." He cleared his throat.

"She was a porn star," Jessica said. "That's why most of the men's tongues were hanging down to their knees last night."

"Our team had no idea about this other line of work that Natalie Stepford was in," Susan said. "She set up this website under a whole different identity—totally disconnected from Natalie Stepford and her catering business."

"Was her husband aware of it?" Jessica asked.

"According to Andy Albert, no," J.J. said. "Andy's wife has no idea either." He gestured at the tablet that Tristan held in his hands. "He found out about Kitty Katt aka Natalie from some friends of his at the gym. Some of her loyal fans recognized her when she was catering a wedding they were attending, and word spread like wildfire. Suddenly her catering business and cooking school were booming."

"It seems that somehow Lee Douglas discovered her real identity, too." Seeing their questioning expressions, Jessica reminded them. "The texts you found on Natalie's phone from a 'Lee,' who insisted that she was 'Kitty.'"

"That's right," Susan said. "She told him that he had the wrong person."

"But he didn't," Jessica said.

"We traced the phone number and account that Lee's texts came from to a Samuel Payne in New Orleans," Tristan said. "He has a stepson named Lee Douglas."

"How did you track them down?" Susan asked.

"I'm rich," Tristan said with a shrug of his shoulders. "I have too much time on my hands and a lot of toys."

"If this Lee is obsessed enough with Kitty Katt to travel all the way from New Orleans to be with her, how do you think he'd take it when she rejected him?" Jessica interjected before Susan could pursue asking Tristan any more questions.

"Her murder does point to a crime of passion," J.J. said.

"And Lee was in the immediate area yesterday when Natalie received those texts last night," Tristan said.

Susan asked, "How do—"

"I wonder if Calvin Stepford became suspicious when his wife's popularity as a caterer suddenly took off?" Jessica interrupted to ask.

"I'd bet he knew who she was all along," Tristan said with certainty. "Who do you think paid for all that plastic surgery? Most importantly, why? He wanted to keep his trophy wife shiny. Why? Because he wanted to show her off to other men and say, look at what I have."

"Not necessarily," J.J. said with a shake of his head. "Wanting a beautiful wife as a status symbol is one thing. Having her take off her clothes and touch herself for the whole world to see for money is an entirely different thing all together."

"Jessica said he was insecure," Tristan said. "Maybe having a porn star all to himself makes him feel like a big man."

"What kind of car does Calvin Stepford drive?" Jessica asked.

With a frown, Susan paused to recall what vehicle she saw in the driveway at the Stepford mansion. "BMW sedan. Late model."

"What color?"

"Metallic blue."

Jessica shook her head. "Natalie's husband definitely wasn't a party in her porn business. He has to be in total control and he's big on pride. But he's also about appearances. He drives a car that exudes his success with a sense of class—"

"And a porn star is not class," Susan said with a nod of her head.

"The guy aspires to be a sophisticated mover and shaker," Tristan said. "What would it do to his image if it got out that his Stepford wife was really a sex kitty?"

"Total devastation," Jessica said. "For him, it would be on par of finding out that he had married a common back alley hooker."

"Would that be enough to make him beat her perfect face in with a meat mallet?" Susan asked.

"You're asking me to analyze someone who I only saw assisting in a cooking class," Jessica said. "All I saw was his public persona, which is very different from his personal one."

"Give us an educated guess," Susan said.

"It depends," Jessica said. "Is Calvin Stepford prone to violence?"

"No history of violence. No reported incidents of domestic disputes."

"Usually, it's been my experience," J.J. said, "that control freaks who are big on appearances are capable of doing whatever they have to do to protect their reputation."

"J.J.'s right," Jessica said. "If Natalie was doing this on the side without him knowing, you have to wonder why? I mean, she was a successful business woman with a good reputation and a husband who spent a lot of money on her—"

"Money that he controlled," Susan said. "We found out during our investigation that he controlled everything in the Stepford home. He put Natalie in business. He managed her money—kept her on a strict allowance. Told her what friends to have. The SUV she has for her catering, he ordered it. Natalie requested the color red on the order. The salesman said that she broke down into tears when she arrived to pick it up and saw that Calvin hand changed the color to white."

"That Nissan we found registered to Kitty Katt is a fire engine red." Jessica pointed at the tablet. "I think Kitty Katt was Natalie's escape from a controlling husband."

"Not just an escape," J.J. said, "but an outright rebellion."

"Ain't it ironic," Jessica said. "A woman beautiful enough to make men drool, married to a very successful man."

"Living in a mansion with servants," Susan said.

"Has a successful business," Jessica said. "She'd acquired the American dream. On the outside looking in, her life was perfect."

"Even if she was half plastic," Susan said.

"But obviously, her life is not really that perfect if she felt the need to act out by taking off her clothes for money," Jessica said. "Since Kitty Katt was a paid website, she was probably making a lot of money that her husband had no control over. That car is registered in Arizona."

"It was delivered here over a month ago," Susan said.

"Maybe we're looking at a wife so miserable that she was planning to run away."

"It would have been only a matter of time before her husband found out about Kitty Katt," J.J. said.

"And what do you think a proud controlling man like Calvin Stepford would have done if he found out that his wife was an Internet porn star and planning to run away?" Susan asked.

"It would have ruined his reputation," J.J. said, "which means a lot to him. Even if he wasn't violent, it may have been enough to make him snap."

"And if Murphy happened to be there when he snapped?" Susan asked.

CHAPTER SIXTEEN

"With all due respect, Captain, I'm beginning to think it was a bad idea to allow you to ride along with me," Boris told Joshua after they had transported the Garlands to NCIS headquarters and placed them in separate interrogation rooms. The heart and liver found in the cooler had been sent to the medical examiner's office.

"I didn't shoot them." Joshua wondered if Boris was going to shut him out of the interrogations.

"No, but you threatened to, and that was bad enough. Dr. Garland peed his pants."

"I never would have threatened to shoot him if I knew he had a weak bladder," Joshua muttered.

Narrowing his eyes, Boris sucked in a deep breath. "Captain, do you really think Stan Garland has what it takes to get the best of your son?"

"Not after he peed his pants," Joshua said while reaching into his pocket to extract his cell phone. "Excuse me. I need to answer this."

As Joshua stepped away, Boris took note that he had another cell phone in a case on his belt.

"Captain Thornton," a sultry voice oozed into Joshua's ear, "have you uncovered any news on Murphy?"

"I've located his cell phone, Ma'am," he said in a low voice. "It had been tossed into a creek and destroyed."

"Are you able to get any data that could help us locate him?" the Phantom commanding officer asked.

"I passed it onto Tristan Faraday. He will see if he can uncover anything, but I'm doubtful."

"Murphy's team is on standby," she said. "As soon as we receive word from you, they'll be mobilized."

"There may be an issue with that, Ma'am," Joshua said. "Since Murphy's navy, NCIS has taken the lead in this case. As soon as they find out where he is, *they'll* be going in. If they encounter a group of secret ops, there's going to be a lot of questions that the Joint Chiefs of Staff are not going to want asked."

There was a long silence from the other end of the line. Finally, she said, "I'll make a few phone calls."

"You can't pull NCIS out," Joshua said in a low voice while checking over his shoulder for Boris's whereabouts. The deputy chief was at the other end of the corridor on his own cell phone. "We're making progress. If they receive orders to back off with Murphy still out there, the NCIS team is going to be very suspicious. You placed Murphy here to work under-cover. He's battled boredom and paper cuts for more than a year. You pull the team out now, then when we find and rescue Murphy, they're going to want to know why. Murphy will lose every ounce of trust that he's built up and most likely you'll have to scrub the mission."

"The Phantoms can't lose Lieutenant Thornton," she said. "We are aware that we may have to pull him out of NCIS. As a Phantom, he's too valuable to our nation's security to take any chances with his life."

"He's worth a lot more to me than he is to the Joint Chiefs," Joshua said through clenched teeth. "Listen. I'm a Phantom. I've led missions and I have the clearances. Pull whatever strings you need to give me the lead of Hamilton's team. When we locate Murphy, I'll direct them to bring him in safely without blowing his cover."

"Captain, do you trust them with your son's life?"

He sucked in a deep breath. "Yes."

The call ended.

Murphy's life is in my own hands. Joshua broke out in a cold sweat as the reality of the weight bore down on him. He checked the time on his phone.

Two o'clock. Murphy had been missing over fourteen hours. Generally, in missing persons cases, the first twenty-four hours were the most crucial. After that, the odds of finding the victim alive dropped significantly.

He heard Boris's heavy footsteps making their way toward him from behind.

"Just got an update," Boris said.

Shoving his phone into his pocket, Joshua sucked in a deep breath and turned around to face him.

"The ME says the heart and liver found in the cooler had been surgically removed," Boris said. "They came from the same person—male. Very poor condition. The heart showed indications of having undergone triple bypass in the past. The liver was diseased."

"Well," Joshua sighed, "that's a relief. Murphy never had heart bypass and his liver is as clean as a whistle."

"Which begs the question, who did the heart and liver belong to and, since you can't live without a heart and liver, whose do they have now?"

Joshua pushed aside the thought of Murphy being killed in order to have his organs harvested to sell on the black market. "What were those organs doing at a private *cosmetic* surgery clinic?"

"Good question." Boris rubbed his chin. "Now, Dr. Caldwell told Murphy that something really bad was going on at a private clinic. I'd put black market organ transplants right up there in the really bad category."

"I thought organ harvesting was more of an issue in poverty-stricken areas like China or Central America," Joshua said, "where people are desperate enough to sell their kidneys to support their families?"

"I can't exactly see folks in northern Virginia selling their kidneys to put food on the table," Boris said. "But I can see some in dire need of a kidney transplant and too far down the waiting list paying big bucks to get one on the black market."

"And Dr. Garland's clinic has the operating room and everything necessary to do those transplants during off hours," Joshua said. "That's why they had those organs. They'd done an organ transplant operation. The heart and liver were the damaged organs they had removed from the patient."

"The bio-hazard service hadn't picked them up yet," Boris said. "Natalie Stepford must have found out about his sideline while having some cosmetic surgery done there. After her murder, they realized that we'd be coming by and had to get the heart and liver off the premises before we found them."

"Which we did."

"Oh, by the way," Boris said, "Archer called. Natalie Stepford had her own side business." He chuckled. "Get this. She was an Internet porn star using the stage name of Kitty Katt—had an Arizona address. I've got Latimore checking it out to see how long she'd been using it. Archer thinks Natalie may have had plans to run away and start over as Kitty Katt."

"Interesting," Joshua said. "Now, my next question is did whoever she was running away from find out about her plans and kill her?"

"Evidence points to her husband, who just got out of emergency heart surgery and is in intensive care," Boris said. "He's in critical condition. Or it could be Dr. Garland. Forensics traced the tracking programs that we had found on Natalie's phone, emails, and laptops back to Calvin Stepford's laptop."

"Insecure husband."

"But, the GPS chip that the medical examiner found in Natalie's arm was transmitting back to Dr. Garland's phone."

"She was being tracked by two men?"

"Apparently Kitty Katt was one popular lady." Boris removed his phone from its case and checked the ID. "I gotta take this. It's the boss."

Joshua took his cell phone from the case. "I'll check in with J.J. Then we'll have a chat with Dr. Garland."

"I'll chat with Garland," Boris said while putting the phone to his ear. "We don't have that many spare uniforms around."

J.J. answered the call on the first ring. "Dad, have you got any leads?"

"We think we know what the private clinic was doing," Joshua said. "Any ransom demands yet?"

"None," J.J. said. "We're thinking Murphy's disappearance has nothing to do with money—at least not for ransom. Tristan has plugged Archer's tablet into a monitor and we're examining surveillance videos from last night to see if we can spot anything."

"Good idea." Joshua saw Boris disconnect the call from his boss. Slowly he turned around to face him. "Let me know if you see anything." Without saying goodbye, he disconnected the call.

"You pulled rank on me, Captain," Boris said. "You used your connections on the Joint Chiefs to get my team pulled out from under me."

"Hamilton, that's not how it happened," Joshua said.

"Do you think my team is a bunch of rent-a-cops?"

"If I did, I would have let the navy chief pull your team out and allow a special ops team to take over," Joshua said. "That's what they wanted to do because of our friendship. But I told them to stand down because your team has made progress and we don't have time to start over. I trust you, Hamilton, and that's saying a hell of a lot considering that it's my son's life on the line here."

"If you trust us so damn much, why did you request that you'd be put in charge?"

"Why do you think? Look, Hamilton, it's your team. You give the orders. We'll keep on just like we have been doing. All I want is to find my son and go home." Joshua held out his hand in a sign of good will.

Boris's tough demeanor dissolved. He grasped Joshua's palm. "Can't say I wouldn't do the same thing if I were in your shoes." He poked him in the chest. "Just don't make Garland pee his pants again." He pushed his way through the door to step into the interrogation room.

Upon seeing Joshua, Stan sat up in the straight-back chair at the table. "I want my lawyer. I did nothing wrong."

"Why would you need a lawyer if you did nothing wrong?" Joshua leaned his back against the wall and folded his arms across his chest.

Boris sat across from Stan. "Tell us about the cooler, Dr. Garland."

"It wasn't ours," Stan said. "Ask Meaghan. She'll tell you. We went to the clinic this morning and found it there outside our door. There must have been a mix-up of some sort and it was delivered to us by mistake. When we saw what was in it, Meaghan and I decided to rush them to the hospital to try to get them where they needed to go. You know transplant organs have a very short period during which they're viable for a transplant."

"Why would someone deliver a *diseased* heart and liver to you?" Joshua asked. "Wouldn't those be taken away by the biohazard service to be disposed of?"

"How would I know they were diseased?" Stan asked.

"You're a doctor," Boris said.

"I'm a cosmetic surgeon."

"With a fully staffed private clinic," Boris said. "Including a complete operating room, which sits unused during the evenings and weekends."

"What are you saying?"

"Cost of living is pretty high in McLean," Joshua said.

"And my patients pay me a lot of money to make them perfect," Stan said.

Boris fingered the edge of a folder that rested on the table in front of him. "You know the old saying. It costs money to make money. Word of mouth. Referrals. You have a lot of high end patients. They come to you because they know you—from golf at the country club, cocktails at the Kennedy Center, vacationing at your beach house at the Outer Banks. By all outer appearances, you're a very successful doctor. But it costs money to keep up appearances to draw in those high-end patients."

"And I doubt if those influential patients are going to go to a plastic surgeon whose office is in a lower priced rent district," Joshua said.

"You needed to bring in some extra money," Boris said, "by taking up a second field of medicine."

"It's not what you think!" Stan said.

"How did it start?" Joshua asked. "One of your rich patients needed a kidney but was too far down on the waiting list? You did some asking around and came up with a donor. Since you had the operating room, you did it yourself and your rich patient paid you—all off the books and non-taxable income."

Stan's face was white. His hands shook. His eyes were wide. "It's not me! You think I'm going to saw open someone's chest and take out their heart? No!"

"Then where did the heart and liver come from?" Joshua charged at the table. "And whose heart and liver does your patient have now?"

Stan let out a yelp. Boris held Joshua back.

"I don't know! I swear!" Stan whimpered. "They left them behind. Meaghan says the surgeon said there was a mix up. He thought his nurse took them to dispose of and she thought he did." He sighed. "I told them from the beginning that I wanted nothing to do with any of it. They gave me this sales pitch about how I would be contributing to the greater good. I'd be doing a public service. Of course, Meaghan saw the huge dollar signs. That woman can nag like no other. Finally, I agreed to let them use my office."

"Not just your office," Boris said, "Your operating room— to transplant human organs bought on the black market into patients."

"I'm just renting it out—off hours. Evenings and week-ends. They bring in the surgeon and staff and patients. Even their own equipment. When me and my staff come in in the morning, everything is to be left like it was when we'd left." Stan waved his hands. "I told them from the beginning that I wanted no part of it."

"If you, a doctor, wanted no part of the black-market or-gan transplant business, how did it begin?" Boris asked.

"Where are you getting the human organs?" Joshua asked.

"They're flown in from Central America," Stan said. "Meaghan organizes the delivery of the organs."

"Your wife dragged you into this," Boris said.

"And Calvin Stepford," Stan said. "He started the whole thing. He was in desperate need of a heart transplant but was too far down on the list. He had the money, but his high blood pressure and other health factors were against him. Somehow, he managed to get a heart. I have no idea where. But he needed a doctor to do the transplant."

When Boris pointed at him, Stan shook his head quickly while holding up his hands. "I am not a heart surgeon. Calvin found a doctor who'd do it, but the only thing was the guy had had his license pulled after they discovered he was a drug dealer. Now they needed a place to do it. Meaghan and Calvin hounded me—telling me that if he died, his blood would be on my hands. Finally, I gave in and let them use my operating room. Things worked out so well that they kept on going."

"How long has this set up been going on?" Boris asked.

"A little over six months," Stan said. "Maybe eight. Calvin got his transplant eight months ago. He was supposed to be out of the woods. I'm sure the shock of Natalie's murder was too much for him."

"How does this setup work?"

"The surgeon's girlfriend is a licensed nurse. She scrounges up the patients, purchases the organs on the black market, and coordinates the surgery schedule. Meaghan makes sure no one is in the building, which is easy since I own it. Meaghan arranges and schedules the transport and delivery of the donations to the clinic." He held up his hands. "All I do is let them use my operating room."

"For a nice piece of the action," Joshua said.

"I'm taking as big of a risk as the rest of them," Stan said. "Before I say anything else, I want a lawyer to make sure I get a good deal."

"Didn't you say Calvin Stepford just came out of emergency heart surgery?" Joshua asked Boris, who nodded his head. "His regular doctor would have had to have noticed that his heart was a transplanted organ during the surgery." He turned to Stan. "That's why you and Meaghan went rushing to the clinic. It wasn't Natalie's murder, but you found out Calvin was in emergency heart surgery. His doctor had to realize he didn't get that heart legally. The authorities are going to be descending on Calvin to find out where he got that heart transplant done and who did it as soon as he is able to talk."

"But Natalie already talked," Boris said. "There's no way her husband got that illegal heart transplant without her knowing about it."

"She was cool about it," Stan said. "It saved her husband's life."

"Are you sure about that?" Boris asked. "How good was Natalie and Calvin's marriage?"

Stan looked from one of them to the other. "How should I know?"

"You were friends," Joshua said. "You were also her doctor. The medical examiner noted that she'd had a lot of work done on her. So obviously you've seen a lot of her throughout the years."

"You should have seen Natalie when Calvin first brought her to me," Stan said. "He had discovered her working as a sous chef at a café someplace. She was young and energetic— and, man, could she cook!" He shook his head with a dreamy expression on his face. "But she was not a lot to look at—at least not in Calvin's circle. A man of Calvin's position among entrepreneurs needed nothing less than the best of women on his arm."

"And you made Natalie into that," Joshua said. "The best of women."

"I did two dozen procedures on her," Stan said.

Joshua groaned. "Basically, you made her a whole new woman."

"Natalie was my masterpiece," Stan said. "My Mona Lisa. Venus de Milo."

"And since you created her, you felt within your right to keep track of her," Boris said. "Our medical examiner found the GPS chip you'd put in her arm."

Stan's eyes dropped to the tabletop.

"Like most artists, you fell in love with your work of art," Joshua said. "How long have you been tracking her?"

"About three weeks," Stan said in a soft voice. "I knew it was crazy when I did it, but I couldn't help myself. Natalie had come in for a laser treatment to tighten up the skin around her throat. While she was under, I placed the chip in her arm. It was so small, just like what they do for pets, she never knew about it."

"Why did you want to keep track of her?" Boris asked.

"Because I wanted to know if what we had was really real or something that I had imagined."

"What did you have?" Joshua asked.

Stan pursed his lips together and focused once more on the tabletop.

"Were you sleeping with Natalie?" Joshua asked.

"Maybe a little."

"How do you sleep with someone 'maybe a little?'"

"She came on to me, I swear," Stan said. "For a week and a half, it was like I was living a dream. Me! I wasn't just watching the angel come to life on a computer screen, but I was really there with her, in that pink bed, with her in my arms, holding her, smelling her, tasting her, feeling every piece of her for real."

"You knew Natalie was Kitty Katt," Joshua asked.

"For ten days, I felt like I was alive," Stan said. "Then, suddenly, it was over. She texted that Calvin was getting suspicious, and she didn't want to hurt him. That was the day after I had inserted the chip in her arm. She wouldn't return my phone calls or texts. I felt like an addict going through withdrawal. I couldn't eat or sleep. I took that cooking class just so that I could be close to her."

Outside in the corridor, Joshua asked Boris, "When was Dr. Caldwell murdered?"

"A month ago today. Shot in the back of the head with a Colt nine-millimeter semi-automatic."

"Any suspects with motives not pertaining to the private clinic?"

"Just yesterday his son-in-law appeared on our radar," Boris said. "Murphy learned from the widow that Woody Harris had three unregistered handguns. We went to question him yesterday afternoon. He confessed to giving away two of them after the shooting because he thought we'd search the house and find them."

"You said three guns," Joshua said. "He gave away two. What happened—"

"Missing," Boris said. "Woody says the last time he saw it was when he moved into the Caldwell home. Oh—and get this. It was a Colt nine-millimeter, semi-automatic."

"That tells me that Caldwell's murderer is closer to home. Maybe Natalie Stepford's murder isn't connected."

"We're certain Natalie was Caldwell's source to the scandal at a private clinic," Boris said. "He talked to her immediately before and after he talked to DHS. Murphy saw Caldwell with her the night before the murder. The GPS chip was inserted in her arm *after* his murder."

"It was inserted during Stan's ten-day affair with her," Joshua said, "which started after Dr. Caldwell's murder."

Boris's eyebrows rose high on his forehead.

"I'm thinking that Natalie wanted more from Stan than his body," Joshua said. "I'm thinking she used her feminine talents to get close enough to him to get actual evidence of the black-market organ transplants—"

"Which she knew about because her husband was their founding patient."

"She had to suspect them of killing Commander Caldwell and the investigator," Joshua said.

"We always felt like she was holding something back when we were able to talk to her," Boris said. "Calvin was like a pit bull keeping us away from her."

"Because he was in on it," Joshua said. "That's probably why he put all those tracking programs on her electronics—to keep her on a short leash. But she couldn't let them get away with murder. She used her assets to get close to Stan to get into the clinic to get evidence to prove what they were doing."

"Archer said they think she was planning to run away," Boris said.

"She was going to blow the whistle on them and then go underground," Joshua said. "Someone figured out that's what she was up to and stopped her."

"But none of that scenario fits with Woody owning a gun the same make and caliber as the kind used to kill Caldwell—a gun that has conveniently gone missing."

"That could be just a coincidence," Joshua said with a shrug of his shoulders, "or maybe not."

CHAPTER SEVENTEEN

"Lee is a good kid," Gladys Payne insisted when Jessica and Susan called to ask about her son's relationship with Kitty Katt.

They made the phone call from the dining room table. Tristan had set out a bowl of tortilla chips, salsa, and chili con queso before he and J.J. went downstairs to study the surveillance videos.

"I admit, I was worried when he told us that he was involved with this Internet model," Gladys said. "She is older and appears to be much more—" She cleared her throat. "—experienced than he is. But based on the emails she's sent him, I can see that she does love him."

"Emails?" Susan asked. "Lee has been exchanging emails with Kitty?"

"And texts," Gladys said.

"Texts?" Jessica asked.

"They text each other all day long," Gladys said with a sigh. "It's a long-distance romance. How else would they have a relationship?"

"Are you sure Lee has been communicating with Kitty?"

"I know," Gladys said. "After seeing Kitty's picture, I was surprised, too. She's absolutely gorgeous. She could have any man she wants, but you can see in her emails that she truly loves Lee for his sensitivity and devotion to her. He would never use or hurt her the way I think other men have."

Jessica wrote a quick note to Susan. "I want to see a copy of those emails."

"What is this about?" Gladys asked while Susan read Jessica's message. "Who did you say you were?"

"Do you know where your son is, Ms. Payne?" Susan asked.

"He's in Washington, DC. He went to meet Kitty. The two of them are running away together."

"Running away?" Jessica asked. "Running away from what?"

Gladys paused before saying slowly, "Lee said that Kitty had gotten mixed up with some dangerous people in Washington who didn't want them to be together. I think they forced Kitty into modeling on the Internet and have made a lot of money from it. But Kitty fell in love with Lee and wanted to give it up to be with him. She doesn't want to do it anymore. He went up to Washington to rescue her and take her away from all of that." Her tone shifted. "What is this about? Why are you asking all these questions?"

"Ms. Payne, do you have copies of those emails between Lee and Kitty?" Jessica asked.

"Who did you say you were again?" Gladys asked with suspicion in her voice.

"NCIS," Susan said. "Federal agents."

"Federal agents? Oh, dear. Lee told me that some very important people in Washington wanted to keep him and Kitty apart."

"Ms. Payne," Susan said, "it is very important that we locate your son. Kitty is dead. Someone murdered her—"

"No!" Gladys said. "That's a lie. You're just trying to trick me into telling you where Lee is so that your agents can capture him and hold him hostage to keep Kitty from working for you."

"Ms. Payne, if you'll just listen to me—"

"I've said too much already!" With a sob, Gladys hung up the phone.

Jessica buried her face in her hands.

"That's what happens when you read too many political thrillers," Susan said. "I'm confused about her saying Lee and Kitty were exchanging emails. Judging by Natalie's responses to Lee's texts, she had no idea who he was. She probably knew he was an obsessed fan."

"Natalie Stepford was smart," Jessica said. "She managed to become an Internet celebrity and set up a whole new identity living on the other side of the country. She wouldn't have risked everything by inviting an obsessed fan into her private world."

"Hey, Archer!" J.J. hurried into the dining room. "What kind of vehicle is Lee Douglas driving?" Carrying his tablet, Tristan was one step behind him.

Susan Archer checked her notes. "It's a 2007 Dodge van."

"White with Louisiana plates," J.J. said.

Tristan laid the tablet down in the center of the table for Jessica and Susan Archer to see.

The gray-scale image on the screen was from a surveillance video for a convenience store service station located directly across the road from Natalie Stepford's Kitchen Studio. The camera's angle offered a view of the gas pumps and the exit out onto the road intersecting with Georgetown Pike. A right turn led to Great Falls' park entrance, intersecting with Old Dominion Road, near Thorny Rose Manor.

The time stamp on the video was twelve minutes after midnight, Saturday morning.

Murphy pulled up to the gas pumps on his motorcycle. He took off his helmet and climbed off the bike. He then proceeded to fill up the gas tank. While the gas was filling the tank, he unzipped his leather jacket and reached inside. Jessica noticed him taking in his surroundings while he fingered the inside pocket of his jacket.

"Now see this," J.J. said. "It's noticeable because after midnight on a Friday night, there are no cars around." He pointed to the screen.

They saw a Porsche convertible with the top up pull into the office park from the main road.

"Is that—" Jessica started to ask.

"No, here," J.J. said. "Check out of the license plate on this van."

A white van pulled up into the foreground as it parked in front of the convenience store. Even with the blurred image, they could see the emblem for the state of Louisiana. A slender young man with thin blond hair climbed out of the van. Casting glances in Murphy's direction, he made his way into the store.

Once Murphy had finished at the pumps, he drove the motorcycle around to park in front of the store and went inside.

"He paid for the gas at the pump with his credit card," Jessica said. "What did he go inside for?"

"Maybe to use the little boy's room," Tristan said.

"He had something in his jacket that he wanted to take care of," Susan said while they continued watching. "He must have just gotten it. He had to have seen Natalie Stepford by this time. It's at least forty-five minutes before the estimated time of the murder."

The young man exited the store and trotted back to the van. Hurriedly, he climbed inside, turned it on, and backed out of the space. He then pulled up to the exit and stopped.

Murphy left the store. After putting on his helmet, he turned the bike on and pulled up behind the van.

"Watch this," J.J. said.

As they watched, Murphy activated his right turn signal. As soon as the signal turned on, the van turned right. Murphy followed it.

Tristan rewound the security footage and played it in slow motion.

"Do you see what just happened?" J.J. asked Jessica and Susan.

"Lee, if that is Lee, is following Murphy, but he's in front of him," Jessica said. "He waited there at the exit for Murphy to tell him with his turn indicator which direction he was going, then he pulled out ahead of him. Since he was driving in front of him, once they got to that deserted stretch of road in the dark, he was able to break down or have an accident to block the road."

"Murphy would have offered to help him," J.J. said. "His guard would have been down. Since he was a kid in front of him, Murphy would never have suspected him of 'following' him."

"But why would this obsessed fan snatch Murphy?" Tristan zoomed in on an image on the tablet.

"Because he's part of the vast government conspiracy keeping Lee and his kitty apart," Jessica said.

"Huh?" Tristan's mouth hung open.

"Murphy is part of what government conspiracy to do what?" J.J. asked.

"To keep the Internet porn star and her lover apart," Susan said.

"And the government cares about the kid and the porn star because?" J.J. shrugged his shoulders.

"Because we have nothing more important to do," Susan said in mock innocence.

"I got the license plate number on the van." Tristan held out the tablet to Susan.

"That image looked too blurry—"

"I cleaned it up."

"With what?" Susan wrote down the number.

"I have a lot of toys on this tablet," Tristan said. "Do you want to run the plate or not?"

Susan picked up her cell phone. "You scare me, Tristan." She hurried into the kitchen to call the license plate number into police dispatch to be on the lookout for the abduction suspect.

"If she thinks you're scary," J.J. muttered, "wait until she meets your butler."

"I heard that," Nigel said, prompting J.J. to look around the room to locate the speaker from which the deep voice, reminiscent of Darth Vader, had been uttered.

"I'm really worried." Jessica wrung her hands. "If it was Lee, and he thinks Murphy was coming between him and Natalie, he'd most likely killed him."

"Murphy carries no less than two weapons on him at any given time," Tristan said.

"But if he let his guard down like J.J. said because he thought Lee was a harmless kid—" Jessica jumped in her seat when her cell phone sounded.

"Blocked number calling," Nigel announced. "Recording and tracing enabled upon connection."

"Your *butler* is tracing your phone calls?" Susan ran into the dining room in time to almost get knocked over by Tristan who plopped down in front of his tablet. "How is—"

Tristan's fingertips flew across the touchscreen of his tablet. Once he had arrived at the desired application, he pointed his finger at Jessica and nodded his head.

J.J. had already connected with Joshua and had the phone to his ear. "Dad, I think this is it. A call from a blocked number is coming into Jessie."

With a swallow, Jessica connected the call and put it on speaker. "Hello."

"Jessica Faraday?" the automated voice asked.

"Yes—"

"Listen to me carefully," the voice said in a hurried tone. "If you want to see your husband again, you'll transfer two million dollars via electronic transfer to this bank account. I'm giving you the bank number now."

Tristan held up his hands together and made a pulling motion—signifying for Jessica to stall him.

"I need to get a pen," she said.

"You must not love Murphy very much if you weren't prepared to write down our instructions," the automated voice said.

"Don't you touch him!" Jessica blurted out.

"As long as you do as we say, we won't hurt a hair on his pretty head." His voice hardened. "Now write down this bank account number." He then rattled off a number, which Nigel and Jessica recorded along with the phone call. "Got that?"

Tristan motioned for her to keep the caller on the phone.

"I want proof that you have Murphy and he's alive," Jessica said.

The caller laughed with a high pitched, computerized sound that added to his eerie tone. "Proof of life? You want proof of life? You don't transfer that two million dollars into that account within sixty minutes and we'll give you proof of *death!*" He laughed again. "The clock is ticking."

The call ended.

Silence echoed from the speaker on her phone.

Jessica slumped in her seat. J.J. wrapped an arm around her shoulders and held her close. He held the phone to his ear with the other hand. "Dad, did you hear that?"

"We're on our way, son," Joshua said. "Don't do anything until we get there."

Susan stared at Tristan who was tapping the touchscreen of his tablet. "Did your *butler* get the location of the caller?"

"Call wasn't long enough to get a precise location," Tristan replied. "But we did get the location narrowed down to the area of Georgetown. Of course, it was a burner phone, and they ran the voice through a filter." With a smirk, he shrugged his shoulders.

"Do you have—"

"Yeah," Jessica cut J.J. off. "Our lawyer Willingham is all ready to do whatever is necessary to bring Murphy home."

"You people have more experience in law enforcement than I have," Susan said. "So I mean it when I say 'with all due respect,' you know that when you pay that ransom, Murphy will be dead and your money will be gone."

Tristan shook his head. "When we pay the ransom, that's when we'll catch the dirty bastards and bring Murphy home." He grinned at each one of them. "Nigel and I have a plan."

CHAPTER EIGHTEEN

"You and your butler have a plan?" Boris narrowed his eyes and arched an eyebrow in Tristan's direction after he and Joshua arrived at the house to listen to the ransom call.

"Well," Tristan said, "it was actually my idea. But Nigel worked out the mechanics of how it would work." He sat at the dining room table with his tablet and a laptop spread out before him.

Bending over Tristan's shoulder, Perry Latimore said in a low voice, "You do know that Nigel is not a real person."

"I'd be careful if I were you, Latimore." Tristan pointed at the control panel on the wall next to the doorway. "He can hear you." He didn't mention that the panel also contained a hidden, motion-activated camera.

Joshua checked the time on his watch. They had less than forty minutes to meet the kidnappers' demand for the ransom payment. He glanced across the room to where Jessica sat at the head of the table. She was chewing on her fingernail, something he had never seen her do before. In the chair next to her, J.J. patted her hand. Her nerves were stretched to near breaking point. "Let's hear Tristan out."

"What's one of the main rules when it comes to zeroing in on your prime suspect in a crime?" Tristan asked.

While everyone else in the room looked at each other, Joshua uttered a sigh. "Follow the money."

"Which is why banks throw dye packs into bags during robberies," Boris said. "And when it comes to ransom demands, many times they'll give money with sequential serial numbers on the bills."

"They're marking the money so they can follow it," Tristan said. "Ideally, it'll lead them to the bad guys. That's what we're going to do."

"We already checked the bank account number the kidnappers gave us," Perry said. "It's in the Cayman Islands. By the time we get the name on the account, the money will have been transferred out of there and probably bounced around to hundreds of other accounts before disappearing."

"Kind of like trying to follow the pea in a shell game," J.J. said. "It's hard to follow several moving parts. You're bound to lose track of it."

"Unless you plant a signal in the pea to tell you where it is," Tristan said.

A slim grin came to J.J.'s lips. "You're going to mark the ransom."

"As soon as I heard Murphy got snatched, Nigel and I went to work on it." Tristan pointed at the laptop screen, which was filled with a complicated diagram which made sense only to him and Perry. "We've developed a code that we're going to insert into the digital ransom. As soon as the money hits the bank account, then it marks the account. Any activity in that account, meaning any transfers or withdrawals, will be recorded. Every account, no matter where it is, will also be marked. All the data from every account that touches any of the ransom, even if only a penny, will be sent back to Nigel's server in real time."

"Works on the same principle as a computer virus," Perry said.

"Exactly the same."

"The ransom payment will be the Trojan horse that's going to take down Murphy's kidnappers," J.J. said.

"Many of the accounts the money will bounce in and out of won't be connected to the kidnappers," Susan Archer said. "They'll be victims of identity theft whose accounts will be used to launder the ransom. Won't the virus infect their accounts?"

"We thought about that," Tristan said. "The virus won't *corrupt* any account it goes into. It's only going to report the data back to Nigel. Plus, it's got an expiration date of seventy-two hours."

"The money will only be in those accounts for a matter of minutes," Perry said. "Maybe even seconds."

"If the kidnappers have any smarts, they're going to know they have to act fast to transfer the money out of that account and move it around," Tristan said. "If the money stays too long, then they'll risk us tracing the ransom to them. The way they see it, we're chasing after them."

"But in reality," Joshua said, "we *won't* be chasing them, we'll be going along for the virtual ride."

"*Eventually*, the ransom will stop bouncing," Tristan said. "It's going to land in a final destination—the kidnapper's account."

"Exactly how many laws are we going to be breaking if we do this?" Perry asked.

"None," Joshua said with certainty. "The kidnappers contacted us. They gave us their account number and demanded that we send an electronic deposit into that account. That acts as their permission for us to send data into their account. As for the subsequent accounts that they send the tracker to," he shrugged with a grin, "that's on the bad guys. We didn't tell them to transfer it. They are the ones initiating and executing the transfers."

"Are you sure about that, Captain?" Boris asked.

"That's my story and I'm sticking to it."

"I don't know," Boris said. "Faraday, have you tested this? If things go sideways, Jessica will be out two million dollars and Murphy will probably get killed."

"I did a test," Tristan said. "I attached the code to a thousand dollars of my own money. I transferred it to my stepmother Archie and told her to arrange a bunch of transfers, without telling me where they were going to go. She set up the transfers, even split the money up and sent it to five different accounts." He grinned. "Nigel reported the movement of the funds to me in real time and I followed every penny. As for losing the money, that won't be an issue."

"What do you mean?" Boris asked. "You're talking about paying two million dollars and trying to follow it. Two million may not be much to you—"

"They asked for an electronic transfer," Tristan said. "We're not counting out dollar bills and packing them into a suitcase. What they're looking for are numbers in a banking account. All we have to do is *simulate* a ransom payment."

"Just like a Trojan virus," J.J. said. "You get an email with an attachment that looks like an innocent baby lamb, when really it's a big bad virus that's going to kill your computer."

"Exactly." Tristan chuckled. "Since they know they'll have to act quickly, odds are they're going to be so excited to get the payment, it will never occur to them that we're paying them off with virtual money from a bogus bank account."

"You've developed digitally counterfeit money?" Boris sighed with a laugh. "I guess it was only a matter of time."

"You're betting your sister's husband's life on them not noticing that the money is fake," Susan said.

"How do we know that he's not already dead?" Perry said.

Susan and Boris shot angry glares in his direction.

Joshua placed a hand on Jessica's shoulder and squeezed it—trying to send strength her way. "Jessie, I'll leave the decision up to you."

"Do it." Fury filled her violet eyes. "I want to bring Murphy home and catch these bastards."

❧ ❧ ❧

"Something isn't right," J.J. whispered to Joshua and Boris after inviting them into the kitchen for a drink while Tristan set up the counterfeit pay-off. "We got surveillance video of who we believe to be Lee Douglas—"

"The license plate of the white van is a match for the van Lee Douglas left New Orleans with," Boris said. "The image of the young man driving it also appears to be a match for the picture on Douglas's driver's license."

"Does Lee Douglas have a bank account in the Cayman Islands?" J.J. poured a full cup of sugar into the pitcher of lemonade. "Is he mentally competent enough to pull off kidnapping a highly trained military officer, who's usually armed, holding him captive, and demanding an electronic payoff?"

"You have two very good points," Joshua said. "Jessica says Lee Douglas is very delusional. If he saw Murphy as a road block between him and Natalie, why the ransom demand?"

"Money for him and Natalie, aka Kitty Katt to make their escape," Boris said.

"Natalie, aka Kitty Katt is dead," Joshua said.

"Maybe he killed her and doesn't remember," J.J. said. "Apparently, this guy is really out there. Archer said his mother claimed he got emails declaring her love to him."

"We asked to see them, but Douglas's mother got spooked and hung up on us," Susan Archer said as she entered the kitchen. "Jessica said it is possible that he wrote them to himself in his delusional state."

J.J. shook his head. "That profile does not fit with this sophisticated ransom demand."

Impatient for the lemonade, Boris reached around J.J. for the pitcher and poured it into the glasses. "The surveillance video only shows Douglas pulling out ahead of Murphy and heading in the same direction that he was going. It doesn't show him abducting Murphy. For all we know, Douglas continued down the road and someone else snatched Murphy."

"No," J.J. said with a firm shake of his head. "Lee Douglas is the one who snatched Murphy. I had a dream last night of Murphy getting abducted and I saw that van."

"You're positive it was that van?" Susan asked.

"Definite. Lee Douglas has Murphy. I can feel it." J.J. shook his head. "But this ransom demand feels out of place. It doesn't fit with what I saw in my dream."

In deep thought, Joshua stared at him before asking, "How did the abductors get Jessica's phone number to call with the ransom demand? Whoever has Murphy must know that his wife has the means to pay a two-million-dollar ransom?"

"Maybe Murphy gave up that information in begging for his life," Perry said from where he had been leaning in the doorway listening in silence.

"Murphy would kill himself before giving up anything," Joshua said in a harsh tone.

"Jessica doesn't give out her phone number to just anyone," J.J. said. "And if Murphy didn't give it to his abductors, that means we have a short list of suspects."

"I'll go ask Jessica to go through her address book to identify potential suspects." Susan grabbed two glasses of lemonade and hurried out of the kitchen.

His eyebrow arched, Joshua shot a glance in Boris's direction. Picking up on the silent message, Boris told Perry, "Latimore, go to the crime lab and check their status on the evidence from the Stepford crime scene."

"But I was going to work with Tristan—"

"I'll work with Tristan," J.J. said since he was aware of the extent of Nigel's capabilities. While Perry had more security clearances than J.J., their sense was that he could not be trusted.

"What experience do you have with computers and the dark web?" Perry asked.

"I'm ordering you to the crime lab," Boris said. "You'll be better able to help us there."

With a huff, Perry spun around and headed out of the kitchen. They heard the door shut when he left.

"Nigel, let me know when Perry Latimore has left the premises," Joshua said.

"Sorry about that, Captain," Boris said as he answered the vibration of his phone.

"He's not coming back to this house," Joshua said. "I won't have Jessica hear talk like that about Murphy."

Boris read the message and uttered a heavy sigh. "The police just found Reginald Baldwin's car. He's the investigator Caldwell was supposed to be meeting with the morning he was murdered."

"The murder that started this whole thing," Joshua said.

"We've had a BOLO out for Baldwin's car since the day of Caldwell's murder. The police just found it parked in one of the long term lots at Dulles Airport." Boris tucked his phone back into the case. "Ransom needs to be paid in less than half an hour. What do you want us to do, Captain?"

Thinking, Joshua looked at J.J. The less Boris and Susan were in on the extent of Nigel's capabilities the better. Even though J.J. only knew as a family member, the Phantoms had been careful to clear him for knowing. There was no telling how quickly the ransom would make its final destination and how long it would take Tristan to identify the owners of the account.

"You and Susan go check out the car," Joshua said. "Stay close to your phones. We'll call you as soon as we get something." He took his cell phone from his pocket and made a call to his CO.

Chapter Nineteen

In the game room, J.J. peered down at Newman, curled and twisted in an unnatural position in the worn recliner. The dog's head was upside-down with his long floppy ears splayed out toward the outer edge of the chair's seat. His jowls hung open to display his teeth.

Not moving, the dog appeared dead.

J.J. was unsure how old Newman was. He was gray when Murphy acquired him—the Bassett-hound-mix came with the condo he had sublet after graduating from the naval academy. Bending over, J.J. peered at the dog's torso to search for any sign that he was breathing.

He saw none.

Damn! First Murphy gets abducted and held for ransom and now his dog dies.

J.J. reached out and placed his hand gently on Newman's shoulder.

With a snort and cry, Newman jumped up from the chair. His eyes bulged.

Equally startled, J.J. leapt back from the chair. "What the hell! I thought you were dead!"

Fixating his gaze on J.J., Newman uttered a noise that sounded like a mixture of a snarl and a snort. He shook himself to regain his composure before rummaging around on the recliner in search of the television remote that had fallen in next to the cushion. Upon locating it, he laid back down on the recliner and changed the station to a Jurassic Park movie.

Carrying a bag of tortilla chips and a tub of salsa, Tristan stopped in the doorway on his way to the control center. He had a tall can of Red Bull tucked under his arm. Following right on his heels, Spencer begged for Tristan to share his chips with her.

Seeing the stunned expression on J.J.'s face, Tristan laughed. "You thought he was dead, didn't you?"

"Does he do that on purpose?"

"He has to amuse himself somehow." Tristan tossed a chip to Spencer, who caught it in her mouth. "I'll give you a hundred bucks to take the remote and change the station."

"He may be old and arthritic, but he still has teeth." J.J. followed Tristan and Spencer down the hallway to the control room. "I'll pass."

❧ ❧ ❧

In the control room, Joshua sat at the counter of the kitchenette and went through Jessica's contact list to uncover potential suspects.

"What about Brett Wagner?" Joshua uttered a sigh filled with frustration.

Brett was the last name on the list and Jessica had cleared everyone else. She insisted she did not give out her cell phone number to anyone she didn't trust. However, as Joshua pointed out, one of those she trusted had apparently abducted her husband and used her cell phone number to make a ransom demand.

Joshua noticed one side of her lip raised in what resembled the beginning of a snarl. "What's wrong with Brett Wagner?"

"Nothing's wrong with him."

Her tone was not convincing. Joshua cocked his head in her direction. His eyebrow arched.

"He's been hitting on me," Jessica said with a sigh.

"I imagine a lot of men hit on you," Joshua said. "You're a beautiful woman. Murphy asked you to marry him less than a day after you two met and I don't see you making a face like that when you hear his name."

"Actually, it was me who proposed to Murphy."

"I stand corrected," Joshua said. "What is it about Brett that makes you snarl?"

"Brett is a player," she said. "He's a trustee baby and has this entitled attitude. Everything's been handed to him—even med school. I don't think he's had to work for anything a day in his life—until recently."

"What happened recently?"

"His girlfriend caught him cheating with Carol's roommate and she kicked him out. Now he's sleeping on a sofa at a friend's apartment."

"If he's a rich, entitled, trustee baby, what's he doing sleeping on someone's couch?" Joshua asked as J.J. and Tristan entered the room and took seats at the bank of monitors.

Jessica had no answer. Slowly, she shook her head. "Brett couldn't have done it. He went with our study group to go see the latest Marvel movie. He called here to invite me to join them."

"And what did you say?" Joshua got up to join Tristan and J.J. at the computer.

"That Murphy and I were spending the evening in—that's what we were planning when Brett called. There's no way he could have pulled off kidnapping Murphy."

She stepped behind Tristan just in time to see him feed a tortilla chip to Spencer. She gave him a head slap. "What have I told you about giving chips to her?"

"She told me that you two had come to an agreement." Tristan rubbed the back of his head.

"She lies. Haven't you learned that by now."

J.J. took several chips from the bowl and dipped one into the salsa. "You have a couch potato who pranks people by playing opossum and another who's a compulsive liar."

"We're just your average dysfunctional American family," Tristan said.

Joshua dipped a chip into the salsa. "You know, Jessie, this Brett could have hired someone to snatch Murphy while he himself established an alibi. What's a better alibi than spending the whole evening with friends?"

She shuddered.

"System is ready for electronic transfer of virtual funds," Nigel said.

The image of a red button appeared on the central monitor. The word "transfer" was written in block letters across the middle of the button. The left monitor displayed two charts. One was of Jessica's bogus bank account, which Tristan had set up in a major banking institution in New York City. He had placed a virtual balance of five million dollars in it. He didn't want the kidnappers to have any knowledge of her actual finances. The second chart was of the bank account into which the kidnappers had ordered the ransom of two million dollars be deposited. The third monitor on the right displayed a map of the world with pin lights indicating banks across the globe for them to follow the phony money.

"Are we ready?" Tristan cracked his knuckles and placed his right hand on the mouse.

Joshua sucked in a deep breath. J.J. took Jessica's hand. He smiled at her.

"Ready," she said in a soft voice.

"Ready," Tristan said. "Set." He pressed the left button on the mouse and clicked on the "Transfer" button. "Go."

"Transfer initiating," Nigel said.

They watched as a progress bar appeared on the left monitor. Gradually, a blue line made its way across the screen. In a matter of ten seconds, the entire line was blue.

"Transfer completed," Nigel said.

"$2,000,000 Deposited" appeared on the lower box confirming the deposit into the bank account in the Cayman Islands.

"Transfer Confirmed," Nigel said.

"Now we will find out if one, the bank realizes that this transfer is not real money," Joshua said, "and most importantly if we're going to be able to trace it."

To answer, Tristan pointed at the world map.

One of the white dots turned blue. Three dotted lines sprouted from the dot. One went to Brazil. Another headed in the opposite direction to South Korea. The third line marked a path to Switzerland.

A spreadsheet beneath noted the country, bank, account number, amount deposited into the account, and date and time of the deposit in World Time Zone. It also noted the name in which the account was listed.

"I don't believe it," J.J. said. "It looks like it's working."

The blue dots and lines multiplied as the ransom was divided and transferred into banks and accounts around the globe. With so much money moving in all different directions, it would have been impossible for a human to follow—but not for Nigel. The spreadsheet below the map filled up rapidly—seemingly at the speed of light.

"Whoever did this has an inside knowledge of the banking business," Tristan said. "This couldn't have been done by hand. Not at this speed. It was set up with a banking program."

"Jessie, do you know anyone with that type of knowledge?" Joshua asked. He ticked off on his fingers. "They have your cell phone number and experience in banking."

"Not just experience," Tristan said, "but access. To do this, they'd have to have access to the international banking network."

"I don't know anyone in banking," Jessica said with a shrug.

In less than five minutes, there was over two-hundred and fifty lines completed on a chart. The monitor was still for so long that Joshua suggested that Nigel had locked up—a comment the AI did not like.

"Please be patient," Nigel said. "After two minutes, if the transfers have ceased, then we may conclude at that point that these two accounts in Hong Kong are the final destination."

Two red dots emerged from the blue nest.

"Transfers completed," Nigel announced.

On each side of the red dots, notes indicated the name of the off-shore bank. The name on one account, which held $500,000, was Selena Parker. Jessica instantly recognized the name on the second account, in which one and a half million dollars of the ransom had been deposited.

"Looks like one of your med school classmates decided to take up felony abduction," Joshua said.

"Wait!" J.J. pointed at the map.

A final blue line crossed the ocean to Washington DC. The total in one of the Hong Kong accounts decreased by nine-thousand-five hundred dollars. The red dot on Washington noted a deposit into the Georgetown branch of a Washington, DC bank.

"Guess who's planning to go out on the town tonight," Tristan said.

"Guess who's going to jail tonight," Joshua said.

Brett Wagner.

CHAPTER TWENTY

"I've got good news," Susan Archer reported to Boris after checking with the head of TSA assigned to Dulles International airport. "They still have all the surveillance videos of the long term parking lots for the day Reginald Baldwin disappeared—including this one."

"What's the bad news?" Boris asked while watching the federal agent examining the lock for the trunk of the car.

"What makes you think I have bad news?"

"Where there's good news, there's always bad news."

"The camera only covers the entrances and exits of the lots."

Susan and Boris observed the area surrounding the car—parked in the furthest corner of the lot located at the outer limits of the busy international airport.

"Which means we won't see who drove this car into the lot and what vehicle they were driving when they left," Susan said.

"He wouldn't have needed a vehicle." Boris pointed over her shoulder at the airport shuttle bus entering the lot. Slowly, it made its way to the stop. A man wearing a backpack and suitcase climbed on board. After the doors shut, the bus looped around the lot and eased back out onto the main road to the airport. "All he needed to do was catch a ride on the shuttle to the main terminal—"

"And then take a taxi back home," Susan said.

The agent working on the trunk wrenched it open. As the lid flew up—a rancid odor hit Boris and Susan in the face. They covered their noses and mouths. Their eyes watered as they peered inside to see what they already knew was there.

It was the decomposed body of Reginald Baldwin.

"Someone really doesn't like loose ends," Susan said.

"Check the surveillance video to pinpoint the time this car arrived here." Boris took his buzzing cell phone out of its case on his belt. "Then we'll check our suspects' accounts. Maybe we'll get lucky and one of them didn't have enough cash to pay the cabbie who took him home."

Boris checked the ID on his phone, which read Captain Thornton. "Yes, Captain?"

"Any good news there?"

"I wouldn't call a dead federal agent in the trunk of a car good, sir. We're having it towed into the lab for forensics to go over for evidence. I hope things are looking better there. How's Nigel and Tristan's Trojan horse doing?"

"Worked like a dream," Joshua said with a smile in his voice. "Send Susan back to the lab to await the results from the victim in the car. Tell them to put a rush on it. I want you to come back to the Thorny Rose Manor—alone."

"Alone, Captain?"

"Alone, Hamilton."

℘ ℘ ℘

"I'm not even going to ask how you and your butler got access to all the world's banking data to set up this program," Boris said after Tristan showed him the charts and data on his laptop and tablet at the kitchen table. He held up his hands in surrender. "Less I know, the better."

"The important point of all this is that we have identified two suspects," Joshua said. "Brett Wagner and Selena Parker. We believe Brett is the brains behind the abduction because he's in Jessica's study group—"

"And has my cell number to make the call for the ransom demand."

"According to my background check, Selena Parker works in international banking for the FDIC," Tristan said.

"Where do you have the resources to run a background check?" Boris asked.

"Google and social media." Tristan shrugged his shoulders. "It's fast and free. She graduated last May with a four-year degree in a double major of finance and cybersecurity and came out to Washington to work with the FDIC."

"So she's not stupid," J.J. said from where he was perched on a stool at the breakfast bar.

"Except when it comes to men," Jessica said. "Selena rented a room from a friend in my study group. She and Brett hooked up and Brett's live-in girlfriend kicked him out. It turns out there was more to the story than meets the eye. Brett led me and everyone to believe that he came from money and was rich. Wore nothing but tailored clothes. Drove a BMW convertible." She shook her head. "Nothing but a cover-up for a sleaze."

"I did some digging around on social media," Tristan said, "and found a feud between Ashleigh and Selena around the time of the blow-up—leading up to Brett getting tossed out. Ashleigh bought Brett that car. It was in her name and she was making the payments. She kept the car and kicked him to the curb."

"I'd gotten the impression that Ashleigh was this young professional," Jessica said. "Turns out she's in her mid-thirties and working as an office manager. He was living off her. She was buying his clothes and paying for his school—all with the expectation of becoming a doctor's wife."

"He was using her," J.J. said.

"Then Brett set his sights on Jessica," Joshua said.

"Because he needed to find someone to support him in the lifestyle to which he wished to become accustomed," Jessica said. "But when he realized I was too happily married to leave my husband for him, he decided to support himself by other means."

"By kidnapping your husband for ransom," Boris said. "Have you been able to find out through your study group where Brett could be keeping Murphy?"

Jessica answered by hanging her head. "Brett has an alibi for when Murphy disappeared. He was out with a bunch of our friends last night. Plus, I know he'd never be able to get close enough to Murphy to touch him."

"He must have hired someone to do it," Boris said.

"Maybe Selena did it," Tristan said.

"She is a petite little thing," Jessica said. "Maybe a hundred pounds. No taller than five feet."

"Helpless woman abandoned on the side of the road late at night with car trouble," J.J. said. "Murphy would've stopped to help her."

"Then she tased and incapacitated him," Joshua said.

"Where do these two live?" Boris asked.

"Brett is sleeping on a friend's sofa in Rosslyn," Jessica said. "Selena is renting a room in Carol's brownstone in Georgetown. Neither of them have a place where they can keep Murphy."

"We have to find out where they've got him," Joshua said.

"Brett called earlier—before the ransom call—to ask how I was doing," Jessica said. "I think he was trying to find out what we know. Anyway, before we hung up, he told me to call him anytime—even if I only needed a shoulder to cry on. Maybe if I called him and ask him to bring his big broad shoulders over here for me to cry on."

"How stupid is he?" Tristan asked. "Now that he thinks he has two million dollars of your money, do you think he's going to go anywhere near you and possibly implicate himself?"

"Then you come up with an idea of how to find Murphy," she replied in an angry tone.

"I've always wanted to try water boarding," Tristan said.

"Water boarding is illegal," J.J. said.

"Only if Brett survives to blab about it." Noticing that everyone was staring at him with their arms crossed, Tristan said, "Hey, I want to get Murphy back, too. *He's* got a sense of humor."

"We'll think of something." J.J. patted Jessica's hand.

"Maybe instead of coming up with some complicated plan of attack," Joshua said, "why don't we go for a simple straight-forward tactic? Jessica just simply calls Brett, tells him what has happened, and asks him for some comforting advice about what to do next. Since he believes he's gotten away with this—"

"He does have an ego," Jessica said. "He won't be able to resist flaunting how smart he is."

"If he's cocky enough, he'll implicate himself," Boris said. "Sounds like a plan to me."

"I still want to try water boarding," Tristan muttered.

"If you insist," J.J. said, "when we get Murphy back, we'll do water boarding—on you."

Joshua moved over to look at the monitors from over Tristan's shoulder. "Where are our suspects now?"

"I wasn't able to pinpoint the location of the computer where the money transfers took place. I'm not surprised. It had to have been heavily encrypted to have been able to pull off all of those transfers the way it did. But, I have been able to track our kidnappers based on Brett's cell phone—not the burner phone he used to make the ransom demand—his official one."

"And Selena Parker?" Joshua asked.

"That was a little harder," Tristan said. "It turns out she's on her parents' family plan. I did a search for the location of all their phones and found one here in the Washington DC area. Both hers and Brett's are in the same area. They must be together."

"Great," J.J. said. "Where are they?"

"They're at the Ritz-Carlton in Georgetown." Tristan chuckled. "They have a room under Brett's name. Checked in without reservations. I'm surprised they got in on the weekend."

Jessica hit the button to connect a call to Brett and put it on speaker phone.

"Keep him talking," Joshua said while the phone rang. "I've had a lot of experience with these types. The more they talk, the more confident they become and the more likely they are to trip themselves up."

"I know what I'm doing," Jessica hissed as Brett connected the call on his end.

"Jessica! I'm so glad you called. I've been thinking about you all day. Any word on Murphy?"

"None." Jessica let out a sob. "We paid two million dollars to get Murphy back."

"Wow. Two mil…"

"It's been over an hour and we still haven't heard anything about where he is," she said. "I've been waiting—Oh, Brett! I'm so scared. I could really use a friend right now." She let out a breathy—and sensual—sigh. "Were you serious when you offered your shoulder to cry on?"

"Of course."

"I could really use a friend right now."

They could hear a curse and thud in the background.

"Excuse me," Brett said before there was silence. They assumed he had muted the call to keep them from hearing Selena in the background.

"I think Selena doesn't want Brett to share his shoulder," Boris said in a whisper.

"Brett, are you still there?" Jessica asked.

Silence.

Glancing at each other, they continued to wait for Brett to return to the phone. Finally, Jessica asked Nigel if she still had a connection.

"Brett has placed the call on hold," Nigel responded.

Abruptly, Brett returned to the line. "Jessica, are you still there?" His usually smooth charismatic tone had become anxious.

"Is everything all right?"

"Yes." He chuckled. "My roommate and his girlfriend got into a fight and I needed to step in. That's me! Always the voice of reason. Things are a little crowded here. How about if I come over?"

This offer was unexpected. Jessica turned to Joshua for guidance. He nodded for her to accept.

"Sure," she said.

"I've got a few things to do here," Brett said. "I'll be there in an hour. Will that work?"

"Sure. Do you know where I live?"

"I'll find you," he said with a laugh.

Brett disconnected the call.

"Tristan, keep tracking Brett's phone," Joshua said. "As soon as he leaves the hotel, block him so that he can't notify Selena and she can't reach him."

"The phone will ring three times before sending them to voice mail," Tristan said. "But they'll actually be leaving a message with Nigel."

"Boris and I will call you when we get to the Carlton." Joshua turned to Jessica and took her into a warm hug. "Jessica, I love you. You're like a daughter to me. You're as smart as you are beautiful. But, I feel I have to tell you this."

"I know. Don't kill Brett," she said.

Joshua nodded. "Don't kill Brett."

"Can we torture him?" Tristan asked.

"No!" Joshua, J.J., and Boris said in unison.

Jessica held up her hands. "I promise no one will lay a hand on him."

"Guys!" Tristan sat up in his seat and leaned over the screen of his laptop. "I think we have a problem."

"What kind of problem?" J.J. hurried around the table to peer at the monitor over Tristan's shoulder.

"It's Selena Parker's account in Hong Kong." Tristan pointed at the monitor. "The one with half a million dollars in it. That money was just transferred from her account over into Brett's."

Joshua joined J.J. in watching over Tristan's shoulder. "The one here or in Hong Kong."

"The one in Hong Kong," Tristan said. "Now Selena Parker's account has been closed. Something is going on."

"Well, Brett did say he had a few things to do before coming over," Boris said.

"Like tying up a loose end named Selena," Joshua said.

"We were on hold for a very long time," Jessica said. "Maybe my call prompted Selena's green-eyed monster to appear and—" She covered her mouth with a gasp. "Do you think he killed her because he decided to ditch her for me?"

"He'd have to be hooked up with her in order to ditch her," J.J. said. "Guys like Brett are users. More likely he killed her because he was always planning to kill her and steal her share of the ransom."

"Break out your top hat, Boris," Joshua said. "We're going to the Ritz."

Chapter Twenty-One

"I've spent my whole adult life working for the government." Boris kept both eyes on the dark twisting road leading to the expressway.

Silently, Joshua prayed.

Darkness had fallen—bringing home that his son had been missing for a full day. Time was moving in closer to the twenty-four-hour mark. With each second that went by, the odds of finding Murphy alive were getting worse.

J.J. insisted Murphy was still alive—he could feel it.

Now that Brett believed he had the ransom, he had no reason to keep Murphy alive. *If* he had him. J.J. insisted Lee Douglas had Murphy. Joshua prayed J.J.'s psychic connection with his twin was right.

Hopefully, Jessica could extract some useful information from Brett. If not, J.J. could be quite persuasive. Joshua had ordered him and Tristan to stay behind to help.

"After retiring from the marines, I was picked up as a department chief at NCIS." Boris cocked an eyebrow in Joshua's direction. "I've met all kinds of people. Seen all types of things. One thing I learned in boot camp that I never forgot—just follow orders and don't ask questions—no matter how weird things appear."

"That's why I've invited you along, Hamilton."

"Murphy is tremendously over qualified for his position as liaison at NCIS." Boris turned the steering wheel to merge onto the beltway.

"He's young. Eager. Full of energy. Always, he was full of energy. That was one way to tell him and J.J. apart when they were kids. J.J. would be playing the piano while Murphy was swinging from the chandelier."

"I heard from more than one source that the SEALS wanted him when he graduated from the naval academy, but *he* turned them down."

Joshua shrugged. "I guess he had his reasons."

"And you're supposed to be *retired*."

"I am retired."

"You don't act like it." Boris cocked his head and looked at Joshua out of the corner of his eye. "You know what else I've heard?"

"What?"

"That there's this ultra—I mean really deep ultra-secret ops group working for the very highest echelons of the military—"

"Do you mean swamp creatures?" Joshua laughed.

"I mean Phantoms."

"You mean like the Avengers?" Joshua uttered a hearty laugh. "I can see Murphy in that Captain America suit."

"Do you remember last fall, when that yacht with four college students broke down and drifted into Mexican territory?"

Joshua nodded his head. "One of the students was a navy reservist, and he had a couple of guns with him. Mexican authorities found guns on the boat and arrested all of them. The guns were all legally registered, but technically they had crossed illegally into Mexico."

"The secretary of state tried to negotiate for their release, but talks had broken down because of a variety of political issues," Boris said. "If the military went into this foreign country to get them, it would have been perceived as an act of war. Politics and diplomacy had tied our hands, leaving these kids and their families twisting in the wind."

"What does this have to do with Murphy?"

"Well, wouldn't you know it," Boris chuckled, "the electricity in the whole area where the jail they were keeping these kids went out. The reports I read said that even the Internet satellite serving that area shut down. Complete communications blackout—during which the kids escaped and returned home."

"The news said the president had negotiated for their release," Joshua said.

"That's what the Mexican authorities said to save face," Boris said. "They didn't want it known that their prison had been infiltrated by some American special ops with the power to black out a whole area."

"And you think my son did that?"

"I think he played a role," Boris said. "Two days before the break out, Murphy abruptly got called out by his CO for a temporary assignment. He returned to NCIS the day after the news broke that the kids had returned home to their families." He chuckled. "That's not the only time, either. Not every case makes the news. A lot of those classified special ops cross my desk and the really bizarre ones seem to happen while Murphy is gone on a classified assignment."

"Couldn't those kids have been smart enough to figure out a way to escape during a freak electrical blackout?"

"Word around the Pentagon is that these lucky instances have been the work of Phantoms."

"The Phantoms are a myth, Boris. They don't exist."

"That's what they say is so special about them," Boris said. "Nobody can confirm that they exist. They work completely without any political or ideological agenda. They answer to no one except the highest powers in the military. Their exclusive mission is to protect our country and its citizens without the interference of politicians or bureaucrats with agendas. Each member of the team is hand-picked—given the best training and—" He cast a glance in Joshua's direction. "—coolest toys to complete their mission. Maybe like an AI named Nigel."

"Can you really see Tristan Faraday being a cloak and dagger special ops guy?"

"No," Boris said, "but that would explain a lot of questions I have about why Murphy isn't out kicking butts and taking names instead of getting paper cuts."

"Well, Hamilton," Joshua said with a drawl, "all I can tell you is what your drill sergeant told you on that first day in boot camp."

"Do what you're told and don't ask questions," Hamilton said before ordering his hands-free phone to connect to an incoming call from Susan Archer.

"Hey, Chief, where are you?"

"On our way to follow up a lead on the ransom demand for Murphy," Hamilton said. "Any news there?"

"Not good news," she replied. "Just got a call from Kendall Harris, Commander Caldwell's daughter. She hasn't seen or heard from her husband since last night."

"That's the son-in-law who had a Colt semi-automatic like the kind used to kill Caldwell," Boris told Joshua in a low voice.

"A gun that is now missing," Joshua said.

"Exactly," Boris said before asking Susan, "Did she say when she talked to Woody last?"

"She said they got into a fight after our investigators left," Susan said. "She confronted him about the missing gun and how he didn't get along with her father. She pointed out that no one knew where he was at the time of the murder. He got in his car and left and never came home. Do you want me to put out a BOLO on him?"

"Wait a minute," Boris said. "If I remember right, didn't the officers who went to meet with Erin Caldwell right after the murder write in their report that Woody Harris arrived back at the house in his car with a kayak strapped across the top and wearing Ross Caldwell's wet suit?"

"Let me check," Susan said.

"He could have killed Caldwell on the way to the river," Joshua said in a low voice, "and went kayaking to establish an alibi."

"Perry checked on Woody's alibi," Susan said. "I have the report right here. Two park rangers identified Woody Harris as a doofus they had to fish out of the river right at seven o'clock. As soon as the park opened, he was one of the first people in the river. Jumped into the river with his kayak—lost control and went flying over the falls. There are several viral videos confirming his alibi on YouTube under the category of sports fails. The park rangers who rescued him have nominated Woody for 'Idiot of the Year.'"

"Ross Caldwell was killed at seven o'clock," Boris said. "If Woody has a solid alibi, why did he run away?"

"Because he's being set up," Joshua said.

As expected, the Ritz-Carlton was hopping. It was Saturday night and the cherry blossoms on the mall were at their height—signifying the arrival of spring. University students from Georgetown, George Washington, and George Mason poured into the city to fill the clubs. Fifteen minutes after the GPS lady announced that they were five minutes away Boris turned his SUV into the hotel's garage.

"We would have gotten here faster if we had abandoned the car and walked," Joshua said when they finally found an empty parking space. "Brett is probably already at the Thorny Rose."

Boris stepped onto the elevator to find that Joshua had pushed the button for the third floor. "They've got a one-bedroom suite on the third floor," Joshua said. "Room three-eighteen."

"Did the front desk tell Tristan that?"

"Something like that."

When the elevator doors opened, Joshua sprinted across the common area and down the corridor. They counted off the numbers on the doors until they arrived at a room toward the end of the hallway.

Joshua pounded on the door. "Federal agents. Ms. Parker open the door."

Boris removed his gun for its holster.

They waited.

There was silence.

While Joshua unholstered his weapon, Boris stepped forward to knock on the door. "Ms. Parker, open the door. Federal agents. We just want to talk."

The doors on either side of the suite opened slightly and curious guests peered out. Boris gestured for them to return to their rooms. While one door shut, the woman in the other room asked, "Is she dead?"

"Excuse me?" Boris asked.

"Did he kill her?" the woman asked in a soft voice while her male companion tried to pull her back inside. "They were having an awful fight. I heard furniture overturning."

Joshua pulled his cell phone out of his jacket pocket and turned on an app to read the security code to open the door.

"I wanted to call the police but my husband—" Her husband yanked her inside and slammed the door shut.

Joshua opened the door and charged inside. "Selena!" He went from room to room within the suite. Feminine personal items were scattered in the bathroom. "Bathtub is still wet." He opened the closet door to reveal women's clothes hung up. He took out the overnight bag to show Boris. "There's two outfits and three pairs of shoes in this closet. Does this suitcase look big enough to carry all that?"

"I'm not certain, but I think this is the scene of the fight the lady next door overheard." Boris stood in the middle of the bedroom that looked like it had been ransacked. Clothes, shoes, and personal items were hurled around the room. A table and chair were overturned. An ice bucket rested on its side. The ice that had been inside was melting in a pool of champagne that had spilled from the open bottle.

Boris picked up the stark white terrycloth robe with the Ritz-Carlton logo on the breast pocket from where it lay across the bed. Joshua found the twisted belt discarded on the floor. While the robe was moist, as if it had recently been put on after a bath, the belt was wet to the point that the fluffy terry fibers were crushed.

"We got strands of hair caught in the belt." Joshua slowly entwined the ends of the belt around his fists. "I think he strangled her."

"But she's not here, Captain. Like you think he strangled her and carried her out of the hotel through the lobby and out into the street filled with clubbers?"

"Something like that." Joshua took his cell phone out of the pocket.

❧ ❧ ❧

"Okay, where do you want it?" J.J. asked Jessica while trying to maneuver his way through the patio door with an enormous potted rose bush in his arms. As if it was not hard enough to peer around the thorny plant, Spencer seemed to be purposely trying to trip him by zig-zagging in front of him.

"Right here." She pointed at a tall table she had placed in the middle of the room and covered with a table cloth.

As soon as J.J. placed the rose bush on the table, Spencer leapt without warning into his arms and licked his face.

"Spencer, stop being a pest," Jessica scolded the blue dog before putting an old apron on over her form fitting spring dress.

"It's okay, I love affection. She must smell Ollie, or Charley, or Gulliver, or Buttercup—"

"Buttercup?" Jessica started at his reference to Murphy's pet name for her.

"She's one of our dairy cows," J.J. said. "She's a favorite. Very sweet."

"A cow? Named Buttercup?"

"Every dairy farm has at least one cow named Buttercup. I think it's a regulation with the department of agriculture."

Her violet eyes grew wide. "Murphy named me after a *cow*?" She picked up the pruning shears from where she had placed them on the pool table.

Clutching Spencer under his arm, J.J. reached into his jeans' pocket for his phone. "Have I shown you a picture of our new baby lamb? We named him Ollie." With one hand, he scrolled for the picture. Unable to find the one he was looking for, he showed her a picture of Izzy, Poppy, and their respective horses, Gulliver, a liver-spotted appaloosa and Comanche, a palomino mare.

"I know what you're doing." Jessica smiled at the image of her fresh faced, curly haired sister-in-law, and Poppy, the lovely horse trainer. With her Irish Setter red hair, and freckles from head to toe, she was as lovely on the outside as she was on the inside. At the farm, she was always surrounded by dogs, horses, and even Charley, the farm's temperamental rooster. "And it's working." With a grin, she handed the phone back to him. "When are you and the beloved Poppy getting together?"

J.J. shoved the phone into his pocket. He extracted a gun from where he had it tucked in the waistband of his jeans and checked the cartridge to make certain it was full of bullets.

"We can either talk about the beloved Poppy or why Murphy selected a cow's moniker for my pet name. It's your choice."

"Why do all the women in my family want to hook me up?" He tucked the gun back into the waistband under his shirt.

"Because we want you to be as happy as we are."

"Yeah, you and Murphy have been really happy since you went back to school."

"He's told you about the fighting?"

"You both have to bend," he said, "and Murphy is not really that flexible. It's always been his way or the highway with him." Seeing the sadness fill her eyes, he stepped forward and took her arm. "But he loves you more than the highway. He's committed to your marriage and when he commits to something, he'll do whatever it takes to make things work—even if it means changing how he is."

Jessica flashed him a smile, which made J.J. smile back at her. She sniffed. "Your smile is identical to Murphy's." She sighed. "Makes me miss him more." She swallowed. "We need to talk about something else. Like you and the beloved Poppy."

J.J. backed up. "I'm not going there."

"You two are together all day every day—"

"Because she's my *employee*," J.J. said. "In today's culture, if I make any movement to change our current relationship in a personal—romantic—direction, and she doesn't reciprocate, then I can kiss my reputation goodbye."

"Maybe that is today's culture, but it's not right," she said. "What if Poppy does feel the same way? Which I think she does. She's told us that until now, she's never spent more than a few months—never more than six months in one place. She's been with you for almost a year."

"The farm," J.J. said. "She's been with the farm—not me."

"She was with you when you got shot," Jessica said. "She took care of you. You two go to church together every Sunday morning and she has Sunday supper with your family. You two go out to dinner together on Friday and she cooks dinner for you on Saturday—"

"That's just an arrangement we have," he said with an air of dismissal.

"Arrangement?" Jessica folded her arms across her chest. "What kind of *arrangement* are we talking about?"

"Poppy puts so much time into the farm and she works really hard with the horses—it's hard physical work—" he shrugged his shoulders. "I take her out to dinner on Friday night to let her know how much she means…" his voice trailed off, but Jessica swore she heard him say "to me."

Clearing his throat, he focused on Newman, who was glaring up at him for making too much noise. The Bassett hound couldn't hear the plan the heroes in the movie he was watching were hatching to escape from the town overrun with zombies.

Jessica resumed. "And she cooks dinner for you on Saturday…"

"Payback for Friday night," he said.

"She cooks dinner for you only because she owes you *payback* for Friday night?"

J.J. nodded his head. "That's all it is. Nothing more."

"And this *arrangement* has been going on for how long?"

J.J. shrugged his shoulders. "Since Poppy came to work for me." He swallowed.

"Almost a *year*."

"Brett Wagner just purchased a one-way airline ticket to Hong Kong!" Tristan yelled while closing the door to the control room. "He's at Dulles International Airport."

"Looks like you got stood-up!" J.J. told Jessica.

Holding his tablet under his arm, Tristan trotted into the game room and perched on a tall stool at the bar. "Josh just called. Looks like Brett and Selena had a royal falling out. He bought the plane ticket after transferring the ransom money out of her account. Josh checked the hotel security and a big suitcase that Selena had when she checked in is gone. Brett wheeled it out with him when he left. Josh thinks Brett strangled her and carried her body out of the hotel in the suitcase."

"If Brett gets on that plane we'll never find Murphy." Ripping off the apron, Jessica ran up the stairs.

J.J. was directly behind her. "We're closer to the airport than Dad."

"I'm driving!" Jessica said.

"I'm driving."

"It's my car."

"I've never driven a Ferrari."

"I'm driving and that's final!"

Tristan yelled, "I'll stay here and—"

The front door slammed to signal their departure.

"Whatever."

Remaining on his stool, Tristan looked at Newman, who peered back at him. The displeasure in the Bassett hound's face revealed his disappointment that Tristan was not leaving with them.

"We live here, too."

Newman shook his head so hard that his oversized ears flew in various directions.

"Okay, I don't live here," Tristan said. "I live in the guest house. But still, I'm higher up in the hierarchy than you are."

With a groan, Newman stretched. When he finished, he looked up at Tristan as if surprised to see that he was still there. The dog seemed to shrug his shoulders with a "*Whatever,*" before returning to his movie.

"What are you watching?" Receiving no answer, Tristan crossed the room to study the scene of a horde of zombies making their way down a street. "Oh, I love this movie. Move over." To Newman's displeasure, he nudged the dog over to one side to squeeze onto the recliner.

CHAPTER TWENTY-TWO

On Saturday night, Dulles International Airport was busy. Jessica raced her Ferrari into the short-term parking lot in front of the terminal. "Nigel, what's the airline and flight Brett's registered to take?"

"American Airlines. One-three-six-two," Nigel reported. "He is leaving in two hours from Gate B-Seventy-Six. His flight is scheduled to depart at eleven-forty-seven."

"Nigel, do you have any way to tell if he's made it through security yet?" J.J. asked.

While Nigel said there wasn't, Jessica turned the sports car into a parking space. "Can't your father order security to keep him off the flight? Keep him from leaving the country?"

"Doubt it," J.J. said. "Every piece of evidence we have against him has been illegally obtained. Basically, he's just some guy who decided to suddenly take a trip to Hong Kong.'

"To spend my two million bucks." She turned the engine off with a vengeance.

"Counterfeit digital bucks." He unbuckled his seat belt. "I'm tempted to suggest we just should let him go. In seventy hours that phony money in his account is going to dissolve into cyberspace and he'll find himself stuck in Hong Kong with no way home."

"And we still won't know where Murphy is." She slid out of the car, slammed the door shut, and pressed the control to lock the car.

"I said I was tempted." J.J. took her hand and led her in a run to the terminal.

Once inside the terminal, they stopped at the top of the escalator on the main level. Upon seeing the line snaking up and down the concourse to go through security, Jessica groaned.

"J.J.!" An unfamiliar feminine voice called out through the crowd of travelers.

"Did someone just call you?" Jessica asked.

J.J. searched the various faces of people moving to and fro around them. "I don't know anybody here."

A slender woman in black slacks and loose-fitting matching jacket broke from the horde to step over to them. "Jessica?" She held up a federal agent's shield for them to see. "Special Agent Ripley Vaccaro. I'm a friend of Murphy's. Captain Thornton sent me. He told me to look for someone who looked like Murphy."

When J.J. and Jessica hesitated, she added in a low voice, "I'm a good friend."

Seeing that they were still questioning, she cleared her throat. "A very good friend."

"Ah!" Jessica and J.J. caught on. Agent Ripley was a Phantom.

"CO has dispatched the team," she explained while leading them toward security. "Our mission is to keep Brett Wagner from leaving the country. Captain Thornton suspects he killed his accomplice and disposed of the body."

"Do you know what he even looks like?" Jessica asked while hurrying to keep up with the agent's brisk pace.

"Nigel forwarded his passport photo to each Phantom." She led them past the travelers waiting in the long snaking security line. "We have agents scattered throughout the airport looking for him."

"On what grounds can the FBI detain him?" J.J. asked. "We have no legally obtained or real evidence to prove he abducted my brother or received a ransom for his release."

"No, we don't," Ripley said. "But we do have a missing woman. Selena Parker. Witnesses reported hearing a loud argument between Wagner and Ms. Parker at the Ritz-Carlton. According to security footage, Brett Wagner was the last person to see her alive. That gives us grounds to hold him as a murder suspect."

J.J. was impressed. "Oh, you're good."

"That's why I'm a Phantom." She held up her badge for the TSA agent and jerked her thumb over her shoulder. "They're with me."

The three of them hurried through the security check point. "His plane is leaving from Gate B-Seventy-Six," Jessica said.

"This obviously was not planned in advance," Ripley said. "He only just booked his flight to Hong Kong."

"That's where the ransom was deposited," J.J. said.

"But he's got to hide out here in the airport for two hours," Ripley said.

"It isn't like this airport doesn't have a lot of places for him to hide." Jessica studied in many faces of the passengers scurrying about with their luggage. "Most likely, he's changed his appearance. If we don't find him—"

"Don't worry," Ripley said. "We've issued a no-fly order for him. He's not getting on that plane."

"Maybe he's getting on another plane," J.J. said. "Jessica, what about private chartered flights? Do they have to go through all the same security checkpoints and luggage procedures as commercial flights?"

"No!" Jessica sprinted up the stairs to the main terminal. J.J. hurried behind her.

"With two million dollars, he could leave on a private chartered flight anywhere at any time." Ripley said into her radio, "Hold all private flights leaving from the airport."

 C/3   C/3   C/3

"Over here!" Joshua gestured for Boris and a couple of airport police officers to join him where he had found the white sedan with Maryland license plates. "This is Selena Parker's car." He peered into the driver's side window. "The seat is all the way back. According to her driver's license, she's five feet tall. She didn't drive this car last."

"Maybe her boyfriend drove it," one of the officers said, "and they're traveling together."

"Her overnight bag is still at the hotel," Boris said.

"We need to look in the trunk." Blocking the officers' view with his body, Joshua held his cell phone in front of the keyless lock and worked the application to open the door.

"Do you have a warrant?"

Boris started to say they didn't when Joshua opened the door.

"Looks like they didn't lock it." Before anyone could object, Joshua peered into the back seat and found assorted items—indications of a messy car owner. He pressed the trunk release button.

"Wait a minute," one of the officers said. "You can't go searching a car without a warrant."

"We have a witness stating that the owner of this car was last seen fighting with her boyfriend," Boris said. "Now she's missing."

"Maybe because her boyfriend gave her a trip to Hawaii to make up for the fight," the other officer said.

"I found the suitcase," Joshua called out to Boris who was holding back the officers threatening to halt them.

"Who goes to Hawaii without their suitcase?" Boris asked.

Joshua pulled the suitcase toward him to lift out of the trunk but found it too heavy. Instead he unzipped it. He threw back the top and groaned.

eɔ eɔ eɔ

Jessica dodged and shoved her way through the throngs of people rushing to flights and searching for loved ones who had just landed. The crowds scattered considerably when she turned a corner to an out-of-the-way section of the terminal.

She shoved her way through the glass doors to enter the world of the rich and privileged. Even the noisy hum and buzz from the international airport terminal knew better than to filter through the heavy glass doors to disturb those waiting for their private flights. The waiting lounge was filled with soft instrumental music meant to soothe the nerves of its guests.

A concierge was serving a sherry on a silver tray to a tiny elderly woman clad in a pink Chanel suit. Wearing a thick diamond collar, her standard white poodle sat in the leather wing-backed chair directly across from her.

"Poor Gigi is in a rather snit today," she warned the server. "We just discovered that her cook has been serving her canned farm-raised salmon instead of fresh wild caught."

Upon seeing Jessica and J.J. burst through the door, the concierge took one look at Jessica with fury in her eyes and sensed that they did not belong there.

"May I help you?" His words offered to assist them. His tone ordered them to leave.

Jessica spotted her quarry scurrying behind the bar. "There you are, you sniveling little worm!" She charged across the lounge.

J.J. had never seen Brett, but his guilty retreat told him that they had found their man.

"Oh, dear!" The woman drinking the sherry shrieked at the sight of the couple hitting the bar from opposing ends. Desperate to escape, Brett went up and over the bar, breaking crystal glassware and sending shards of broken glass flying. J.J. and Jessica attempted to grab him by the ankles as he tumbled head first to the floor.

Landing in the broken glass, Brett cut his hands and cheek, but even that was not going to stop him from claiming his fortune. Seeing J.J. coming at him, he jumped to his feet and yanked a gun from where he had been concealing it in the waistband of his slacks. "Get back!"

J.J. jumped in front of Jessica.

The concierge ushered the elderly woman out of the chair and across the room to safety. "We can't leave Gigi!" She called to the poodle who remained in her chair.

Ripley burst through the door with her gun drawn. "Drop it, Wagner! There's no way out!"

"Oh yes, there is! I have my ticket and my plane is leaving in twenty-eight minutes!"

"We just want to know where Murphy is," Jessica said. "I paid the ransom."

"I'll send instructions once I get where I'm going."

"Some place where there's no extradition," J.J. said.

"Exactly," Brett said.

"You're not leaving here!" Ripley said.

"Then Jessica is going to end up being a widow," Brett said with a chuckle.

"You are an awful man!" the elderly woman said. "That young lady paid you what you asked for. You promised to give her back her husband and now you won't." She shook her finger at him. "An honorable man keeps his word."

"I never said I was honorable."

"You're not only dishonorable, you're a bastard," Jessica said.

"I'm a rich bastard," Brett said with a chuckle.

"Somebody needs to teach you a lesson about manners, young man," the elderly woman said.

Brett aimed the gun at her. "How about if I teach you a lesson about minding your own business, you old biddy?"

Before anyone had time to react, Gigi launched seventy-five pounds of fur, teeth, and diamonds to connect with Brett's lower body—directly between the legs.

With his testicles caught in what felt like a bear trap, Brett dropped onto his knees. Still the poodle refused to let go. Dropping the gun in his anguish, Brett screamed like a wounded animal and attempted to pry the poodle's jaws open to free his family jewels.

"I told you Gigi was in a snit," the woman said.

Ripley joined J.J. in trying to remove the dog. Upon seeing airport security arrive with Joshua and Boris, the elderly woman clapped her hands. "Gigi, time for us to board our jet for Paris. You may release that nasty man now. I think he's learned his lesson."

Immediately, Gigi released her hold on Brett and trotted over to her master.

The concierge took the woman's arm to escort her to the gate.

"Oh, is the shrimp on the plane fresh?" She patted Gigi on the top of her head. "Gigi likes her shrimp fresh."

"What Gigi wants, Gigi gets."

Once Brett was cuffed and deposited in a chair, Joshua grabbed him by the front of his shirt. "Brett Wagner, we found the suitcase that you left in the trunk of Selena's car.

You know the one. The one in which you had stuffed her body after killing her."

Brett chuckled at him.

Joshua lifted him up and slammed him back down into the chair. "Where's my son?"

"Lawyer," Brett said.

ɞ ɞ ɞ

"We've got you for killing Selena Parker," Joshua told Brett Wagner.

Desperate to find Murphy, Special Agent Ripley Vaccaro finally consented to Joshua interrogating Brett in the conference room where they held him while preparing to transport him back to Washington.

She only agreed to allow him in with the promise that he would not touch Brett. Just to ensure that Joshua wouldn't strangle their suspect in a fit of rage, she and another agent remained in the room as well.

J.J. was watching the interrogation through the window between the two offices when he felt a sharp pain on the right side of his head—directly above his ear. His head throbbed. The room swirled around him.

"J.J., are you okay?"

He turned to Jessica only to see two of her swimming before his eyes. He reached out to her, but had difficulty determining where she stood before him.

Jessica grabbed his hand when she saw him becoming unsteady on his feet. "What's wrong?" She helped him sit in a chair.

"It's Murphy," he gasped.

"You've got nothing on me," Brett said with a cocky grin.

"How about brandishing a firearm in an airport—for a start?" Ripley asked.

"We have witnesses who saw you and Selena Parker check into the Ritz-Carlton together," Joshua said. "Witnesses in the suites on either side of yours heard the two of you fighting. We even have hotel surveillance video of you leaving the hotel with her suitcase. Plus, we have garage footage of you taking her car—the same car where we found her suitcase in the trunk and her nude body in it."

The smirk on Brett's face sickened Joshua. He was going to offer them a deal—Murphy's life for his freedom.

"It's not too late," Brett said. "Let me get on a jet and fly out of here. Once I reach my destination, I'll call Jessica with the location of where she can find Murphy."

Joshua slammed his hand down flat on the table. "You—"

The door opened, and Jessica stepped inside. Furious by the interruption, Joshua shot a glare in her direction.

"We need to talk," she said.

"You do that," Brett said. "Talk some sense into your old man."

"Big talk for a guy who got taken down by a poodle." Jessica led Joshua and Ripley into the office down the hall where Boris and J.J. were waiting. J.J. held his throbbing head in his hands.

"I know what you're going to tell me," Joshua said to Boris. "I'm too personally involved."

"Hey, you're getting results, Captain."

"We still don't have Murphy's location."

"Brett's bluffing." J.J. sat up in his seat. "He doesn't have Murphy."

Joshua cocked his head at him.

"Excuse me," Ripley said. "The ransom money ended up in a Hong Kong account with Wagner's name on it. He booked this private flight one-way to Hong Kong so that he can get that money. What makes you think he doesn't have Murphy stashed someplace?"

"J.J. had a vision," Jessica said.

"J.J.… had a vision? You called us out of an interrogation for a *vision*?" Ripley laughed. "Excuse me. I don't believe in psychics."

"I'm not a psychic," J.J. said. "But Murphy and I do have a special connection to each other."

Ripley turned to Joshua who nodded his head. "They do. They can feel each other. Some of their experiences have actually been written about in medical journals."

"During my sophomore year in college, I went skiing with my roommate and some friends," J.J. said. "The first night at the lodge, I had too much to drink and tripped over a seeing-eye dog."

Ripley giggled. "You tripped over a service dog."

"I was looking straight ahead, and he was below my—"

"Was he out on the slopes or—"

"He was in the bar with his handler and it was dark and the music was real loud, and it was crowded—the point is I broke my leg."

"After tripping over a service dog," Boris said with a smile.

Joshua said, "Murphy limped for four weeks—actually sat out two games with the navy football team because his leg hurt so bad."

Speechless, Ripley and Boris stared at Joshua, who nodded his head.

"Was it sympathy pain?" Jessica asked.

J.J. shook his head. "Murphy was in bed in his dorm when I fell. His roommate said he woke up screaming out of a sound sleep. He told the medic that it felt like he was being stabbed in the calf—same place in his leg where I broke mine. They took him to the hospital for X-rays to see if he had somehow broken it in his sleep."

"But his leg was fine?" Boris said.

"They found nothing," Joshua said. "The naval academy called me the next day to tell me that my son was in sick bay. Five minutes after I talked to them, J.J. called to tell me that he had a broken leg. I compared the times and realized that J.J. broke his leg at exactly the same time Murphy woke up with a mysterious pain in his leg."

"Was it the same leg?" Jessica asked.

J.J. nodded his head. "He limped for a full month—until my leg healed."

"Twin telepathy?" Jessica murmured.

J.J. shrugged his shoulders. "Maybe. Maybe not. Some psychiatrists claim it is empathy—"

"But Murphy woke up screaming before he knew that you had broken your leg," Jessica said.

"Exactly," J.J. said. "So, if Murphy felt it when I tripped over that dog and broke my leg, I should definitely sense it if he's still alive in a motel room some place—and not being held captive by Brett Wagner or some crony of his."

"You're certain Brett didn't have anything to do with Murphy's abduction?" Ripley said.

"We were so jacked up trying to catch this guy that I didn't think of it until just now," J.J. said. "Brett didn't react when he saw me."

"He didn't?" Joshua asked.

"When Jessica and I ran into the private jet lounge, Brett reacted to Jessica, but not to me," J.J. said. "If he played a role in Murphy's kidnapping, his first response upon seeing me would have been to think Murphy had escaped. But he didn't do that. Then, when Jessica demanded he tell her where Murphy was, he fed her the same bull he's telling you. If he had kidnapped Murphy, then he would have pointed at me and said, 'There he is.'"

"He has a point," Boris said.

"Brett has never met Murphy," Jessica said. "He doesn't know what he looks like. Obviously, he still doesn't because he didn't react when he saw J.J."

"He could have hired someone to kidnap Murphy for him," Ripley said.

"Even then, the gun for hire would have wanted to know what his target looked like," Boris said.

"True. If you're going to arrange someone's kidnapping, you'll need to know what they look like to make sure you get the right guy," Ripley said.

"He's pretending he knows where Murphy is because that's the only leverage he has left to get out of the country," J.J. said.

"And escape a murder charge," Joshua said.

"What do you want to do, Captain?" Ripley asked Joshua. "Call his bluff?"

Joshua turned to J.J., who was rubbing his aching head. "Are you certain about this?"

J.J. nodded his head.

"Arrest Wagner for extortion and the murder of Selena Parker," Joshua said.

A wide grin filled Agent Ripley's lips. "With pleasure."

Through the office window, they watched Ripley sashay through the door.

Confident, Brett Wagner sat up. "I see Murphy's old man decided to give up. I guess he's smarter than he looks."

His smile fell when he saw two agents, donning jackets with FBI written across the back, step in behind her. With a toss of her head, Ripley ordered the men to take Brett to FBI headquarters for processing.

"What the hell are you doing?" Brett struggled as the two agents lifted him out of the chair.

"Brett Wagner," Ripley said, "you are under arrest for fraud, extortion, and the murder of Selena Parker." She went

on to explain his rights while he fought to escape the agents—
a fruitless endeavor since his hands were cuffed behind his
back.

"You're going to regret this, Jessica! Murphy's as good as
dead and it's all your fault! He's as good as dead! I hope you're
happy, you selfish little bitch!"

Jessica blocked out his threats by focusing on J.J. who
pressed his hands against his aching head. He squeezed his
eyes shut to stop the room from spinning around him.

"If Brett Wagner didn't take him," Boris voiced the
thought running through everyone's mind, "then where is
Murphy?"

Chapter Twenty-Three

The blast of a semi-truck's horn jolted Murphy to consciousness. With a jump, he sat up to find his hands bound behind his back. The warm metal dug into his wrists to tell him that they were cuffed.

The sound from the deep sigh he uttered was muffled by the thick tape across his mouth. He fell back onto the bed.

This is not good. Not good at all. Cuffed. Mouth taped shut.

The walls spun around him—making it nearly impossible to distinguish his surroundings. Pushing past the pounding inside his head, he squinted up at the ceiling dancing above him.

Come on, Thornton. Focus.

He closed his eyes and tried to remember what had happened.

The throbbing on the right side of his head brought forth the flash of a memory.

Here you go, he recalled saying to someone. *All done.*

Thanks a lot for your help, a young man said as he took the tire iron from Murphy's hand and swung it.

All went black.

Hey, your buddy's bleeding! Murphy remembered an old man's voice while being carried. Bright lights from road signs flashed before his eyes.

That's what he gets for getting wasted, the same young man had said with a laugh. *He's gonna have a real headache in the morning. Just drop him on the bed over there.*

Murphy felt himself begin to drift off back to unconsciousness. The sound of a truck horn jarred him back to consciousness.

You can sleep later, Thornton. Right now, you have to get out of this. What's your situation? You're handcuffed. Most likely yours. That means whoever it was searched you.

He rubbed his ankles against each other. His ankle holster and weapon were gone.

Yep, he's got your weapons.

Lifting himself up off the bed, he rubbed his bound hands against his back. His utility belt with the cell phone and gun that he wore under his jacket were missing.

The darkened room continued to bounce around him. His brain throbbed against his ears and the back of his eyeballs.

Most likely a concussion. Okay, Thornton, where are you?

He focused on the surrounding noises. Truck horns. The sound of fast moving cars—a lot of them. He recalled the bright lights as he was being carried in a parking lot.

He took in a deep breath and like a wine taster doing a blind test, he separated the various smells in the room. Stale cigarette smoke. Booze. Cheap cologne—both men's and women's. Sweat liberally mixed with other body odors. Overpowering room freshener in an attempt to cover it all up.

Bingo! Motel next to an expressway.

He felt a thump against the wall which bumped against the bed's headboard. A woman's muffled giggle turned into a low moan of pleasure, which was soon joined by a man's grunting. Murphy could hear the rhythmic creak of their bed as plain as if it were in the same room.

Yep, Thornton. You called it. God, please don't let there be bedbugs. Those things are nasty.

Fighting vertigo, he sat up to find a way out of his situation. He vaguely remembered a young man—little more than a teenager—who had knocked him out with the tire iron.

How did that happen? I was handing the tire iron to him. Why? Closing his eyes to stop the room from spinning, he pushed the question from his mind. *Focus on getting the handcuffs off and calling home.*

Remembering his encrypted cell phone, Murphy looked down at his leather jacket to see if he still had it in his pocket. If so, then help would be coming soon. He couldn't feel the stiff square shape of the device. He groaned. His lifeline to the Phantoms was gone.

Okay. I'm on my own. How long have I been here? He saw a sliver of light peeping between the heavy curtains. *Daylight. It is at least the next day. Jessica had to have noticed that I'm missing.*

The thought of Jessica and their last words before he left made him sick to his stomach—or maybe it was the concussion.

Got to get home. Got to apologize—let her know how much I love her. Can't let her last memory of us be a fight. What were we fighting about?

He couldn't remember. But he could recall her scent and the love in her eyes when she'd brushed her fingertips across his cheek. He could almost feel the touch of her lips on his.

The swirl of the key card mechanism on the door pulled him out of his thoughts. The doorknob rattled as it was turned. Murphy dropped back down flat on his back and closed his eyes—playing opossum until he could plan his escape.

Formerly muffled noises from the outside burst into the room when Murphy's captor opened the door and stepped inside.

"Excuse me," the voice of what sounded like a young woman called out. "Hello?" Her voice drew closer. "I've got some coupons for you. Johnny's Pizza. We're across the street. We deliver."

"Thank you." Murphy recognized the voice. It was the same young man to whom he had handed the tire iron.

"Is this your first time to Washington?"

Silence.

"I see that your van has Tennessee plates on it."

Tennessee? Why would someone from Tennessee want to abduct me?

"Yeah." He sounded hesitant.

"Are you here to see the cherry blossoms? They're—"

"I came to pick up my fiancée." There was a note of great pride in his tone when he said 'fiancée.' "We're going to elope."

"Oh, how romantic."

"She's gotten mixed up in a really bad situation," he said. "I've come to rescue her. We're going to run away and start all over someplace else. I'm taking her far away from Washington and the evil power brokers who think they can take whatever they want just because they want it."

"I see." There was tangible fear in her tone. "Well, if you and your fiancée get hungry for some pizza while trying to break away from the Washington swamp, here's a buy one large, get a second for fifty percent off coupon."

Oh great! I've been abducted by a lunatic. Keeping his eyelids shut, Murphy rolled his eyes. *If he was a terrorist or enemy spy, I'd be able to out think him with logic. Psychopaths are not logical. There's no predicting what they'll do next.*

He heard the door shut, the click of a light switch, and the shuffle of footsteps move toward him. Murphy could feel his captor bend over where he lay motionless on the bed. Murphy resisted the urge to hold his breath—reminding himself that if he was indeed unconscious, he would be breathing easily.

"He's still not awake, Kitty. He's not dead. I can see him breathing. I guess I hit him harder than I thought."

His captor stood up. The rustle of paper near Murphy's ear indicated that he had tossed the coupons onto a table next to the bed. Murphy heard the brushing of fabric and the creak of a bed. Since he didn't feel anyone sitting next to him, he realized that the motel room must have had two beds.

The television clicked on. In a loud overly enthusiastic voice, a woman declared how switching to a new laundry detergent had saved her life.

"Kitty, I waited for you at the Capital Wheel for hours," he said in a mournful tone between the familiar noises of dropping items on a table. "Why didn't you come?" Abruptly, his tone shifted. "Oh! I see now why you didn't text me. The battery on my cell phone died."

There was a flurry of movement across the room, which Murphy concluded had to do with him plugging in his cell phone to charge it up.

"Welcome to Action News Tonight!" an announcer on the television sang out.

Murphy sensed the young man turning to look in his direction. "Did they stop you from coming?" Murphy heard footfalls move in his direction. "Maybe I should've killed him and left his body on your husband's doorstep. Then, they'd know better than to keep us apart."

"Have you been to the mall to see the cherry blossoms, Lee?" the news anchor asked her colleague.

Murphy held his breath while waiting for his captor to carry out his threat. He strained his aching ears and body space to gauge where he was. While his hands were bound, his legs were free to deliver a kick, but that would be useless if he couldn't tell where his target was.

The room was silent except for the chatty news hosts.

"Is that where you want me to go, Kitty? Won't they find us so close to where they live?"

"The Mall is the place to be tonight, Lee," the woman on the television said seemingly in response to the question in the motel room. "Of course, it's crowded with sightseers from all over the world converging on the capital to see the cherry blossoms, which are so gorgeous right now at their peak—"

"That's right. We'll get lost in the crowd," he said. "You're so smart, Kitty. Beautiful, sexy, and smart. That's why I love you. I'll do anything for you, Kitty. But then you know that."

"There will be a band playing on the steps of the Capitol at eight o'clock," the anchor said.

"Eight o'clock," he said. "Got it. I'll meet you on the Capitol steps at eight o'clock. I'll get it right this time, my love."

Is he really having a conversation with the news anchor on television?

"They tried to trick me today, Kitty. Before I got your message to go to the Capital Wheel, I went to your place and there was all this yellow crime scene tape there. A bunch of their spies in the coffee shop told me that you were dead. Someone killed you. But I saw right through their lies. I didn't believe them for a minute. Good thing I didn't because then I wouldn't have gotten your message across the radio. I may have messed up and gotten it wrong about the Ferris wheel, but I know I've got it right this time. I'll get this yet. Be patient with me, Love. I'm still learning how to connect with you on a deeper level. But I'll get it soon. I will find you and take you away from all these horrible vulgar people and we'll be together always."

Murphy heard the heavy thud of a weapon connecting with a tabletop—most likely one of his guns—now in the hands of someone who was mentally unstable.

Murphy could feel him moving in closer to where he was bound on the bed.

"I promised you, Kitty, that I would rescue you. That I would do whatever it took to stop those awful men who were too perverted to see beyond your beauty on the outside to see you for the beautiful woman you are on the inside."

It took every ounce of his control for Murphy to not flinch when he felt the cold metal of the muzzle of his gun press against his cheek.

"I love you, Kitty. I love you so very much," he said with a heavy breath. "I'll even kill for you."

The buzzing of the phone made Murphy's captor jump. Luckily, he was so distracted hurrying for the phone that he didn't notice Murphy let out a sigh of relief when the muzzle of the gun was released from his cheek.

"Mom, what are you doing calling me?" he chastised the caller. "They're tracing our calls. I told you."

"Lee, dear, I know but I had to tell you they called me." Murphy heard the excited muffled voice on the phone.

"Who called you?"

"I didn't get their whole name. Some government agency. Two women. They sounded real official. I think they were the police."

"Kitty's husband," Lee said.

"They told me that Kitty is dead."

"No!"

"She was murdered, Lee."

"They're lying!"

"That's what I told them, but dear. The more I think about it. Maybe—"

"No, Kitty's not dead. If she was, she wouldn't be sending me messages. She just now told me to meet her at eight—" He stopped.

"Eight what? Eight o'clock? Where are you meeting her, Lee?"

Lee cackled. "Good try, but I'm not going to fall for it, whoever you are!" He screamed into the phone. "I'm not going to fall for your tricks!"

"Lee, you're scaring me," she said. "I'm your mother!"

"No, you're not. You're one of them pretending to be my mother," he said in a low voice that grew increasingly excited. "I'm going to find Kitty and we will be together even if I have to kill you and everyone trying to keep us apart!"

Murphy heard the phone fly across the room.

Lee's cry sounded like that of a wounded animal. He fell to the floor and wailed.

"Kitty. My kitty," he murmured while he regained his composure. "I'll show them. You're alive. You've been calling to me—begging me to help you. I'm the only one who can save you. You can count on me, Kitty. I'm coming."

Murphy heard the door open and close. Right outside the door, he heard the van drive away. Straining his ears, he listened to the engine blend into the mass of roaring vehicles on the nearby expressway.

Lee had gone in search of his kitty and taken at least one of Murphy's weapons with him.

CHAPTER TWENTY-FOUR

Lying motionless in the dimly lit motel room, Murphy wordlessly counted. He bided his time to ensure Lee had left in his quest to find his kitty and wouldn't return immediately. He intended to count to three hundred. He only made it to ninety-eight.

The impact of a body against the wall behind him jarred Murphy awake.

"You don't tell me what to do!" a man screamed in the next room.

"And you don't touch me!" was the slurred reply from a woman, followed by a crash.

Murphy wondered if they were the same couple who he had heard having sex earlier.

Remembering what he had been doing before drifting off, he opened his eyes and sat up straight.

No, no, no, no, no! I didn't! How could I have fallen asleep? How long—

He searched for a clue of the time to determine how long he had been asleep. His heart fell when he saw darkness through the sliver between the heavy curtains.

Lee was going to meet Kitty on the mall at eight o'clock. The clock radio read ten-forty-seven.

I've got to get out of here before he gets back!

There was a crash against the wall and the sound of breaking glass. "Do you want a piece of me?" the woman dared her companion.

The lamp on the table between the two full-sized beds was on. The light pierced through Murphy's eyes to send a sharp pain to the side of his head where the tire iron had connected with his skull.

Before his eyes, the single lamp turned into two and began to dance around him. The motion made his stomach turn. Nausea washed over him. Shutting his eyes to stave off the nausea, he dropped back onto the bed.

Get the cuffs off, Thornton. Get them off now. It'll be easier once your hands are free.

Years of training—including yoga—had made his body flexible. He hunched over and pushed his cuffed wrists down toward his rump. Pulling his knees up to his chin, he slipped his wrists past his hips. Within minutes, he was in the fetal position with his cuffed hands behind his knees. Then, it was a matter of slipping his feet through his hands.

Once he had slipped the cuffs around to his front, Murphy peeled the duct tape from his mouth and let out a breath.

Now to call for help.

He reached for the hotel phone on the night table.

At the same moment, the swirl of the keycard in the lock signaled Lee's return. Glancing toward the door, he saw a glimpse of the white van through the opening of the curtains.

There was not enough time for him to get his hands back behind his back. Murphy rolled across the bed and dropped down to the floor on the other side.

The door opened.

Immediately, Lee saw that his captive had broken free. He slammed the door shut and took the gun out from under his shirt. "Come out, come out, wherever you are." Aiming the weapon across the room, Lee stepped toward the bed.

Holding his breath, Murphy tried to see beyond the double vision to pinpoint Lee's exact location. The double vision and handcuffs had him at a physical disadvantage.

But then, Lee's delusions put him at a mental disadvantage.

Lee jumped around the corner of the bed and aimed the gun at him. "Gotcha!"

Murphy recognized the weapon as the Ruger he usually kept holstered on his hip. Holding up his hands in front of him for Lee to see, he eased to his feet. "You do realize that killing me isn't going to make any difference. They'll only send others."

Lee looked uncertain. "Well—"

"The Big Guy won't stop until he has what he wants," Murphy said with a crooked grin. "He never does. He always gets what he wants, and he stops at nothing. I was sent with my orders—to keep you and Kitty apart. That's my job. I only follow orders."

"That's why I have to kill you." Lee cocked the gun and moved in closer.

"Sure, you can kill me," Murphy said with a shrug, "but they'll send someone else. And you can kill him, too. Then, there will be another and another. You and Kitty will always be looking over your shoulders because the Big Guy will never stop—not until he has Kitty all to himself."

Murphy saw both Lees waver. The gun shook in his hands.

"But I can help you, Lee. You can end this here and now."

"Why should I believe you?"

"If we take out the Big Guy together, then you can take his kitty. She'll be all yours." Holding up his cuffed hands for Lee to see, Murphy moved in closer to the gun. "I can take you to him. I'll take him out and then you and Kitty will be free to run away together. With the Big Guy gone, no one will stop you from being together."

"Why would you help me?"

Murphy had to think fast.

He had succeeded in grabbing Lee's attention. All he needed was to get just another foot closer. Then, he would be within reach of the gun. Even with his hands bound, if he moved fast enough, he could disarm Lee.

Suddenly the words were there—from a movie he had seen long ago. It was some black and white gangster flick that he and Jessica had watched late one night.

"Because no one works for the Big Guy because they want to. We work for him because we have to. He owns everyone and everything. I'd be glad to help you take him out. Not only would that set Kitty free—Hey, I like Kitty. She's a nice kid. You seem like a nice kid, too. It would make my heart glad to see you two kids get together."

Tension filled the room while Lee seemed to weigh Murphy's offer. While waiting, Murphy inched closer to him—and the gun.

Just a couple of inches closer.

The pounding on the room door made both men jump.

Springing several feet back, Lee tightened his grip on the gun and held it up—aimed at Murphy's face.

"Open up! This is the police!"

Lee spun around and aimed the gun at the door and the police officers on the other side. "You'll never keep me away from my kitty!"

"Gun!" Murphy bellowed while dropping to the floor behind the bed. One of Lee's first shots hit the lamp which fell into many pieces. The bulk of it landed in Murphy's head.

The gun fight was over in a matter of seconds. The last thing Murphy recalled was Lee's declaration of love for Kitty as the police officers' bullets ripped through his body.

CHAPTER TWENTY-FIVE

Even with his eyes shut, Murphy recognized Jessica's lovely sweet scent when she leaned over him. Feeling the touch of her soft hand in his made him instinctively entwine his fingers with hers.

"He's waking up," she whispered.

He opened his eyes. Two blurry Jessicas floated before his eyes.

"Murphy," she said in a low voice. "I'm here. Are you okay?"

"No," he murmured. "I got hit in the head with a tire iron and now there's two of you."

He heard J.J. chuckle from somewhere in the room. On the opposite side of the bed, Joshua grasped his arm. "The double vision will clear up over time, son. You've got a fractured skull and a concussion."

Murphy sensed rather than saw that he was in a hospital. "How long have I been here?"

Jessica perched on the foot of the bed. "It's Monday. They found you at a seedy motel on Saturday night. We didn't know where you were for like twenty-four hours."

"We'd gotten quite a few false leads." Joshua pulled a chair in close to the side of the bed.

"None of them leading to that motel in Falls Church," J.J. said.

"How did the police end up there?" Murphy asked.

"Answering a domestic disturbance call in the room next door," Joshua said. "We had put a BOLO out on Douglas's van as a suspect in Natalie Stepford's murder. The officers saw the white van with Louisiana plates that matched the BOLO and knocked on the door to take Douglas in for questioning."

"You saved those two police officers' lives," Jessica said. "They knew Lee was wanted for questioning, but the order said nothing about him being armed. You warned them that he had a gun just in time."

"Natalie Stepford is dead?" Murphy let out a breath.

"We think Lee Douglas killed her," Joshua said.

"The guy who snatched me. He was from Louisiana?"

"From New Orleans," J.J. said.

"The police killed him?"

"They had no choice," Joshua said. "He fired on them through the door."

"With my gun." Murphy shook his head. "Why?" Gradually, he remembered the conversations Lee was having with the television about Kitty. "What did Natalie Stepford have to do with this Kitty he kept going on about?"

"Natalie had a double life," Jessica said. "She was an Internet porn star named Kitty Katt. Do you remember the red sports car in the parking lot? The one you said you saw Ross Caldwell get into with Natalie?"

"Vaguely," Murphy said. "*Everything* is a blur, including you." He reached out to take her hand—not so much as to touch her, but to place where she was.

"Natalie had a paid station on the Internet, which seemingly was more popular than her cooking videos," Jessica said.

"Let's just say Lee Douglas was her biggest fan. He thought they had some sort of relationship going on. Do you remember the night of the cooking class? She made some comment about someone texting her and not believing her when she said she didn't know him?"

Slowly, Murphy nodded his head. "He was having a conversation with the television in the motel room. But he kept calling her Kitty. He thought there was some big conspiracy to keep the two of them apart. Why did he target me?"

"He must have followed you when you left her cooking studio," Joshua said, "and concluded you were part of the conspiracy. When he found your military ID—"

"After hitting me with a tire iron," Murphy said, "I still don't remember what happened—how I allowed him to get that close."

"He had a fresh tire on the van and a flat one in the back," J.J. said. "The flat one had a puncture wound in it—like he had stabbed it with a knife. We have him on a surveillance video pulling out in front of you at the service station after you'd left Natalie's studio on Friday night—"

"What was I doing there?"

"She called you," Joshua said. "Do you remember her calling you?"

Murphy shook his head.

"Anyway," J.J. said, "we believe he pulled out ahead of you. He sped up to get far enough ahead to stop, block the road, and flattened his tire. Since he blocked the road and looked helpless, you—"

"He said he didn't know how to change a tire," Murphy recalled. "I changed it for him. Then, when I handed the tire iron back to him, he slugged me with it." He dropped back on the bed with a sigh. "What a newbie mistake. Just because he looked like an innocent dumb kid, I let my guard down. I even handed the weapon to him."

"Don't beat yourself up, son."

Murphy wouldn't have it. "Dad, I could have been killed. He took my weapons. He fired at those police officers with my Ruger. If they had been killed, it would have been their blood on my hands."

"Then you'll know better next time," Joshua said. "Yes, you've made a mistake. Learn from it and don't let it happen again." Casting a glance in Jessica's direction, he rose from the chair. "I have a lot of paperwork to complete and turn into the police and CO before J.J. and I head back home. We'll let you have some time alone with your wife before they chase us out of here to let you rest."

After Joshua stepped aside, J.J. grabbed Murphy's hand and patted him on the shoulder. "Glad to see you made it out in one piece, brother." He tapped the bruise that took up the right side of Murphy's face. "At least now people can tell us apart—temporarily."

Murphy squinted up at him. "You look different."

"I got a haircut."

"No, that's not it," he said. "Who's minding the farm?"

"Poppy. Who else?"

"Ah, the beloved Poppy." Murphy chuckled.

"But they're not dating," Jessica said in a low voice.

"Do we really have to have this conversation now?" J.J. asked with a heavy sigh.

"Okay, don't tell her how you feel," Murphy said. "But what if you run into some lunatic with a tire iron and get your brains bashed in on the way home? Then you'll be dead, and she'll spend the rest of her life thinking that she was nothing more to you than a horse trainer."

"I'm going to dismiss this to the pain killers they have you on." J.J. turned to walk away.

"One thing I clearly remember from that night is fighting with Jessie," Murphy called to him while looking into her tear-filled eyes. "And the number one thing that made me want to come home was to tell her how sorry I was for leaving the house without telling her how much I love her."

J.J. watched Jessica wrap her arms around Murphy to give him a deep kiss before closing the door to the private room on his way out into the hallway.

Downstairs, he found Joshua talking on his phone. As he approached, Joshua held up his finger to indicate that he would be a moment longer.

Stepping out into the hospital courtyard, Murphy's warning repeated itself in his mind.

The number one thing that made me want to come home was to tell her how sorry I was for leaving the house without telling her how much I love her.

Seemingly everyone knew how he felt about Poppy—except Poppy. How? He had no idea. Since the day he'd met her, they had nothing but a professional relationship. Well, maybe not entirely professional. They talked. They laughed. They even hugged. As Jessica had noted, based on Izzy's reports to the family, he and Poppy spent a lot of time together.

Not all of that time was spent working.

Possibly, they had moved too quickly into the friend-zone. J.J. had been in a relationship with his first love—Suellen Russell, the owner of Russell Ridge Farm and Orchard. Suellen had hired Poppy to rebuild the Russell's once prestigious quarter horse farm. Suellen died shortly afterwards and J.J. was devastated.

If it hadn't been for Poppy's friendship, he doubted if he could have gotten over the loss and learned how to keep Russell Ridge running. Raised on either military bases or in the suburbs around the globe, J.J. had no farming experience. Poppy had taught him about the joy that comes from the sweet taste of a luscious juicy peach picked straight from the tree, the ticklish touch of an appaloosa chewing on a stray lock of hair, and the natural beauty of a bright smile from a freckle-faced redhead.

At what point did his feelings of friendship for Poppy turn into love? He had no idea. And how was it that everyone could see it? The point was, he had come to depend on Poppy, not just personally, but professionally. He couldn't risk losing her by revealing his feelings for her—only to discover that she did not feel the same way.

What if I run into some lunatic with a tire iron and get my brains bashed in on the way home? Then I'll be dead, and Poppy'll spend the rest of her life thinking that she was nothing more than a horse trainer.

J.J. looked down at the phone in his hand. *What if she does feel the same way? As Murphy says—No guts no glory.* He pressed the speed dial button.

The phone rang three times before Poppy's voice sang out, "Hello…"

"Hi, Poppy, it's me—"

"Sorry I missed your call. I'm either on the other line or busy with a critter or two or three or four. So—well, you know what to do. Go right ahead and have a blessed day."

Beep.

"Hi, Poppy, this is me—Ah, I mean J.J. I'm just calling to tell you that I love you—I mean, I don't love you. No, I take that back. I don't mean that I don't love you. I mean that I do. I do love you. But, what I mean is that when I say I love you, I'm not saying it like 'I love you, guy!' as in I like hanging out with you and drinking beer—"

Beep.

"If you would like to continue your message, press two," the automated voicemail lady said.

"Dammit!" J.J. pressed the button.

"Please continue with your message."

"Poppy, I don't want to hang out with you and drink beer! That doesn't mean that I don't like hanging out with you and drinking beer. I love hanging out with you and drinking beer. The thing is that I would rather hang out with you than anyone else and drink—"

Beep.

"URGH!" J.J. shook the phone and cursed.

"If you would like to continue your message, press two," the voicemail lady instructed him.

J.J. pressed the number as she had instructed.

"Please continue with your message."

"I love you, Poppy! There! I said it. And I hope you love me, too. But not just to drink beer with. I mean, if you want to get together and drink beer, then that's fine. But I was hoping that you would maybe like to get married and have a bunch of kids toge—"

Beep.

"What the hell!"

"If you would like to continue your message, press two," the voicemail lady instructed him.

J.J. stabbed the number two with his finger.

"Please continue with your message."

"We don't have to have the whole bunch of kids all at once. My mom had Murphy and me all at once and Tracy came the year after that." He laughed. "She about tore out her hair. We should space them out a few years apart. I mean, if you don't mind raising a houseful of kids with me."

Beep.

Before the voicemail lady could say anything, J.J. pressed number two.

"Please continue with your message."

"If you don't want to marry me and have my children, then, that's okay. I'll just go away and blow my brains out. Not, that I want to put you under any pressure. There. I said

I love you and I mean it. You can go back to what you were doing now. Goodbye."

He disconnected the call.

You, idiot!

℘ ℘ ℘

"I am… so very… sorry," Jessica told Murphy between kisses. "You are not my errand boy.… I've been taking you for granted.… I never should have treated you that way… And I never will again."

He was so busy enjoying her scent and the soft touch of her lips on his that he didn't care what she was saying. It was heaven enough just being alive to touch her again—even if the sight of two of her bouncing before his eyes made him nauseous.

"I love you." She pressed her face into his neck and held him as close as she could—practically climbing into the bed next to him.

"I don't believe the lieutenant's doctor has approved sexual activity yet?" a woman announced in a good-natured tone from the door.

The woman's abrupt tone forced Murphy to open his eyes which set the room spinning again. He laid his head back.

"What about cuddling?" Jessica asked.

"Lieutenant Thornton, I'm Lieutenant Libby McAuley with the navy's medical corps." He felt her grasp his hand to shake. "Your CO requested that I consult with your attending physician here at Inova to make sure you're getting all the attention you need."

"CO was the one who insisted you have a private room," Jessica whispered to Murphy, who was not surprised. As a Phantom, a private hospital room was more for security than a perk.

Murphy squinted to see through the double images dancing in front of his eyes. All he could see was a mass of blond hair. He saw that she was wearing a black navy jacket with rows of ribbons on her chest.

"Do you still have the vertigo?" She shone a pen light into his eyes.

"And double vision," he said. "Do I know you?"

She flashed him a grin. "I saw on your record that you graduated from the naval academy. I did my internship there the same year that you graduated." She moved around the bed to examine the bruises, cut, and fracture on the right side of his head and face. "The MRI does show significant bruising and swelling of the brain. That's resulting in poor eye teaming which is causing the double vision."

"Eye teaming?

"Eye teaming occurs when the eyes align to focus on the same point on an object, resulting in a single image and depth perception," Jessica said. "If both eyes are not pointed at the same spot, the brain won't be able to combine the images, so the images are doubled."

"Exactly," Libby said.

"I'm going to medical school in Georgetown," Jessica said with a sense of pride.

"Looks like our lieutenant is in good hands."

"You worked with Commander Caldwell during your internship, didn't you?" Murphy asked.

Jessica saw Libby's smile fall for just a split second before she forced it to return. "Yes, he was a wonderful doctor and a good mentor," she said while fingering a charm hanging around her neck.

Despite his blurry double vision, Murphy saw the ugly dark scar on the back of her right hand with which she was fingering the medallion. "He died recently."

"Yes," she said softly. "I heard. It was awful."

"I saw you at his funeral," Murphy said.

"No, I don't think so," Libby said. "I wanted to attend, but, unfortunately, my schedule wouldn't let me."

Murphy wanted to argue, but could see that by doing so, she would only dig in her heels.

"It was a huge turnout." Jessica tried to be nonchalant about moving in closer to see that Libby was fingering a medal worn on a chain around her neck.

"I'm sure it was." Libby resumed her examination, checking Murphy's heart beat and breathing.

Finally, Jessica caught a glimpse when the medal slipped out from under her shirt when she had bent over to look once again in Murphy's eyes.

It was a Saint Luke's medal—the patron saint of doctors.

But there was something else she noticed as well. Libby had a long severe looking scar under her collar bone. Jessica only saw it due to the angle from which she was sitting next to the bed.

Even in the short amount of time that she was able to observe it, Jessica could see clearly that it was not a surgical scar. It was too brutal—purple and jagged—not unlike the scar on her hand.

Both were healed over stab wounds.

"You're really in very good shape, Lieutenant," Libby said upon concluding her examination. "I'm going to concur with your attending physician's assessment. If you continue with your progress, you can be released to go home tomorrow."

"What about my double vision and vertigo?"

"They'll go away in time," she said. "It all depends on how quickly your brain injury heals."

"And how long is that?"

"Weeks," she added in a soft voice, "Could be months."

"During which—"

"You'll be on medical leave," she said. "You can't return to active duty until I release you."

"I hate being cooped up at home."

"We'll make the most of it," Jessica said. "I'll be your naughty nurse. We'll have fun."

"And with my double vision, it will be like having two naughty nurses," Murphy said.

"That's the spirit," Libby said.

The doctor finished her examination and Jessica followed her out into the corridor.

"The best thing for him right now is rest," Libby told Jessica. "He needs to allow his brain time to heal. A fractured skull and brain injury is not something to mess with."

Agreeing with a nod of her head, Jessica asked, "Why did you say you didn't go to Commander Caldwell's funeral?"

With a gasp, Libby cocked her head. "I didn't."

"With all due respect, Murphy said—"

"Murphy has a head injury," she said. "His eyesight is shot right now."

"He saw you well enough to recognize you."

"From Annapolis." Libby jammed her pen light into her breast pocket. "Even if I did go to Ross's funeral, what does that matter?"

"He was murdered. His family wants closure. They can't have that unless we find out what happened."

"I suggest you ask them." Libby turned around and marched down the corridor.

Chapter Twenty-Six

"Jessica paid two million dollars to get me back?" Murphy's mouth hung open upon hearing J.J.'s account of Brett's ransom demand during his disappearance.

Jessica had gone to school to meet with her professors and arrange to study remotely. Murphy's double vision and vertigo made it difficult for him to get around by himself. Despite Murphy's objections, she insisted she was going to take as much time as needed to care for her husband. While waiting for the doctor to release Murphy to go home, J.J. kept his brother company.

"Didn't Jessica tell you?" J.J. asked about his surprise.

"She told me Brett, a jerk in her study group, led you in a totally different direction during my disappearance."

"That's for sure."

"But she said nothing about paying two million dollars to get me back."

"Why are you so surprised?" Squinting his eyes, J.J. cocked his head. "Wouldn't you pay two million dollars to get her back?"

Murphy felt his cheeks turn a bright pink.

"Don't get cocky about it." J.J. shrugged his shoulders. "It was only phony digital money. It didn't come out of her account. In fact, it was Tristan who set it up, and he pressed the button to do the transfer."

"What did Jessica do?"

A slim grin crossed J.J.'s lips. "She invited Brett to bring his big shoulders over to cry on, which prompted him to strangle Selena and stuff her body in a suitcase."

"All this happened while I was drifting in and out of consciousness while listening to a hooker doing business in the next room."

"Breakfast." A chirpy orderly sailed through the door carrying a meal tray. Upon seeing the two attractive men, she stopped. "Are you two identical twins?"

"Identical?" Murphy jerked his thumb in the direction of the young man sitting in the chair next to his bed. "Do you really think he looks like me? I'm *much* better looking than that."

"He's messing with you," J.J. said when she stopped and struggled to come up with a response.

While the orderly didn't have a verbal comeback, the breakfast she delivered did offer a payback. As she breezed out the door, Murphy removed the cover to reveal a chicken fried steak, scrambled eggs, hash browns, sausage gravy, toast, and a fruit cup. The only thing the pescatarian—a vegetarian who ate fish—could eat was the fruit cup and toast.

Hesitant, Murphy examined the wrapper on the orange juice to discover that his double vision made reading impossible. "Does this have sugar in it?"

J.J. glanced at the label. "Fifteen percent sugar."

Murphy tossed the orange juice to him.

"Payback's a bitch, isn't it?" Chuckling at Murphy's displeasure, J.J. took the tray, minus the fruit cup and toast, and settled down to eat breakfast.

"Have you talked to Poppy?" Murphy asked while sniffing the fruit cup for any sign of other items on his "don't eat" list.

"I talk to her every day." J.J. dumped the sausage gravy on the hash browns and steak.

"I meant last night." Declaring the fruit cup edible, Murphy took a bite of pineapple.

"What do you mean last night?" J.J. took a bite of the lukewarm steak.

Murphy looked at him out of the corner of his eye.

J.J. continued to eat until the silence became too loud to stand any longer. "Ollie has imprinted himself on her." He flashed a grin in his direction. "Follows her everywhere."

"Did someone tell him to get in line? Every animal on that farm has imprinted himself on Poppy—including you."

"I'm not going to have this conversation with you."

"If you're not going to have it with me, who are you going to have it with?"

J.J. shook his fork at him. "Ever since you met Poppy, you've been poking at me like a kid with a stick—"

"And you've been acting like a bear getting poked with a stick when she comes up." Murphy chuckled. "That's what makes it so much fun."

"You do know that it's dangerous to poke a bear with a stick?" J.J. set down the fork and knife. "You were always the bold one when it came to women."

"You may not have been as bold as I was, but you weren't scared like—"

"I'm not scared." J.J. stirred the scrambled eggs into the hashbrowns. "Poppy and I have a good thing going right now just the way it is."

"If you're so content with the status quo, why are you so frustrated?"

"I'm not frustrated." J.J. focused on the food on the plate to avoid Murphy's prying eyes. No one could read him easier than his twin. "Did Dad tell you that Dana Tucker died?"

It took Murphy a full moment to remember the high school classmate with whom he and J.J. had graduated. "No," he said while recalling a fun fresh-faced girl who had excelled in cheerleading and sports. "What happened?"

"Drug overdose. Last week, her husband tried to get her up to get the kids ready for school and she was dead. Left three little kids behind."

Memories of youthful outings flashed through Murphy's mind. "Drug overdose?" He shook his head. "No, that's not possible. Dana never even drank when we'd go out. I know she didn't do drugs."

"Not in front of us," J.J. said. "But the autopsy revealed stage two cirrhosis of the liver. Prolonged alcohol and drug abuse. They found bottles of booze hidden all over their house. Laundry room. Dana always carried a dark water bottle around with her. I'd seen it myself. I thought it was water. Turned out to be black sambuca, an Italian liquor. Smells like liquorice. Everyone thought the smell on her breath was from candy."

"If she was drunk all the time—"

"She had developed a tolerance to it," J.J. said. "She was drunk but appeared to be stone sober because that was her natural state. She was a stay-at-home mom, so there was no matter of missing work. She managed the home's finances. Her husband noticed a lot of money being spent on household expenses, which she would explain away. Since he worked all the time—"

"He wasn't seeing what was really going on," Murphy said. "Didn't the kids see anything?"

"They had to have seen something," J.J. said. "Who knows at this point what they saw. She'd had a couple of car accidents in the last year. One time, she hit a tree. The second time, she overturned her car and landed upside down in a ditch. Both times, she told the police a deer had jumped out in front of her car. No one had reason to doubt her. She wasn't a regular in the bars. She hung out with middle-class upstanding folks. But, I think Cameron sensed something was up."

Murphy wondered why their stepmother, a homicide detective with the Pennsylvania State Police, would notice what no one else saw.

"About a month before Dana died, Cameron was talking to Dana at a church fellowship dinner. Afterwards, she asked me about her home situation. Of course, I told her that she was a stay-at-home mom—maybe a bit stressed with three little kids." J.J. shrugged. "Cameron replied that something seemed off about her. I forgot all about it until Dana took an overdose of opioids and the medical examiner told us she was a closet addict."

"I guess if anyone is going to pick up something like that, Cameron, a recovering alcoholic herself, would have," Murphy said.

"Dad looked at the police reports and interviewed the officers for the two accidents she'd had," J.J. said. "In both cases, they saw no sign of intoxication. No smell of alcohol. No booze in the car—that they saw. No stumbling."

"Plus, Dana's reputation of being a straight up girl who had everything together," Murphy said.

"Married to a great guy with a good job," J.J. said. "Three beautiful kids. Middle class home. Active at church and non-profits."

"Sounds like our mother," Murphy said.

"Our mom wasn't a closet alcoholic," J.J. said. "Whoever would have thought that underneath that smiling, confident, pretty face, there was a terrified, insecure sick woman guzzling booze and popping pills just to make it through the day?"

"On the outside, life was perfect," Murphy said, "but inside, her life was rotten to the core."

"That's the case more often than you think."

Murphy watched his brother finish eating his breakfast in silence. When he returned the empty plate to the tray, he said, "Jessica would say your fear of taking your relationship with Poppy to the next level is rooted in guilt over Suellen."

"Give me a break." With a sigh, J.J. dropped his head.

"She's only been gone ten months. The time you two had together was so short."

J.J. plopped down into his chair. "Do we really need to talk about this now?"

Murphy dropped back onto the pillows and stared up at the ceiling—two of them spinning above his head. He closed his eyes to ward off the vertigo that threatened to upset his stomach. "I have to give you credit, man. I don't think I would be able to keep it together the way you have if anything happened to Jessica."

"Appearances can be deceiving." J.J. picked up the copy of a daily newspaper that he had purchased in the gift shop on his way to Murphy's room. "I thought it would be easier because we knew she was going to die. Time to… prepare but …" His voice trailed off.

"Does it ever get easier?" Murphy turned to look at him.

"Easier isn't the word." J.J. said. "Maybe it is guilt. Suellen left her family farm to me—the biggest dairy farm in the area." His eyes met Murphy's. "I'm not even thirty and my assets are worth over a million dollars."

"I had no idea it was worth that much."

J.J. sat back.

"Hey, man, did you see where I live? If I hadn't married Jessica, I'd be living in a condo. That'd be all I could afford on my salary."

"Back when Dad was our age, he was married with three kids, fourth on the way, and we were all squeezed into a three-bedroom rancher at Pearl Harbor," J.J. said.

"But we were happy," Murphy said.

"It isn't that I'm not happy," J.J. said. "I love that farm. Growing up all over the world the way we did, I never would have imagined—I can't imagine living anywhere else. It's home. I've put down roots."

"But you feel guilty because it was handed to you," Murphy said. "Every morning, you wake up feeling like you have to work twice as hard as everyone else to prove you're worthy of the life that you've been blessed with. That's why you get up at five o'clock in the morning to shovel manure out of the horse stalls."

"No, I get up at five o'clock in the morning because I can't wait to see Poppy." A slow grin came to J.J.'s lips.

The two men laughed.

"If I married Poppy and we—"

"Whoa, man!" Murphy sat up. "I said nothing about getting married."

"You didn't, but I did."

Murphy turned to him. "Have you asked her?"

J.J. shrugged his shoulders. "Kind of."

"How do you kind of propose marriage?"

"I kind of blurted it out."

"And she said—"

"Nothing."

"Nothing?"

"I had left it on her voice mail. We've talked three times since then and she's said nothing about it except that she'll talk to me when I get home."

Murphy cringed. "Ah, man. That's not good."

"This is all your fault."

"Why is it my fault?"

243

"You told me that if I got killed on the way home without telling her how I feel that she'd be miserable thinking she was nothing more than a horse trainer to me. So, I called—"

"I meant for you to tell her how you feel," Murphy said. "I expected you to take her out to dinner and then—if things went well and she felt the same way—maybe get a little busy when you got home. I didn't tell you to *propose marriage* to her."

"Well, once you got me started, then everything that I've been thinking about her came out. I told her that I loved her and wanted to marry her and have a bunch of kids." J.J. opened the cup of orange juice.

"You mentioned kids?"

"A bunch of kids."

"Well, after hearing that in her voice mail, if she hasn't left the state by the time you get back, then she must be in love."

J.J. drained the juice, crushed the plastic cup in his fist, and shook it at him. "If I lose her, I'm going to kill you, Murphy."

Nodding his head, Murphy said, "Europe is quite nice this time of year."

CHAPTER TWENTY-SEVEN

That afternoon, Tristan, Joshua, Susan, and Boris rushed out onto the front porch, with Spencer leading the way, to welcome Murphy home.

There were still many questions they had about Natalie Stepford's murder. Murphy had no memory of seeing Natalie after the cooking class. The last thing he clearly remembered was his argument with Jessica and leaving to go for a ride on his motorcycle. The doctor offered some hope that parts of his memory would return over time.

With Jessica at the wheel, the SUV rounded the circular drive to pull up to the bottom of the steps. Tristan scooped up Spencer just in case she chose to welcome Murphy with a body slam.

J.J. slid from the rear seat to help Murphy climb out. With an arm around his brother's waist, J.J. ushered him up the steps to the porch. Jessica hurried around the SUV and trotted ahead.

Exhausted from his weekend, Murphy took a seat on the loveseat in the living room to rest up before going upstairs. As soon as she was within reach, Spencer licked his jaw before cuddling against him.

"Spencer really missed you," Jessica said. "She loves your runs together."

"Not when we run into a killer." Murphy recalled the two of them encountering Ross Caldwell's suspected killer on the trail.

Instantly, he experienced a quick flash of memory. Like a single frame of film in a movie—for an instant it was there and just as quickly, it was gone again.

"Where are you on the Commander Caldwell murder?" Murphy asked them.

"We're at a crossroads," Boris said. "Calvin Stepford and the Garlands are ripe for killing him. They had motive coming out of their ears. Yet, Caldwell's son-in-law had ample motive as well."

"Woody," Murphy said. "Married Ross's youngest daughter just last fall."

"He had a nine-millimeter semi-automatic Colt," Susan said. "Now it's missing and so is he. Caldwell's daughter says he disappeared right after they had a huge fight where she accused him of killing her father."

In silence, Murphy stared at Spencer.

"Are you remembering something?" Joshua asked.

"It's right there at the very edge of my memory," Murphy said slowly. "But I can't quite grasp it."

"It will come to you."

"We're just glad you're home." Jessica slipped into the loveseat on his other side and wrapped her arms around him. "Especially me."

"Susan and I didn't come here because we like you or anything," Boris said with a wicked grin. "We're here because we're still investigating Natalie Stepford's murder and you're a witness—even if you can't remember anything." With a frown, he rubbed the back of his neck.

"I wish I could help you," Murphy said. "I've been doing nothing but trying to remember what happened that night."

"You may never remember," Jessica said.

"Do you have any memory of going to Garland's clinic?" Joshua asked. "Your bike's GPS indicates that you had been there."

Pressing his fingers against his throbbing forehead, Murphy shook his head.

"According to your phone, that's where you were when Natalie called you," Boris said.

"I don't even remember talking to her."

"Would it help to jog your memory if you saw the surveillance video from the night of the murder?"

"Tristan—" Jessica started to object, but everyone else was instantly on board—especially Murphy.

Tristan hurried into the kitchen to get his tablet. He opened the video to the beginning of the recording and handed it to Murphy, who hit the play button. Even though she had seen the video before, Jessica rested her head on his shoulder to watch it once more.

"That's me on my motorcycle," Murphy muttered.

"At least his brain has healed enough for him to recognize himself," J.J. said with a smile.

"On second thought, he kind of looks like you, J.J." Murphy flashed his twin a grin.

"Good to see that the blow to the head didn't stop you from being a smartass," Joshua said.

"I told you Murphy has the better sense of humor," Tristan said.

"This is helping," Murphy said. "It's coming back to me. I had just come from seeing Natalie when I stopped to get gas."

"Watch what you're doing while filling up your tank," J.J. said.

Murphy squinted as he watched himself unzip his leather jacket and reach inside.

In the back of his mind, it started as a whisper—sensuous—but also desperate.

"People have died because of that quack!"

He saw Natalie rip the cord of the video camera from the wall in her studio and roll it up. "But do any of them care? Calvin says he feels bad, but it's not their fault. Their patients know the risks going in." Her sapphire eyes flashed with anger. "Dr. Caldwell didn't."

"If you're so appalled, why don't you stay and testify against them?"

Dressed in skinny jeans with four-inch heel ankle boots, she was literally on her way out of town. Two big suitcases rested next to the door. A stack of packing boxes contained studio equipment.

The gourmet cooking equipment was untouched. It was staying.

"I'm done with my life here," she said.

"We can't prosecute them without evidence. We need proof."

She spun around from where she had shoved the cord into a box and strutted to her bag on the counter. She reached inside and extracted a thumb drive, which she shoved into Murphy's hand. "This is everything you need."

Murphy looked down at the thumb drive. "One more thing."

"I'm not staying. Tomorrow, Calvin will report me missing. When I walk out that door, Natalie Stepford will be no more."

"Fine. But before you disappear, tell me which one of them killed Dr. Caldwell?"

"That, I don't know."

Murphy watched his own image fingering the object inside his jacket while glancing around.

The thumb drive that contains everything we need. Where did I put it?

Murphy handed the tablet to Jessica, who continued to watch the recording to see a Porsche convertible with the top up pull into the office park from the main road. Once again, she was startled to recognize the vehicle. Next to her, Murphy bent over and proceeded to yank a boot off one of his feet.

"What are you doing?" Joshua squinted at Murphy who was prying the heel off the boot that he had removed.

"Tristan was right," Murphy said.

"About you having a sense of humor?" Tristan said. "Or is it something else? I can be right about so many things."

"About the video jogging my memory," Murphy said. "When Natalie called, she said I had to see her right then and there because she was leaving town. She was going to disappear. I had only one shot to get this." The outer edge of the heel snapped off into Murphy's hand to reveal a hollow compartment inside. A grin came to Murphy's lips as he turned the heel over, shook it, and a thumb drive fell out into the palm of his hand.

"That's what you went into the men's room for," J.J. said. "To hide that."

Murphy held the thumb drive out to Joshua. "It's everything we need to close down the black-market organ transplant clinic. Patient records. Information about the doctor and surgical teams. The suppliers in Central America who they buy the organs from. Even the pilot who smuggles the organs into the country."

Joshua took it from him. "Good job, son."

"She was adamant about not sticking around to testify," Murphy said. "She was planning to disappear. She said to expect her husband to report her missing the next day."

"Because she was running away to Arizona to start under a new identity," Tristan said. "She had a condo, driver's license. All she had to do was jump out of Natalie's life and land in Kitty's."

"And she would have succeeded if Lee Douglas hadn't caught up to Kitty and killed her," Susan said.

"That doesn't make sense." Murphy looked at each of their faces. "What about Commander Caldwell's murder? If Lee Douglas killed Natalie because he thought—No."

"What doesn't make sense, son?" Joshua asked.

"In the motel room, Lee got a call from—I think it was his mother. She told him that Kitty was dead."

"We told her that Kitty had been murdered and we need-ed to find Lee," Susan said. "She didn't believe us."

"Well, she believed you enough to call Lee and warn him. He insisted it was a lie. Apparently, he had been hanging out around the Kitchen Studio while the investigation was going on and some people told him that Natalie had been killed. He went nuts—I mean nuttier than he had already been. He insisted that this woman on the phone was not his mother and that she was trying to trick him to make him go home. Everyone was conspiring to keep him and Kitty apart." Murphy shook his head. "That doesn't make sense though. If he was the one who had killed her then—"

"Darling, in his mental state, he could have killed her for rejecting him." Jessica handed the tablet back to Tristan. "Then, because he couldn't handle the guilt, he replaced the memory of killing her with the whole conspiracy theory against the two of them."

"Our forensics people found phony accounts on his lap-top and phone. He had sent emails and texts from Kitty to himself to feed his fantasy," Susan said.

"Let me ask you two ladies a question." Joshua cleared his throat. "If some person who you had never met showed up claiming to have a relationship with you, would you open the door and invite him inside?"

"Or course not," Jessica said.

With a heavy sigh, Susan shook her head while taking in Joshua's smirk. "There was no evidence of forced entry at the Kitchen Studio."

"Natalie opened the door to allow her killer inside," Joshua said.

"And the estimated time is after one o'clock in the morning," Boris said. "She trusted whoever it was or, at the very least, knew them."

"This all happened *after* Murphy had left." With one eyebrow arched, Tristan plopped into a chair and reviewed the security video once more.

"Natalie considered Lee to be a nut when he was texting her and refusing to believe that she didn't know him," Jessica said. "If he showed up at the door, she would have bolted it shut and called the police."

"Not only that, but I think Lee Douglas has an alibi for the time of the murder." Tristan held up the tablet with a still image of the white van in the security video. "Murphy says he went straight from the studio to the service station across the street. Lee pulled in right behind him and they basically left together. We can assume that Lee had stopped Murphy a few minutes later. That was all a little before one."

"According to the motel manager, Douglas asked him to help carry his drunk friend out of the van and into the motel room *after* one o'clock," Boris said. "The motel is almost a half hour away—inside the beltway."

"And the coroner puts Natalie's time of death between one and two o'clock," Susan said.

"That means Lee Douglas was kidnapping Murphy during the time of Natalie's murder," Joshua said.

"It could have been another obsessed fan," Susan said. "Natalie certainly had more than her fair share of obsessed admirers. Dr. Garland micro-chipped her like a pet."

"Micro-chipped her?" Murphy asked.

"The ME found a GPS tracking chip in her arm," Susan said. "He did it during her last surgery."

"Who was monitoring her phone and emails?" Murphy asked.

"That was her husband," Boris said. "Calvin Stepford is still in the hospital recovering from heart surgery, during which they discovered that his heart was not an original body part. He was the one who started this whole illegal organ transplant stuff that Garland had going on at the clinic. Stepford had bought a heart on the black market. He found a disgraced surgeon willing to do the transplant but who needed an operating room to do it in."

"Natalie called him a quack," Murphy said. "That's what made her call Caldwell. She'd overheard conversations between Meaghan Garland and Stepford about patients dying on the table."

"What did they do with deceased patients?" Joshua asked.

Slowly, Murphy shook his head. "I don't remember whether she told me that or not."

"Hopefully, that information will be on this thumb drive." Joshua handed the thumb drive to Tristan to plug into his tablet.

"They talked Dr. Garland into allowing them to use his clinic and a criminal enterprise was born," Joshua said. "Meaghan and the transplant surgeon's nurse arranged the surgery scheduling and acquisition of the organs. According to Garland, Calvin Stepford was a full financial partner in the operation—supplying plane and pilot to go wherever they needed to pick up the human organs."

"Where did they get them?" J.J. asked.

"Mostly Central America," Boris said. "Everyone involved was making a fortune. Well over a million dollars in a few months."

"They all had reason to kill Natalie for blowing the whistle on them," Murphy said. "Calvin Stepford was tracking her technology and realized what she was doing, so he killed Commander Caldwell and intercepted the investigator from the health department. Did anyone find the investigator?"

"Reginald Baldwin was shot in the head—execution style," Boris said. "Most likely the same day. Police found his car in long term parking at Dulles Airport. His body was stuffed in the trunk."

"But if Stepford knew Natalie was selling them out, why let her live?" Murphy asked.

"Calvin Stepford didn't want to lose her," Jessica said. "He figured if he scared her enough by killing two men, that he could control her and keep her in line."

"Obviously, he couldn't since she was an Internet porn star behind the scenes and arranging to run away," Tristan said.

"Looks to me like she just *pretended* to stay in line," Jessica said. "She was obviously very smart and had a devious streak considering this alternate identity and life she had created."

"From what Stan Garland has told us, she used his obsession with her to seduce him into an affair to gather evidence of the black-market organ transplants," Joshua said.

"And it looks like she got a lot," Tristan said while eying the files on the thumb drive. "There's a whole folder here with patient records, financial registers, release forms. This criminal organization was *organized*." He ejected the thumb drive and handed it back to Joshua. "Nigel backed it up just to be safe."

"Between Stan Garland's testimony, the heart and liver found at the clinic, and this thumb drive, this whole operation will be shutting down real fast." Joshua handed the thumb drive to Boris. "Get your team together. I'll get warrants for everyone and we'll have ourselves a party."

"We still don't know which one of them is a murderer," Murphy said.

"All in good time, dear," Jessica said. "All in good time."

⁓ ⁓ ⁓

"Are you sure you can't clean it up any better?" Jessica peered at the still image of the Porsche entering the business park in the security video. "I think that's a 'G' at the beginning of the license number, don't you?" She moved so close to where Tristan was sitting at the bank of computers in the control room that they were shoulder to shoulder.

"Or it could very well be a 'C'." Tristan slumped. "The service station set up the camera to catch people in *their* parking lot, not the road next to them. The angle is all wrong."

"And since it's black and white, we can't get the color of that Porsche. Does it look like it could it be a dark red to you?"

"Or dark gray," he replied. "Even if you don't have the color or the license plate number, we do have the time that our suspect drove into the business park where Natalie was murdered. Plus, we have a picture of the car. I can tell you what type of Porsche and the year. How many of our suspects are driving a hundred-thousand-dollar car that model and year?"

Jessica scoffed. "Tristan, have you looked at where we live? *Everyone* drives a Porsche."

"I don't. You don't. Murphy doesn't."

"My point is that without the license plate number, we can't prove beyond a reasonable doubt it was him. There has to be some way we can prove it's him."

Tristan minimized the security video. "How about a shot from a different angle?"

"That would be fabulous."

Tristan's fingers flew across the keyboard while he spoke, "Do you know how many times a day the average person is caught on CCTV?"

Jessica rolled her eyes. "Several?"

"Seventy." He went on. "Places of business. Traffic lights. You name it." He shot her a grin. "That's why I make it a policy to only scratch myself at home."

"What a guy," she muttered.

Tristan maximized a screenshot of the dark red Porsche driving through an intersection. "Looks like our guy was in such a hurry to kill Natalie that he ran a red light."

Jessica moved in closer to identify the building in the background of the picture. "Is that the library?"

"Yep." He zoomed in on the license plate. "That is the intersection at the corner of the business park. Guess he thought since it was after midnight and no one was around that he could run it without anyone knowing. But the traffic cam knew and took a picture of the car and the license plate."

Jessica grinned. "We have the car, the license plate, and the time that he was there—which is right at the time of the murder. We got him!"

They bumped fists.

Cell phone in hand, Joshua stepped into the control room so fast that Tristan let out a shriek. "There you two are. I've been looking for you. Where's Murphy?"

"He took Spencer for a walk," Jessica asked.

"He's got double vision!"

"J.J. went with him," she said. "You know Murphy. He insists on pushing himself. He thinks that if he just ignores the double vision and vertigo that it will cease to exist."

"Kind of like the parallel universe," Tristan said.

Narrowing his eyes to blue slits, Joshua cocked his head at him. "Parallel universe? There's no parallel universe."

"Are you sure about that?" Tristan asked. "Maybe you just believe it doesn't exist because you pretend it doesn't. Thus, making it cease to exist. But, does it really cease to exist just because you pretend it isn't there?"

"Kind of like the question—if a tree falls in a forest, does it make a sound?" Jessica asked.

"Exactly." Tristan sucked in a deep breath when he noticed that Joshua had folded his arms across his chest. His eyes bore through the young man. "As much as I would love to continue this discussion, I can see that you are more interested in locating Murphy, who is walking Spencer, with J.J.'s assistance."

"What's up, Josh?" Jessica asked.

"Boris called." Joshua held up his phone for them to see. "Commander Caldwell's daughter shot her husband."

Chapter Twenty-Eight

The night sky was lit up with multi-colored lights from the wide variety of emergency vehicles. As Boris led Joshua, Murphy, and J.J. through the convoy of law enforcement vehicles, he explained what information he had gathered before their arrival.

"We've had a BOLO out on Woody Harris since last night when he took off after having a fight with Kendall. She called our office and told Archer that she believed he killed her father because he blamed him for breaking up their marriage. Apparently, he came back tonight to resume their fight. He brought the gun he had used to kill the commander, and she killed him in self-defense."

A uniformed state police officer held the front door open for them to file into the elegant foyer of the mansion.

"He's back in the kitchen." Boris led them through the spacious home toward the gourmet kitchen in the rear.

Only a month had passed since Murphy and Boris had attended a funeral reception in the elegant mansion. Once again, it was a venue for death.

Erin Caldwell was holding her sobbing daughter, who was huddled in the corner of the sofa. When Murphy paused to squint beyond the double vision to observe them, Daniel Caldwell stepped into the doorway.

"Kendall is really too upset to talk right now."

"We're going to need to get a statement from her," Boris said.

"We'll have no problem giving you a statement after she's had time to gather her thoughts," Daniel said.

"Can't you see she's lost both her father and her husband?" Erin said.

Boris gestured for Murphy, with J.J. acting as a human guide with his hand on his arm, to move on to the kitchen.

Woody Harris's body was sprawled out in the middle of the kitchen floor next to an overturned table and chair. "Shot three times in the chest and mid-section," Joshua noted for Murphy's benefit. "Where did she get the gun?" he asked Boris.

"It was one of her father's. Nine-millimeter Berretta semi-automatic. Military issue." Boris squatted down to point out a semi-automatic resting on the floor under an antique break-fast table. It was tucked against the wall. "One of the forensics folks found it while examining Harris. It's a nine-millimeter Colt semi-automatic."

"The same type of gun used to kill Caldwell," Murphy said.

"I thought Woody claimed it was missing," Joshua said.

"Woody *claimed* it was missing." Boris said. "We'll need to test it to see if it was the gun used to kill Caldwell, but considering that he brought it here tonight…"

"Did you test his hands for gunshot residue?" Joshua asked.

"He got one shot off. It hit the top of the cupboard." Boris pointed to the cupboard next to the sink. "She got off three."

J.J. stuck his fingertips in the sink which contained some dishes. He found the water was still warm. "Who was doing the dishes?"

"Kendall was," Boris said. "Her mother was taking a nap."

Joshua checked the time, which was eight o'clock. "What time was the shooting?"

"An hour ago," Boris said.

"Mom and I had just eaten dinner. I was cleaning up."

They turned to find Kendall leaning against the doorway—seeming to hold herself up. Her mother supported her with her hand around her waist. Kendall wiped her face with a worn tissue.

"Kendall," Daniel said, "You don't have—"

"I want to get this over with," she said in a strong voice.

Murphy moved over to the sink and bent over to peer inside at the dishes stacked up at the bottom of the sink filled with water.

Hugging herself, Kendall stared at the dead man, laying in a pool of his own blood, while recounting in a monotone voice. "I hadn't heard from him all day. After yesterday, I assumed he had left and was getting as far from here as he could. He knew I was going to go to the police. There was no way I could protect the man who killed my daddy. I was washing dishes and I could just feel someone watching me. I turned around and there he was. His eyes had such hatred in them. He raised his arm. At first, I didn't see the gun. I thought he was pointing at me. I didn't realize what it was until he pulled the trigger. I felt the bullet fly right above my head."

She pointed toward the ceiling above the sink where a hole in the crease between the ceiling and wall marked the spent bullet's location.

"I don't even remember doing it," Kendall said. "I grabbed Dad's gun from the counter, aimed it at him, and pulled the trigger until he hit the floor and I knew he was dead."

Murphy squinted his eyes to peer up at the bullet hole in the wall two feet above his head. "Man, you sure are lucky. I mean, he had the drop on you. He fired a shot while you were up to your elbows in soapy water. He misses by a country mile. And then, you manage to pick up your gun, with soapy hands, and fire off three shots—each one hitting its mark—before he can pull the trigger a second time."

While her face conveyed distress, Kendall's eyes were filled with icy malice directed at Murphy.

"Did Woody say anything before he fired his weapon?" Joshua asked her.

Kendall shook her head. "We both said all we had to say yesterday."

"Then I guess he told you yesterday why he wanted to kill you," Joshua said.

"He felt like if I loved him, that I'd protect him after he killed my dad."

"Did he tell you why he killed your father?" Murphy asked.

"He blamed Dad for our marriage breaking up," Kendall said. "Dad never did like him. I married Woody on a whim. I realized I had made a mistake. Woody saw where we were heading, and he thought that if Dad was out of the way that maybe our marriage had a shot."

"Which it didn't," Erin said.

Murphy could see dark circles and bags under Erin's eyes. Her complexion was pale. Her pale complexion was a sign of the emotional toll that the last several weeks had had on her.

"Did you see or hear anything, Ms. Caldwell?" Joshua asked Erin.

"I didn't feel well," Erin said. "I haven't felt well since Woody took my Ross away. Kendall gave me some medication to help me sleep. I woke up to the gunshots and called the police. I knew it was Woody. Kendall had told me earlier that she was afraid he'd come back."

"That's why I kept Dad's gun close by," Kendall said.

"Didn't you just say that you assumed Woody had left for good and was getting as far from here as possible?" Murphy asked.

"Yes," Kendall said, "I did say that. But I meant that if he was smart, he would get as far from here as possible because he knew I was going to the police."

Daniel Caldwell gestured at Woody Harris's lifeless body. "Obviously, Woody was not smart enough to stay away, and he paid a price for his stupidity."

CHAPTER TWENTY-NINE

"The doctor gave strict orders for you to rest," Joshua said when he climbed into his SUV the next morning to find Murphy in the back seat with Jessica.

"You always told me to never start something unless I intended to finish it." Murphy winked at him. "I started this. I'm going to be there to finish it."

Joshua shot a glance at Boris, who rolled his eyes, in the passenger seat. "You have a *brain* injury."

"So I've been told," Murphy said.

"We have to hurry," Jessica said. "We have to get back in time for me to take Murphy to the hospital to see Lieutenant McAuley."

"Do you still have double vision?" Joshua asked him.

"A little. Now the two of you are overlapping."

With a heavy sigh, Joshua turned his attention to Boris. "Have we got the arrest warrants?"

Boris kissed the folded paper in his hand. "Signed. Sealed. And delivered."

"Let's go arrest ourselves a killer."

Morning rush hour was on the decline, which made it a quick trip from the Thorny Rose Manor to the Garland estate in Lansdowne, a community west of Great Falls. Like a neon marker, the dark red Porsche convertible rested in the driveway of the manicured lawn of a large two-story red brick colonial home.

"Lieutenant Thornton," Joshua said in a deadly serious tone as he turned into the driveway behind the Porsche.

"Yes, sir," Murphy replied in a meek voice.

"You are on medical leave. I am only allowing you to tag along as an observer. You are not to take any active role in this. As a matter of fact, Lieutenant," he turned around in his seat. "I'm ordering you to stay in the car."

"Stay in the car?"

Joshua narrowed his eyes in response to Murphy's harsh tone.

"I mean 'stay in the car, *sir?*'"

"It's the only way to can make sure you stay out of trouble, Lieutenant." Joshua climbed out.

Murphy turned to Jessica, who kissed him on the cheek. "I'll roll down the window a little so you can get some air." She hurried out of the vehicle to join Joshua and Boris on the walkway leading to the front door.

Meaghan threw open the door and met them on the front stoop. "You can't talk to us without our lawyer."

"We're not here to talk." Boris extracted the warrant from his breast pocket. "We're here to arrest your husband."

"For what?" she replied. "The twerp has been cooperating with you."

"For the murder of Natalie Stepford," Joshua said.

"Are you serious? Have you met my husband? That weasel doesn't have the balls to—"

Abruptly, the side door leading into the garage flew open and Stan Garland ran out.

"Not again," Joshua groaned.

"I'll get him." Boris gave chase.

Blubbering, Stan ran to his Porsche only to find that it was blocked in by Joshua's SUV. Desperate, he sprinted down the driveway. As he passed the SUV, the rear door flew open to whack him in the face. Stan dropped to the pavement—flat on his back—knocked unconscious.

Boris cuffed the unconscious man's hands behind his back.

Joshua peered into the back seat where Murphy sat back with his fingers laced behind his head.

"I stayed in the car as ordered, *sir*."

ᘓ ᘓ ᘓ

"How's the headache, Lieutenant?" Libby McAuley asked while shining a pen light into his eyes.

Murphy had removed his shirt and sat on an examination table. While the rest of his vitals were normal, his primary concern was the head injury. In the two days since Lee Douglas had fractured his skull with the tire iron, the vertigo had subsided. But he still had the double vision and headaches.

After dropping Stan off at the NCIS office, Jessica had driven Murphy to the hospital for his appointment with the medical corps doctor. While the doctor examined him, Jessica remained in the waiting room to check in with her professors and field questions from her study group about Brett Wagner's arrest for murder.

"Pretty bad," Murphy said in response to the doctor's query about his headaches.

"Scale of one to ten?"

"Eight. Yesterday it was a twelve."

"Then it's getting better," Libby said with a grin of encouragement.

Murphy noticed that she didn't smile very often.

She held up her hand with the index finger pointing upward. "Don't turn your head and follow my finger with your
eyes."

Watching her finger, Murphy saw that the scar on the
back of her hand was also on the palm. The wound she had
suffered had gone through her hand.

"Very good." After she had finished testing his peripheral
vision, she returned to her laptop to mark down the results.

"What happened to your hand?" Murphy asked.

Almost as a reflex, she grabbed her hand and held it close
to her chest.

"I'm sorry," Murphy said. "I don't mean to be nosy. It just
looks like quite a serious injury. Looks like a puncture wound.
The scar is both on the back and the palm—"

"I was stabbed." She pulled the collar of her medical jacket and shirt to expose her left shoulder. There was an equally
nasty, jagged red scar under her collar bone. "Like you, I'm
lucky to be alive."

"I'm sorry."

"Don't be." She returned to making notes on his case.
"You can get dressed now."

Murphy slipped off the table and removed his shirt from
where he had draped it across the back of a chair. "Did they
catch whoever did that?"

"Yes."

"Why—"

"She was mentally disturbed."

"Like the guy who abducted me." Noticing that she had
referred to her attacker as "she", he said, "A woman did that
to you?"

"Really, Lieutenant? Women can be just as dangerous as
men. They have the added advantage of being underestimat-
ed—especially when they're extremely manipulative."

He finished buttoning his shirt. "Then you knew your attacker?"

"Yes." Libby stood up. "I've issued a prescription for a pain medication for your headaches." She headed for the door. "I want you to make an appointment to come back in one week for a follow up."

"When are you going to release me to return to duty?" Murphy tucked his shirt tail into the waistband of his jeans.

"We'll see how you are in a week." She stopped with her hand on the door knob. "I can't release you as long as you have double vision." She opened the door—allowing the noises of the busy military clinic to flow into the examination room. "Any other questions?"

"Why didn't you want anyone to see you at Dr. Caldwell's funeral?"

Libby stood up straight. Her mouth tightened. "That is none of—"

"I saw your hand," Murphy said. "That was before I got hit in the head. I know it was you. You didn't want someone to see you. Was it Commander Caldwell's wife? Did you have an affair with—"

She closed the door to allow them privacy. "I did not have an affair with Ross."

"I notice you refer to him as 'Ross,'" he said. "Not 'Commander.' That indicates a personal, not professional, relationship. Were you hiding from his widow at the funeral?"

"Why—"

"We're trying to track down Commander Caldwell's killer," Murphy said. "Now it is obvious that you cared deeply for the man. You cared enough about him to sneak to his funeral to say goodbye. Yet, you refuse to offer any help in catching his killer. Why?" He looked into her face and saw the answer.

Fear.

"You're afraid. You believe—no, you *know* that the same person who stabbed you murdered Commander Caldwell."

"I don't know that for a fact," she said.

"Who attacked you?"

She turned back to the door. "I'm not saying anymore." Murphy objected as she stepped out into the corridor where she turned back to him. "I hadn't seen Commander Caldwell for years before we both ended up assigned to this hospital. After what happened in Annapolis, we kept our relationship strictly professional. We never discussed our personal issues. As far as I know, our past had absolutely nothing to do with his murder. That being the case, it would be inappropriate for me to implicate someone in his murder without evidence."

℺ ℺ ℺

YOU don't believe it? Jessica texted to her friend Carol, Selena's landlord. *I'm the one he tried to extort $2 mil from.* When she saw Murphy return to the waiting room, she kept one eye on the phone to await Carol's response while gathering her belongings.

Murphy stepped up to the medical assistant at the reception desk and flashed his brightest smile—putting both dimples on full display. "Excuse me, but Lieutenant McAuley, I swear I know her from someplace—"

The medical technician melted. "She did her internship in Annapolis."

"Ah," Murphy said, "that must be where I knew her. The chief medical officer on base there—"

"Commander Caldwell." She let out a mourned-filled breath. "He passed away recently."

"Back in Annapolis, I heard a rumor that he and Lieutenant McAuley—"

"No." She lowered her voice. "I don't think they even liked each other." She paused. "Who knows? Maybe they did have a fling. If so, it didn't end well."

"Maybe."

Jessica slipped her hand through his arm. "You do an awful lot of flirting for a married man." When she saw the confusion on his face, she asked, "What's wrong?"

"Lieutenant McAuley."

"What about her?"

"The lady doth protest too much."

⌘ ⌘ ⌘

"This is ridiculous!" Calvin Stepford's lawyer uttered a hollow laugh in a poor attempt at bravado upon reading the arrest warrant that Joshua had handed him. Since his client was still hospitalized after cardiac surgery he would be delegated to having armed guards stationed outside his door and being handcuffed to his bed. "Ridiculous and cruel!"

In the busy corridor outside his client's room, the lawyer did not care about disturbing anyone with his scene in defense of Calvin Stepford. "For one, my client could not have killed Natalie as you say he did. If you don't believe me, look at the blood test results for when he was brought in here."

"What about them?" Joshua asked.

"Stepford had heavy doses of benzodiazepines in his system. Sleeping pills. Not good for a bad heart. The doctor says that is probably why his heart gave out."

Boris started to ask, "What does that—"

"If Calvin Stepford's heart is as bad as his doctor is claiming," Joshua said, "and he had been taking—"

"Given," the lawyer snapped. "Big doses, too."

"The stress of committing murder would have killed him," Joshua said.

"My client's heart couldn't have withstood the stress of pulling the trigger on the gun, let alone putting a dead man in the trunk of a car."

"Then he couldn't have done it," Joshua said.

"The doctor will swear to it in court. Calvin Stepford had been given sleeping medication on a regular basis. His heart has been irreparably damaged. He was not physically able to have murdered anyone without killing himself, too." The lawyer threw up his finger into Joshua's face. "Notice that I said 'given.'"

"I did notice that," Joshua said.

"Because my client did not take sleeping pills. He's never taken sleeping pills in his life. Someone has been slipping him medication without his knowledge." The lawyer stopped to catch his breath. "And it is said sleeping pills that my client has been given without his knowledge and permission that will most likely sign his death warrant. The cardiologist believes that the sleeping pills have damaged his heart so badly that there is nothing more they can do."

The weight of what the lawyer was saying hit Joshua. He turned to Boris to see that it had also hit him.

Calvin Stepford was dying.

"How long does he have?" Joshua asked in a whisper.

"Days. Maybe a week."

The full force of the personal tragedy for the man in the hospital room behind the door washed away their professional differences.

"Mr. Stepford must have some suspicion of who did this to him," Joshua said.

The lawyer looked down at his hands. "Yes."

"Natalie," Joshua mouthed.

"Look at the times she filmed and uploaded her little performances," the lawyer said. "Always in the evening. Stepford told me that for more than a year, he couldn't make it past eight o'clock in the evening. He thought it was because of his bad heart. Turns out his bad heart was because of the sleeping pills Natalie was slipping into his dinner so that she could go to the studio to make her one-woman porn shows." He shook his fist at them. "My client gave Natalie everything she ever asked for. A successful business. A gorgeous home. The perfect face and body. He gave it all to her. How did she thank him? She stripped him of his reputation, honor, and his very life."

Joshua paused to take a deep cleansing breath. "Explain to me how your client's credit card was used to pay for a cab ride from Dulles International Airport to Starbucks in Reston." He brought up a picture of the digital payment on his phone and showed it to the lawyer.

"That receipt says the credit card is registered to Stepford Enterprises," the lawyer noted.

"And Calvin Stepford is Stepford Enterprises," Joshua said.

"Calvin Stepford has over a thousand employees who work for him," the lawyer said while referring to notes on his tablet. "He's got dozens of credit cards in company names that are used by various departments and employees doing business in his name." He chuckled. "Okay, I just looked up the credit card ending in those four digits. That credit card is actually a debit card that has been issued to Calvin's accountant to take care of online accounts."

"And who is Calvin Stepford's accountant?" Boris asked.

"Meaghan Garland."

Joshua and Boris spun on their heels and ran to the elevator.

"What am I supposed to do with this arrest warrant?" The lawyer waved it over his head.

❧ ❧ ❧

"I thought it was settled," Jessica said while maneuvering Murphy's SUV through city traffic to merge onto the beltway to take them home. "Woody Harris killed Commander Caldwell."

"I'm not buying it, my love," Murphy said. "At the funeral reception, Daniel Caldwell said Woody did not have enough initiative to commit murder. I'm sorry to say I agree with him."

"If it wasn't Woody, then that takes us back to Stepford and the organ transplant business," Jessica said. "Calvin Stepford had been monitoring Natalie's electronics and found out that she had been selling them out to Commander Caldwell. He followed Caldwell to Great Falls and killed him. Then he ran to Starbucks to intercept the investigator, Reginald Baldwin, and killed him."

"Where did Stepford run to?" Murphy asked.

Her eyes wide, Jessica turned her head to look at him where he was seated in the passenger seat.

Receiving no answer, Murphy repeated his question. "After Calvin Stepford killed Ross Caldwell in Great Falls and I saw him take off down one of the trails, where did he run to?"

Jessica returned her focus on the traffic ahead.

"I saw the killer, Jessie," Murphy said. "He was on foot. He was running—fast. Calvin Stepford had heart transplant surgery less than a year ago and he's still got a bad heart. A run through Great Falls Park would have killed Stepford."

She glanced over at him. "Are you thinking it was Libby McAuley?"

"I'm thinking she knows who killed Caldwell." Murphy took his cell phone from his pocket and hit the application to connect him to Nigel. "She was closer to Caldwell than she wants anyone to know."

"Hello, Murphy," Nigel said. "How was your doctor's appointment?"

"It went fine, Nigel. I need—"

"I've been talking to the OMPF database—"

"What's OMPF?" Jessica asked.

"The Office of Military Personnel Files," Nigel said. "OMPF isn't very chatty. They don't want her to be, considering the personal data that she is responsible for organizing and guarding. But, she did tell me about the consistently impressive numbers on your blood work. Good job, Murphy."

"Thank you, Nigel," Murphy said. "Now, can you—"

"Jessica, OMPF told me that you do need to do a little work on your cholesterol," Nigel said. "I could help you with that. Would you like me to delete all desserts from your shopping list?"

"No!" Jessica almost drove off the expressway at that offer. Once she had regained control of the SUV, she turned to Murphy. "We need to tell Tristan to turn Nigel's social skills down a notch."

With a grin, Murphy said, "Nigel, I need a background check on Lieutenant Libby McAuley, United States Navy, Medical Service Corps."

"What are you looking for specifically?" Nigel asked.

"Police reports," Murphy said. "She has a couple of healed over stab wounds. She has been the victim of an assault. I'm particularly interested in during her internship at the naval academy in Annapolis."

"There is an incident report on record at the naval academy involving Lieutenant McAuley," Nigel said. "Unfortunately, I am unable to divulge the details of that report. It is sealed. Lieutenant McAuley is the daughter of Admiral Clarence McAuley, retired."

"I know Admiral McAuley," Murphy said in a low voice. "He's known as Pit Bull McAuley."

"Because he's tough?" Jessica asked.

"Because he's got a hair trigger temper. You never know when or what will set him off."

"Anger issues," she said.

"Textbook case."

"I can tell you that Lieutenant McAuley had a restraining order issued against her four years ago when she was doing her internship at Annapolis," Nigel said.

"A restraining order?" Jessica asked. "That's interesting."

"It had been requested by Erin Caldwell," Nigel said. "Would you like me to access the application Ms. Caldwell had submitted to the court?"

"Yes, Nigel," Murphy said.

"That was four years ago," Jessica said. "This couldn't possibly be relevant to Dr. Caldwell."

"Maybe. Maybe not."

"According to the application," Nigel said, "Lieutenant McAuley was stalking Commander Caldwell. Erin Caldwell ordered Lieutenant McAuley to back off. The lieutenant refused and assaulted Ms. Caldwell. Lieutenant McAuley was arrested, but the charges were dropped. Commander Caldwell requested a transfer out of Annapolis days after that."

"No trouble since then?" Murphy asked.

"Are you aware that Lieutenant McAuley has been receiving death threats?" Nigel said. "Four to be exact."

"No," Murphy said while exchanging glances with Jessica.

"She reported them to NCIS," Nigel said. "They started Friday night. Phone calls. Dead roses and rats on her door step. You know. The usual."

"That started last Friday?" Jessica asked. "Caldwell died over a month ago. Doesn't sound to me like these death threats against McAuley have anything to do with him. She must have gotten someone else mad at her."

"We didn't know she was even connected to Commander Caldwell until I ended up in the hospital and recognized the scar on her hand." Murphy dropped back against the seat and closed his eyes. "I feel like I'm forgetting something. Something that hit me right before…" His voice trailed off.

"Perry Latimore is the case officer heading this investigation," Nigel said. "Would you like me to connect you to him?"

"No," Murphy said. "Thank you, Nigel. Send what you can from her file to my email."

"Okey dokey."

Jessica and Murphy exchanged glances.

"Tristan definitely needs to make some adjustments," Murphy said.

CHAPTER THIRTY

"You went to see Natalie that night."

Joshua and Stan Garland sat across from each other at the table in the same interrogation room where Stan had revealed the illegal organ transplant operation. This time, Stan had his lawyer with him.

Boris Hamilton was watching the interrogation from behind the two-way mirror.

"I think you realized that night that she had used you and went to confront her after the cooking class." Joshua fingered the closed folder he had in front of him. "When you got there, you saw that she was leaving. Not only had she used you to bring down everything that you had worked for, but she was leaving. You were never going to see your Venus de Milo again. You had created this beautiful perfect woman and now she was just going to walk out of your life. You picked up the meat mallet, and you broke her face—the face that you had created, and you killed her."

"You have everything right up to where I picked up the meat mallet," Stan said. "I would never hit Natalie. I loved Natalie. And you're right. I made that face. She was my creation. I loved her. I could never do anything to hurt her."

"Do you have any evidence to place my client at Natalie Stepford's Kitchen Studio at the time of the murder?" his lawyer asked.

Joshua opened the folder and slid the still photograph taken by the traffic camera. "The approximate time of the murder is one o'clock Saturday morning. Your client was in such a hurry to stop Natalie that he ran a red light at the intersection next to the business park. The traffic cam took this picture when he ran the light at twelve-forty-seven. It's his car. The license plate is in plain view."

The lawyer studied the photograph.

Seeing it, Stan's eyes grew wide.

The lawyer slid the picture back across the table. "The license plate may be in plain view, but the driver is not. You can't see who's behind the wheel of that car." He shot Joshua a smug grin. "Maybe his car was stolen."

"Yeah," Stan said, "my car was stolen. That's not me."

"Your car was stolen," Joshua said, "driven from Lansdowne to Great Falls, to the same area where your ex-mistress was murdered, and then returned."

"That sounds good to me." The lawyer sat back and folded his arms. "Unless you can place my client, not just his car, at the scene, we're walking out of here."

ტ ტ ტ

Jessica was so worried about Murphy that she had trouble concentrating on the road as she maneuvered through city traffic to NCIS headquarters. After their discussion about Lieutenant Libby McAuley, Murphy pushed his seat back and closed his eyes. Jessica could see that he had fallen asleep. Worried that he would slip into a coma without her knowing it, she kept glancing over at him. Finally, in desperation, while keeping one eye on the road, she reached over and slapped him in the face—her knuckles connecting with the bridge of his nose.

With a yell, he jumped up and glanced around to get his bearings. "What did you do that for?"

"I wanted to make sure you were all right. I was worried."

"If you were any more worried, I'd be back in the ER." Rubbing his nose, he sat back in his seat. "Something's not right. I'm forgetting something important."

"Well, your father called while you were asleep," she said. "Calvin Stepford has a bad heart."

"We know that," Murphy said.

"So bad that he isn't strong enough to have outrun you on a trail in Great Falls Park. Someone else had to have killed Commander Caldwell and the HHS investigator. Guess we're back to Woody for Caldwell's murder. Face it. He had a motive. He blamed Caldwell for breaking up his marriage. He had the means. The gun. And the opportunity. The Caldwell home was within running distance of the scene of his murder."

"Can you really see Woody running through Great Falls to kill Caldwell and then running back?" Murphy scoffed. "Can you see him being clever enough to escape detection?"

"He wasn't clever enough to pull it over on his wife," Jessica said. "She figured it out, and he admitted it to her. That's why he came back to finish her off and got killed."

"Funny how that worked out," Murphy muttered.

"What do you mean?"

"Well…" Murphy struggled to keep his train of thought on path. The single piece of information was lurking at the edge of his memory once more—just beyond his grasp. "I mean. If we hadn't found out about Woody's guns, and Kendall hadn't figured it out and confronted him about it— we'd never know…" His voice trailed off.

"Know what?"

"Hope they know to look close to home?" Murphy recalled Kimberly one of his friends saying at the funeral.

"If Stepford was too ill and weak to have killed Caldwell and the investigator, then he must have had someone do it for him." Jessica took out her and Murphy's identifications to drive through the security gate. "Your father's getting a warrant for Calvin Stepford's phone records."

Murphy stared out the passenger side window while Jessica drove the SUV through the lot to take him to his reserved parking space—one of the perks of being a Phantom.

What am I forgetting? Mentally, he replayed everything that had happened since that evening he had bumped into Commander Ross Caldwell.

"Well, I see someone's pretty face ain't so pretty anymore." Perry Latimore said with a chuckle upon seeing Murphy's bruises after they walked into the staff's office.

"Bruised or not, we're just glad to have you home." Susan stepped in front of Perry to give Murphy a warm hug.

"So am I." Jessica kissed him on the cheek.

"Latimore," Murphy said, "I have a few questions about a case you've been working on."

"I thought you were on medical leave," Perry said.

"This will only take a minute," Murphy said. "My doctor, Lieutenant Libby McAuley has been receiving death threats." He gave a casual shrug of his shoulders. "Just wondered what the status was on that case."

"I gave her an update this morning." Annoyed, Perry shook his head. "She saw you were assigned to NCIS and decided to sic you on me."

"No need to be paranoid, Latimore," Murphy said. "She's a nice lady. I saw she was upset about something and offered to help."

"I've got this case under control, Thornton."

"Good," Murphy said. "Fill me in. Who's your suspect?"

"Herself," Perry said.

"Herself?" Jessica repeated.

"She may be a big fancy doctor and her father may be a big retired admiral, but she's a whack-job. She did three stints in drug rehab as a teenager. Erin Caldwell filed a restraining order against her after McAuley assaulted her. Commander Caldwell requested a transfer to get away from her."

"If he was so afraid of McAuley, why did he request her for his staff up here in Washington?" Murphy asked. "His request is in her personnel file."

Perry was silent.

"Latimore," Susan said, "Murphy asked you a question."

"Considering that McAuley and Caldwell had a connection," Murphy said, "isn't it possible that the death threats against McAuley are connected to Caldwell's murder?"

"The death threats didn't start until last week," Perry said. "Commander Caldwell died over a month ago."

"Lieutenant Thornton."

Joshua's voice from behind them made Murphy physically jump. He whirled around and stood at attention.

Joshua folded his arms across his chest and looked Murphy square in the eyes. "Did Lieutenant McAuley release you for active duty, Lieutenant?"

"No, sir."

"Then what are you doing here, Lieutenant?"

"I want to know what's happening, sir. This is my case."

"I'll tell you when we make an arrest," Joshua said. "You are dismissed. Go home, Lieutenant."

"We ran into a snag on Natalie Stepford's murder." Boris stepped up to tell Murphy from over Joshua's shoulder before he had an opportunity to leave. "The traffic cam picture doesn't show who is behind the wheel of the Porsche. Garland's lawyer is claiming the car was stolen, driven to the crime scene at approximately the same time as the murder, and then returned home."

"That's crazy," Jessica said. "No jury will believe that."

"Without more evidence, we won't even get an indictment," Joshua said.

"Did you get the ballistics report back on the bullets that killed Baldwin, the HHS investigator?" Murphy asked Boris.

Boris nodded his head. "Yes, and they do not match the bullets the ME took out of Caldwell's head. We're still waiting for a ballistics report on Woody's Colt that we found last night."

"That means the same gun wasn't used to kill both Caldwell and Baldwin," Murphy said.

"Which means it could very well be a different killer," Joshua said.

"The two murders may not even be connected," Murphy said.

"Woody Harris killed Caldwell and Stepford's hired gun killed Baldwin," Boris said.

"We still don't know who killed the kitty cat," Jessica said.

"We'll know more as soon as we get the ballistics report on the Colt." Joshua took Murphy by the arm. "Now go home."

Ignoring him, Murphy turned back to Boris. "How did the killer know Caldwell and I were going to be at the park? We only decided to go running the night before."

"Go home, Lieutenant. That's an order."

With a laugh, Boris turned to Jessica. "Do your husband a favor and coax him into that Ferrari of yours and take him to dinner before the captain knocks him along the other side of his head."

"I'm not driving my Ferrari," Jessica said while extracting her keys from her purse. "I'm driving his SUV."

Stunned, Joshua stared at the keys she was holding up in her hand. "Excuse me. What did you just say?"

"I'm not driving my Ferrari, I'm driving Murphy's SUV."

"And you have *his* keys on *your* key chain," Joshua said, "which gives you access to his vehicle."

"And he has my keys on his key chain," she said. "Don't most couples do that?"

Joshua looked past Murphy and Jessica to Boris. "I believe they do."

CHAPTER THIRTY-ONE

"Thank you for coming in, Ms. Garland," Joshua said in a cheerful tone as he burst through the interrogation room with a folder tucked under his arm.

Her face filled with boredom, Meaghan shot a glance at her lawyer. "Let's get this over with. I've got an appointment with my massage therapist in one hour."

"Shouldn't be any problem getting you out of here in time for that." Joshua tossed the folder onto the table and dropped down into the chair across from her. He rubbed his hands together and then placed them flat on the table.

On the other side of the two-way mirror, Murphy whispered into Jessica's ear. "And so the fun begins."

Joshua opened the folder to expose a report. A blank blue sheet of paper concealed the statement underneath. He lifted the page only enough to check the details himself. "As you are aware, Ms. Garland, we arrested your husband this morning for the murder of Natalie Stepford."

"And I told you this morning, Stan doesn't have the balls to kill anyone."

"Maybe not to plan and execute a murder." He dropped the blue sheet down. "However, the medical examiner believes

Natalie was killed in a fit of anger. Not pre-meditated. That would make it second-degree murder."

"You plan on charging my client's husband for murder," the lawyer said. "What does that have to do with my client?"

"He's denying that he did it."

"Of course."

"Stan admits to being at the Kitchen Studio on the night of the murder," Joshua said. "He's stated that he had confronted Natalie for using him only to get evidence of the black-market organ transplant operation that your client was involved in. He also discovered that she was leaving and that he'd never see her again. He was obsessed with her—so obsessed that he had implanted a GPS tracking device in her arm so that he could keep track of her."

"Sounds like grounds for an insanity defense," the lawyer said with a laugh.

"Should be easy to prove," Meaghan said.

"Only problem is that Stan is insisting that all that happened much earlier and that when he left, Natalie was still alive." Joshua slid the photograph of the Porsche at the traffic stop across the table. "But we have evidence that he was there later. This traffic camera recorded his car at the intersection next to the business park where Natalie's Kitchen Studio is located around the time of the murder."

Meaghan stared down at the picture of the Porsche.

"Then you got him," the lawyer said. "Again, what does that have to do with us?"

"Unfortunately, this picture does not show who is behind the wheel of your husband's car," Joshua said. "We have no evidence that he actually murdered Natalie."

The three of them sat in silence.

In the interrogation room, Murphy whispered to Jessica. "Here it comes."

Joshua sat back in his seat. "Now, we do have a lot of incriminating evidence against you, Ms. Garland, for operating an illegal organ transplant business."

"My client was providing a valuable life-saving enterprise," the lawyer said.

"I'd rather talk about murder," Joshua said.

Meaghan's eyes narrowed.

"I can't believe that your client did not see or hear anything that night," Joshua said. "Stan had become obsessed with Natalie Stepford. He considered her to be his Mona Lisa. She had used him, was going to destroy everything he had, and then walk out of his life. I can't believe that he killed her and then calmly returned home and went to bed." He leveled his eyes on her. "You tell us what you know, testify in court against your husband, and maybe all this other stuff might just go away."

The lawyer held up his hand to silence her. "We want that in writing."

Joshua's eyes held hers. "Before we put anything in writing, I need to know if it's worth the paper it will be written on."

"He killed her," Meaghan pointed at the picture. "He did tell you the truth about going over there earlier. All of that is the truth. She broke him. I knew about his obsession with her. He was so proud of the work he had done. And it was good. You should have seen Natalie the first time Calvin brought her in." She scoffed. "No one turned heads like Natalie did after Stan went to work on her." She tapped the table top. "My husband made her." She sniffed. "And how did she thank him? She crushed him like a bug under her heel."

"What happened that night?"

"Stan came home after seeing Natalie," she said. "I'd never seen him like that. He told me everything. The whole time he was drinking—trying to drown the pain, I guess."

284

She clutched her chest. "I know he cheated on me, but I was heartbroken for him. He was in such pain." She wiped away an imaginary tear. "The more he told me about how she had used him and what she was going to do—to not just him, but us. We haven't been doing these organ transplants for money—we've been doing it to save lives. Anyway, the moe he drank, the madder he got. Until finally, he was drunk with booze and fury." She shook her head. "I tried to stop him, but I couldn't. He went running out of the house." She tapped her finger on the table top. "Check my phone records. You'll see that around midnight, I called Natalie to warn her. But she didn't believe me. She didn't think Stan had enough guts to go over there again—this time to kill her." She sighed. "But he did. When he came back home, he was covered in her blood. Then, he passed out in the bed. He told me that next morning, when I told him what happened, that it seemed like it was all a dream to him."

Sitting back in her seat, she gazed from one of them to the other.

Joshua stared at her.

Pleased with his client's story, the lawyer asked, "Do you think that's good enough for a deal?"

"And you're willing to stand up in court and tell a jury that?" Joshua asked. "You'll send your husband away for life."

Meaghan again dabbed at another imaginary tear. "Frankly, Mr. Thornton, I've never seen my husband like that. He scared me. Since that night, I have lived in terror for my life. I mean, so much fury. Suppose he gets angry with me." She nodded her head. "I think I should have police protection. Don't you?"

"Do we have a deal?" the lawyer asked.

"If your client testifies against her husband, then we have a deal." Joshua stood up and went to the door.

Congratulating each other, Meaghan Garland and her lawyer stepped out to come face to face with Stan Garland, Boris, Murphy, and Jessica.

With a gasp, she jumped back, colliding with Joshua.

"I believe you know Dr. Stan Garland," Joshua told her. "He's been claiming that his car was stolen that night, and he doesn't know who killed Natalie Stepford."

"Of course, he'd say that." She glared at her husband.

"Is that still your story, Stan?" Murphy asked.

"No," Stan said. "It was true only up to a certain point. We both were drinking that night. Meaghan was the one who got madder and madder about Natalie screwing all of us. Around midnight, she called Natalie drunk and the two of them got into a huge fight. Natalie hung up on her and Meaghan became so enraged she ran out. I tried to stop her, but I was too drunk to even get to the door. I passed out drunk in the foyer."

"Shut up, Stan," Meaghan said.

"Now we have two different stories with two different killers," Joshua said. "Who are we supposed to believe?"

"Stan admits he was drunk," the lawyer said. "He was having an affair with the victim and admits she ruined him. My client—"

"I have proof Meaghan killed Natalie," Stan said.

"He's bluffing," the lawyer said.

"Meaghan was covered in Natalie's blood when she came home," Stan said. "She passed out drunk in bed. Got it all over the sheets. She was afraid of the police finding trace evidence. She wrapped it all up—sheets and all—in a plastic bag and hid it in a vent in the basement." He looked at her. "I knew I couldn't trust her, so I took it out and put it away, some place safe, just in case I needed it."

"Which is now," Jessica said.

They all looked across at Meaghan, who fumed.

"I think we've got a winner," Murphy said.

❧ ❧ ❧

"You have a lot of explaining to do, Ms. Garland," Joshua said. "Let's start at the beginning—with Commander Caldwell's murder."

They had returned to the interrogation room—Meaghan, her lawyer, Boris, and Murphy, who had been ordered to remain quiet since he was still on medical leave.

"It wasn't me."

Joshua opened the folder and slapped a print out onto the table. "Calvin Stepford's phone records. He had been tracking his wife. Apparently, Natalie was very popular."

"Yes, she was," Meaghan said with a sigh.

"Her husband had been tracking her electronics—emails, texts, and phone calls," Joshua explained. "When you put his phone records together with hers, you get a picture. She had been in contact with Commander Caldwell. They had met when Natalie catered his daughter Kendall's wedding last fall. She contacted him about your criminal enterprise—"

"Natalie was okay with it," Meaghan said. "She loved the dough. But then, Dr. Lou slipped up one night and someone died." With an eye roll, she threw her hands up in the air. "Stuff happens. You know."

It took Joshua a full moment to regroup, shake off her toxic indifference, and get back on track. "Natalie's husband, Calvin, knew that Commander Caldwell was going to meet and pass on information about your black-market organ transplant clinic on Saturday morning. Murder wasn't something that he would do himself. That was the type of thing he passed on to his subordinates. He ordered you to take care of it. That morning, you went to Great Falls and killed Commander Caldwell while he was waiting for Murphy to go running."

Meaghan shook her head so hard her hair swung off her shoulders. "I did not kill him."

Joshua pointed at the line in Calvin Stepford's phone records. "Stepford called you from his cell phone on Friday night—two minutes after Caldwell texted Natalie saying that he was going to meet Reg, from HHS at Starbucks at eight-thirty. Are you telling me that he called you after reading that text to discuss the weather?"

Her lawyer whispered into her ear. Letting out an exasperated breath, she said, "But I didn't kill him. I didn't kill either of them." She leaned across the table to make her point. "The HHS agent was expecting to meet a man. Dr. Lou went to intercept him. He pretended to be Caldwell and then took him someplace and offed him."

"Dr. Lou is the surgeon who does the actual transplants," Boris said.

"He's an excellent surgeon," Meaghan said.

"Wasn't his medical license pulled because he was a drug dealer?" Joshua said.

Meaghan's eyes grew wide. "I have no idea what you're talking about?"

"What do you do with the patients Dr. Lou kills?" Joshua asked.

"He doesn't kill them," Meaghan said. "So a few of our patients have died on the table. It isn't like they were healthy coming in. If Dr. Lou didn't operate on them, they were going to die anyway."

"I don't imagine you give the patients' families any refund when they die, do you?" Murphy asked.

"Again, what do you do with the bodies of the patients who don't make it?" Joshua asked. "We will find out and when we do, you and your partners are looking at negligent homicide charges. And that's a best-case scenario."

"His—" With a heavy sigh, she shook her head. "Dr. Lou has a friend who runs a crematorium. The patients sign an agreement that if they die on the table, they'll allow their bodies to be cremated—"

"To get rid of the evidence," Boris said.

"Dr. Lou pays a doctor friend of his to sign the death certificate," Meaghan said.

With a shake of his head, Joshua said, "Let's get back to Calvin Stepford's order to take care of Dr. Caldwell. Who ordered Dr. Lou to get Reginald Baldwin out of the way?"

"Stepford."

"How did he do that?" Joshua showed her the phone records. "Stepford never called Dr. Lou after discovering what Natalie had been up to. The only contact Stepford had during that period was you. Do you know what I think?" He chuckled. "Stepford told you about the meeting that Caldwell had set up with Baldwin—and told you to take care of it. You called Dr. Lou, which I'm sure your phone records will confirm, and you ordered him to take care Baldwin."

"You have zero evidence that my client organized a hit on a federal agent," the lawyer said.

"Yet," Joshua said. "We're collecting your client's phone records now—with a warrant. If she tells us what she knows, then we can make a recommendation to the prosecutors. Let's start at the beginning. What happened with Commander Caldwell?"

"I didn't kill him," Meaghan said. "That doctor was killed in a park. I didn't know he was there. I was waiting for him at his house."

His theory validated, Murphy jerked his head in Joshua's direction.

Joshua ignored him. "What were you waiting for at Caldwell's house?"

"Calvin Stepford ordered me to kill him." She slumped. "He was going to ruin everything. I thought Natalie needed to be taken care of, too. But, Calvin was head over heels in love with her. He insisted he could control her and since he owned a controlling share of the company, then we had to listen to him."

"Tell us what happened at Caldwell's house," Murphy said.

"I had parked in one of those turnoffs in the woods and hiked to Caldwell's house," she said. "I wanted to do it early and get it over with. I was hiding behind a tree close to the property line. Just as I got there, I saw a car pull out of the garage and leave. So then, I'm waiting and waiting. Some guy comes out of the house to the garage. I know it's not the doctor because this guy looked like some MTV reject. After a few minutes, he drives off in his car. It had a kayak tied to the top of it. After that—we're talking a long time—some woman comes out yelling, 'Woody.' She goes into the garage and I hear all this yelling. She was mad about something. Then I heard her screaming, 'Ross.' She comes running out of the garage back to the house. That's when I realized she was talking on the phone to the guy I was supposed to shoot. She's hysterical—saying that she's going to call the police. I decided I had to get out of there. I took off like a bat out of hell back to the car."

Joshua looked over at Murphy and Boris.

"You're saying," Murphy said, "that you were in Great Falls Park at the time of the murder, intending to kill the victim, but you didn't do it?"

"Would I make something that crazy up?"

"That's almost as good as the one about the car being stolen, driven to the murder scene, and then returned," Boris said.

"Did anyone see you at the Caldwell home at the time of the murder in the park?" Murphy asked. "Or did you see anyone?"

She started to say no, but then grinned. "There was a runner. I was so busy looking behind me running away from the house that I bumped into her. We both got knocked off our feet. I didn't say a word to her—and she didn't say anything to me either. We both just jumped up and ran like hell out of there. I looked over my shoulder and she was running across the back yard to Dr. Caldwell's garage."

"What did she look like?" Murphy asked.

"She was wearing a blue running suit," Meaghan said, "with a hood. She was young. She had really short red hair."

"Why should we believe you?" Joshua asked.

"Because I'm telling you the truth."

લ લ લ

Meaghan was taken to be locked up in a holding cell. While Perry and Susan went to the Garland home to retrieve the clothes that she had worn the night she killed Natalie Stepford, Murphy, Joshua, and Boris met in the deputy chief's office.

"Do we believe Meaghan Garland or not?" Boris asked.

"The information about the blue running suit was not released to the media," Murphy said. "That means Meaghan Garland is either the killer or an eye witness who saw the killer."

"But which is she?" Boris asked.

"Meaghan's description matches Kendall Harris, Caldwell's youngest daughter to a 'T'," Murphy said.

"Why would she kill her father?" Joshua asked.

"I don't know," Murphy said in a soft voice. "But I think I know who to ask."

Chapter Thirty-Two

Dr. Libby McAuley pulled her car into the garage of her townhome. She climbed out and hit the button to close the garage door. With her valise slung across her shoulder, she went to the door leading into her home. Once inside the kitchen, she propped the door open with her foot and jiggled the key to get it out of the lock.

Creak.

She stopped when she heard the creak of a floorboard.

She listened.

Silence.

She had heard that creak before. It was the third step from the top of the stairs leading to the second floor.

"Hello?" she called out. "Is anyone there?"

Silence.

She wanted to dismiss the noise, but the beating of her heart would not let her. "Hello?" Moving slowly, she reached inside her valise and wrapped her hand around the grip of her small semi-automatic. She never went anywhere without it—not since that night she almost died.

"Is anyone there?"

292

She lowered the valise to the floor and holding the gun straight out, her finger on the trigger, she eased through the kitchen to the living room. Her eyes darted around to search every corner and shadow for the intruder she knew had to be in her home.

Creak!

This time it was the creak of the bathroom door opening or closing in the master suite.

Libby spun around and aimed the gun up the stairs. The sound of footsteps in the bedroom were unmistakable.

It was not her imagination.

"I know you're up there!"

Beads of cold sweat dripped down her back.

The dongs of the doorbell scared her like an electrical shock throughout her body. She shrieked with fright before running to the front door and peering through the peep hole. She recognized Lieutenant Murphy Thornton and his wife, but not the two men behind him. She yanked open the door.

Seeing the gun in her hand, Murphy's hands shot up. "We've come in peace!"

"There's someone in my house." She pointed the gun in the direction of the stairs. "I heard her on the stairs and moving around in the bedroom."

"Murphy, you stay here with the lieutenant and Jessica," Joshua ordered while pulling out his weapon and following Boris up the stairs.

"But—"

"You're still on medical leave!"

"You're still on medical leave," Murphy muttered in a mocking tone.

"But you are," Jessica said before turning to Libby, who had lowered herself into a chair. "Who is it?"

The doctor was focused on the scar on her right hand.

293

When Libby didn't respond, Jessica repeated the question.

"Excuse me?" Libby asked.

"Who is it?"

"Dr. McAuley," Joshua yelled from upstairs, "we need you up here now! Murphy, call emergency! We need EMTs and an ambulance!"

Murphy took out his cell phone to place the call while following Libby and Jessica up the stairs to the master suite. They found Joshua and Boris standing over Erin Caldwell stretched out across Libby's bed. She was barely conscious.

"Stay with me, Ms. Caldwell." Boris patted her cheeks to keep her awake. "Stay awake."

Joshua handed an empty prescription bottle to Libby. "She appears to have taken these."

"These are meds for bipolar disease." Libby sat on the bed to examine Erin. "How many pills did she take?"

"We have no idea," Joshua said. "We found her like this."

"Medics are on the way," Murphy said.

"They better get here fast." Libby took her hand. "Erin, why did you do this?"

"Payback." Erin's words were slurred. "You took my Ross."

"I did not!" Libby squeezed. "Your husband and I were friends. Nothing more! I was trying to help."

"You took his love from me."

"No! I told you before—"

"Lies. Kendall told me about seeing the two of you to—" Erin's voice trailed off. Her eyes closed.

"Libby, what's she talking about?" Jessica asked. "What did Kendall see?"

"It's no use. She's unconscious," Libby said while checking Erin's pupils. "Whatever Kendall told her was a lie."

❧ ❧ ❧

After following the ambulance to the hospital, they were surprised to discover J.J. and Tristan in the emergency room waiting area.

"What are you doing here?" Joshua shook his head with annoyance.

J.J. wordlessly responded by pointing to Tristan. That was when they realized he was sitting in a wheelchair with one of his legs raised up and resting on a cushion.

"What happened to you?" Jessica dropped into the seat next to the chair.

"I was in the kitchen," Tristan said, "making a batch of Buffalo wings to enjoy with this totally awesome zombie marathon we found on the sci-fi channel and—"

"He tripped over Newman," J.J. said with a chuckle.

"I don't need you to answer for me." Tristan turned to Jessica. "I tripped over Newman."

"Is Newman okay?" Murphy asked.

"Do you see Newman in a wheelchair?"

"It was terrible," J.J. said. "Buffalo sauce all over the kitchen. But that's okay. Spencer was cleaning it up when I carried Tristan out to the car to bring here."

"You allowed my dog to eat Buffalo sauce!" Jessica's eyes were wide. "Do you know what Buffalo sauce does to a dog's digestion?"

"I had to take care of Tristan," J.J. said. "He was crying like a baby."

"Some of us have lower pain thresholds than others," Tristan said.

"How did you trip over Newman?" Jessica gasped. "He's so slow. It isn't like he'd dart in front of—"

"He may be slow, but he's got the heart of a ninja lurking deep in his evil little heart," Tristan said. "I know he did this on purpose. He's had it out for me ever since I accidentally deleted his copy of *Friday the 13th*."

"Not only do you have a low pain threshold, but you're paranoid, too," Joshua said.

"What's Newman doing now?" Murphy asked. "Are you sure he's okay?"

Tristan raised his eyes up to Murphy's. "I don't know for certain what he's doing, but there is one thing I do know for sure—He's not sitting in a wheelchair in the ER!"

Next to him, J.J. covered his laughter with his hand over his mouth. "Last I saw him, he was back in his recliner watching *Invasion of the Body Snatchers.*"

"The original one or the remake?" Joshua asked.

"Is anyone going to ask about my broken leg?" Tristan asked.

"You're not a Bassett hound," Jessica said.

Dr. Libby McAuley drew their attention from Tristan's leg when she stepped through the doorway.

"How's Ms. Caldwell?" Murphy asked.

"We've pumped her stomach, but we won't know for certain until the morning," Libby said. "Our office has notified her family. They're on their way. I've transferred this case to another doctor. He will be meeting with them when they get here."

"Because you don't want to see them," Murphy said. "Why is that?"

"This really is not any of your business, Lieutenant." She turned to leave, but Murphy sidestepped to cut her off.

"Commander Caldwell was your friend. You cared deeply enough to sneak into his funeral to pay your respects—even though I believe you were afraid for your safety. That means a lot. Your friend's wife is grieving so badly that she attempted to kill herself in your bedroom."

"Obviously, she did that to send a message," Jessica said.

"She's the one who was sending death threats to you," Murphy said.

"Erin Caldwell is deeply disturbed," Libby said. "She needs help."

With a flash, Murphy remembered an incident from the day he had been abducted. "After Ross Caldwell's funeral, Kendall told me that her father had a stalker in Annapolis."

"I was not stalking him!" Libby said.

"Caldwell's brother said the same thing."

"And we found no complaint of stalking during our investigation," Boris said.

"Daniel Caldwell also told me that Kendall had an active imagination—"

"A polite way of saying she's a liar," Libby said.

"I dismissed the claim of a stalker," Murphy said. "But then, on Friday, a month later, I ran into Erin Caldwell and asked her about it. She said she had seen the stalker only recently here at the hospital."

"It's not true," Libby said.

Murphy held up his hand. "At the time, she couldn't remember your name. But then, I think it came to her. She asked her daughter Kendall about it, and Kendall told her that you had returned to Caldwell's life and the two of you had had an affair. That is when the death threats started."

Libby's voice was weak. "Ross and I did not have a love affair."

"I believe you."

Libby raised her eyes to meet his. "None of this has anything to do with Dr Caldwell's murder."

"Let us be the judge of that," Joshua said.

Exhausted, Libby eased down into a chair. Her face was pale. Her eyes sad. "Ross Caldwell and I were colleagues—and friends. He was my mentor. But—" She let out a breath.

"His wife thought it was more," Jessica said.

"And Kendall fed that suspicion because she had her own agenda."

"Is Erin the one who stabbed you?" Jessica asked.

Shaking her head, Libby rubbed the scar on the palm of her hand. "Erin was too imbalanced to believe Ross when he told her that our relationship was not what she thought. What didn't help was…" Her voice trailed off.

"Was what?" Joshua asked.

"Ross came to me for help with a personal problem. He didn't want anyone to know about it." She sucked in a deep breath. "It had to do with Kendall."

"Kendall has a drug problem," Murphy said.

"How did you know?" Jessica said. "At the funeral, she seemed so normal."

"But she isn't. Something struck me as just off." Murphy turned to J.J. "Kind of like a friend of ours who recently passed away. Everything looked good on the outside—but inside, she was rotten to the core."

"That's Kendall all right," Libby said. "Not only is she hooked on booze and recreational drugs, but she's also a dealer. In Annapolis, she dealt drugs in high school. Being a doctor, Ross saw the early warning signs—"

"And you had a personal history with drug addiction," Murphy said.

"Rehab three times before I was eighteen," Libby said without any shame. "Ross invited me to his house and different activities so that I could observe Kendall. He wanted me to confirm his suspicions, which I did. Then, I tried to get close to her to help."

"And Erin thought you were hanging around to put the moves on her husband," Jessica said.

"Yes," Libby said. "When Kendall realized our real agenda, she manipulated her mother into thinking I was a stalker. Kendall is Erin's baby and her favorite. She's completely incapable of seeing Kendall for the monster she really is."

"Tell us about the assault," Murphy said.

"Erin attacked me during one of her manic episodes," Libby said. "I defended myself. She wouldn't stop coming at me and ended up bearing the brunt of it. Ross sent me home. An hour later, the military police were at my door. Erin wanted to file assault charges. Ross told her not to, but Kendall convinced her mother that she had to fight for her man if she wanted to keep him."

"And since Ross was Erin's husband," Joshua said, "he ended up in the middle. Based on what little I've seen of Erin's mental state, if he defended you, she'd see that as betrayal on his part against her."

"He finally did convince Erin to withdraw her complaint," Libby said. "Then, he sent Kendall away to rehab and transferred out of the area. He hoped that a change of scenery, different school, new friends, would help get Kendall on the right track, and maybe undo the damage she had done to his marriage."

"Boy," Tristan said, "if I were you, I'd stay as far away from that family as possible."

"Who stabbed you?" Murphy asked.

"Kendall is a highly functional closet addict." Libby rubbed the scar on her shoulder. "Not all addicts are street people unable to hold jobs. She went to school—socialized—had friends and was very popular. Erin never realized that Kendall was popular because she was the high school drug dealer. Kendall also stole booze from her father's liquor cabinet, pills from her mother's medicine cabinet, and money. Ross took steps to cut her off. One night, I was driving past the medical office on base and saw a light on. I went in to see what was going on. Kendall jumped out of the shadows and stabbed me with a pair of scissors. She had used her father's security pass and keys to get in to steal pills out of the pharmacy. Base police were called. Out of respect for Ross, I agreed not to press charges. I knew that if that ended up on Kendall's record it would ruin her future, and I didn't want to hurt Ross's career. So, I asked my father to use his influence to cover it up. One week after that, Kendall was at a rehab facility up here in Washington."

"Did you and Dr. Caldwell remain friends?" Murphy asked.

"Not publicly," Libby said. "He requested me here on the staff at the hospital because I specialize in addiction. The opioid addiction crisis has become a serious problem. I thought long and hard about it when he contacted me. I was scared. But he said that our personal problems were secondary to helping service members and their families suffering from addiction." She fingered the Saint Luke's medal she wore around her neck. "He was right. It made me remember why I decided to specialize in addiction issues. I set my fears aside and came here."

"Did Dr. Caldwell give you that medal?" Jessica asked.

Her eyes moist, Libby nodded her head. "The last day we saw each other in Annapolis. He gave it to me as thanks for trying to help him and his family."

"You're a brave woman," J.J. said. "Most people wouldn't have been able to do what you have accomplished."

"If I've accomplished so much, why do I feel like a failure?" Libby pointed at the room down the hallway where Erin Caldwell was recovering from her suicide attempt. "Kendall won. Look at what she did to her own mother. She practically destroyed her parents' marriage—all because she didn't want to give up her addiction. Erin hardly trusted Ross after Annapolis. To this day, she thinks I tried to kill Kendall to get back at Ross for rejecting me."

"What motive would Kendall have to kill her father?" Murphy asked.

"He was going to send her back to rehab," Libby said. "Four years after she got out of rehab, she was right back to where she was before—only now she's more devious. She's dealing to the local rock groups downtown."

"She's kept it well hidden," Murphy said. "Manipulates those around her to cover for her."

"Exactly," Libby said. "She's got a job. Never misses a day of work. On the surface, she looks like any upper-middle class daughter. But behind the scenes, Ross noticed that booze, pills, and money were disappearing. He finally concluded that Kendall never got clean. She just said and did all the right things to fool those around her. For example, she gets dressed to go running, takes a water bottle filled with booze and goes out on the trail. Then she finds a secluded spot to drink."

"Did Ross tell you what color her running suit was?" Boris asked.

Libby shook her head. "Erin actually thinks her daughter is a marathon runner because she spends so much time out on the trail."

"What was the catalyst to make Kendall kill her father?" Joshua asked.

"The day before he was killed, Ross showed me a brochure for a rehab facility out west," she said. "He was going to tell Kendall that night that he was kicking her husband out of the house and sending her back to rehab for three months."

"And if she said no?" Jessica asked. "She is over eighteen. Legally, she could refuse to go."

"Then he was going to kick both her and her husband out and cut them off completely."

Seeing someone approaching from down the corridor, Libby rose to her feet. "If you don't mind, I would like to go home now. I really prefer not to have any part of this upcoming conversation." She hurried out the opposite door as Erin's three daughters stepped into the waiting room.

Kendall was dressed in multi-colored leggings and a tunic top. She carried an oversized bag and a water bottle from which she took frequent sips. Having become aware of her addiction, they realized that the water bottle which she constantly kept in her grasp most likely contained something other than water. It contained something with an odor which she covered up with breath mints.

The eldest daughter, Heather recognized Boris as the lead investigator for her father's murder. After a warm and awkward greeting, she said, "We received a call that our mother has been brought in for a drug overdose. Do you believe this has something to do with our dad's murder?"

"Of course not," Kendall said. "Woody killed Dad because he blamed him for me ending our marriage. Mom's suicide attempt is because she can't live without Dad."

With a frown, Boris slightly nodded his head. "Your mother did attempt suicide."

"In Lieutenant Libby McAuley's home," Murphy said while keeping a close eye on Kendall's face. He saw only a flicker of recognition at the mention of Libby's name on Kendall's face.

Meanwhile, Heather and her other sister, Cynthia, exchanged long glances. "That name sounds familiar," Heather finally said.

"Should," Murphy said. "She's the woman Kendall stabbed four years ago."

Heather and Cynthia turned to look at their younger sister.

Kendall took a drink from her water bottle before saying, "In self-defense."

The doubt in the sisters' eyes as they exchanged glances revealed that Kendall had less influence over them than she did her emotionally vulnerable mother. "I told you all about that night. Lieutenant McAuley was chasing after Dad. They had a one-night stand and Mom found out about it. He realized he had made a mistake and ended it, but McAuley refused to let him go. She told him that she was not going to let him ignore her. But Dad didn't want to lose Mom. She decided to get even by killing me. She lured me to the base medical office. I walked in and she attacked me with a pair of scissors. It was only by luck that I was able to get them off her and stab her."

"I think Newman and I saw that movie last night," Tristan said. "Only the mistress was a vampire."

Heather and Cynthia regarded their sister with disdain.

Kendall took a big sip from the bottle and wiped her mouth with the back of her hand. "I'm lucky to be alive."

"You certainly have a lot of good luck," Heather said. "Lieutenant McAuley tries to kill you, but you get the better of her and stab her. Woody sneaks in and tries to shoot you—hitting the ceiling instead—"

"And only gets off one shot," Cynthia said. "Then, you're able to dry your hands, grab Dad's service weapon, and fire three shots, which all hit their target before he can fire off a second one."

"Didn't you go into drug rehab directly after that incident with Lieutenant McAuley, Kendall?" Murphy asked.

"Yes, she did," Cynthia said. "Mom bought her story about Lieutenant McAuley attacking her, but Heather and I knew the truth. We all knew she was an addict."

"So I liked to cut loose and have fun back then," Kendall said. "I worked hard. I kept my grades up. I went to school every day."

"Because you had a thriving drug business," Heather said. "All you learned in rehab was what to say and do to make everyone think you're a pure drug-free angel. You may have fooled Mom, but you didn't fool Dad."

"Which is why you killed him," Murphy said. "He was sending you back to rehab. If you refused, he was going to disown you."

Clutching each other's hands, Heather and Cynthia backed away from their sister. Kendall took another long drink from her bottle.

"I notice no one is saying 'she couldn't have,'" Tristan said.

"Woody killed Dad," Kendall said. "After I called him out, he came back to shoot me with the same gun he used to kill Dad."

Boris nodded his head. "Yes, the bullet we found in the kitchen ceiling was a match for the bullet that killed your father. That gun was found at the scene of Woody's shooting."

"But Woody didn't shoot your father," Murphy said. "He couldn't have."

"Because…" Kendall asked.

"He had a solid alibi for the time of the murder," Boris said. "Two national park rangers. Woody decided to go kayaking down the Great Falls rapids in your father's kayak, which he had found in the garage. Unfortunately, he had zero training. He was there right at seven o'clock when the park opened and just about drowned minutes later. Some tourists shot videos of it on their cell phones. Over half a million people have seen it and Woody became a front-runner for the National Park Service's Idiot of the Year Award."

"Woody couldn't have killed your father," Murphy said. "That leaves—"

"I couldn't have done it," Kendall said with a loud laugh. "I was at work that morning. I clocked in at six o'clock. Dad was shot at seven o'clock. I didn't leave until after Mom called to tell me what happened."

"We checked with your manager," Boris said. "You clocked in right before six o'clock. At around six-thirty, you left for a cigarette break. Your office manager told us that you go for a cigarette break every hour on the half hour, so it was no big deal. But she remembers that particular morning because she didn't see you for a full hour. When you returned, you told her that you had just gotten a call from your mother saying that your father had been shot. You explained your absence on crying in your car."

"We have a witness who saw you in a blue running suit behind your house and going across the back yard into your garage shortly after your father's murder," Joshua said.

Kendall took another drink from the bottle. "Your witness is wrong. I never wear blue."

"You have a tell, Kendall," Joshua said. "It's your drinking. Every time you lie, you need to take a drink. I imagine it's for liquid courage."

"Why—" Unable to find the words, Heather stopped and swallowed. She and Cynthia clung to each other while staring in horror at their sister.

"Dr. McAuley specializes in substance abuse," Murphy said. "She and your father were working together to help your sister. But she didn't want help. She wanted to continue taking drugs and drinking. She did everything she could to sabotage them like feeding your mother's insecurities to pit her against your father and Dr. McAuley."

"You practically split Mom and Dad up, you little bitch!" Heather tried to lunge at her sister, only to have Boris and Cynthia hold her back. "You drove Mom to suicide."

"They moved up here to Washington to get Kendall help," Murphy said, "but it didn't work. I imagine your father saw that it was worse than ever before. Not only were you using, but you were dealing, as well."

Kendall scoffed. "You don't know what you're talking about."

"That's how you met Woody," Murphy said. "Your uncle told me that you had a growing promotion business with the local independent rock groups. Could some of that popularity be due your drug connections?"

She glared at him in silence.

"We talked to the Washington D.C. police," Boris said. "They know all about you, Kendall."

"You had two growing businesses," Murphy said. "Music promoter and drug dealer. Both would have been shot to hell if your father succeeded in sending you back into rehab. But that's what he intended to do. He was sending you far away from here—out west. Dr. McAuley said that he had told her that he was telling you that Friday night—the night before he was murdered."

"One of the numbers on your father's list of phone calls was to a substance abuse counselor in Arizona," Boris said while checking a text on his cell phone. "We called him about an hour ago. He had made arrangements to send Kendall there. She was supposed to check in the Monday after his murder." He nodded his head at Murphy.

"They found it?"

"Yep," Boris said.

"We sent investigators to your home after you left this evening," Murphy told Kendall. "They have a warrant. They searched the bins in the garage and found the blue running suit with hoodie that you wore the morning you killed your father. You said you never wore blue. But Heather did. You took it out of the clothes she stored in the garage. That's why your mother found them dumped all over the floor that morning."

"You wore my clothes to kill Dad!" Once again, Heather lunged for Kendall, but was held back by Cynthia and Boris. But she was able to reach out with her hand and slap her across the face. Kendall tried to retaliate, only to have J.J. hold her back.

"You knew your father was going running through the park that morning," Murphy said. "So before going to work, you dug through the bin of Heather's old clothes for a running suit. Your style is very different from your sister's and you wanted to conceal your own appearance. Based on conversations with Dr. McAuley, I suspect it was no mistake that you took one of Woody's unregistered handguns. The first time I met you, you called Woody 'your mistake.' You were going to take care of two problems at one time. Kill your father and frame Woody."

"You're a monster," Cynthia said in a low voice. "My own sister is a cold-blooded monster."

"By clocking in at work, you gave yourself an alibi," Murphy said. "Then, when you went for your first cigarette break, you drove back home and parked down the road. You put on Heather's running suit and ran through the woods to the park that was only a few minutes away. You shot your father with Woody's gun and then ran back home. You kept the gun because you wanted the police to find it in his possession to frame him. You had to go back home and into the garage where you took off the running suit and mixed it back in with your sister's old clothes. You then ran to where you had hidden your car and went back to work, where you said you had just received news that your father had been murdered."

"According to your mother's phone records, she didn't call you until after eight o'clock, when you were on your way home," Boris said.

"Do you know what gave you away?" Murphy asked.

Kendall glared at him in silence.

"You told me that you were there at the funeral reception," Murphy said. "It didn't hit me until much later when my wife mentioned how I take Spencer running with me. You mentioned that at the reception—how lucky it was that me and my dog encountered the killer on the running trail after he'd killed your father."

"You're wrong," Kendall said. "I didn't say anything about your little blue dog."

"How did you know she was blue?" Murphy asked.

"That's right," Jessica said. "You never met Spencer."

"Unless you were at the park that morning and tried to escape on the same trail we were on after you'd shot your father," Murphy said.

With a smirk, Kendall took a drink from her bottle. "You can't prove I was the one who shot him. It was Woody's gun. He had it when he came in last night and tried to kill me."

"He didn't try to kill you," Murphy said. "You set him up."

"He had three guns and got rid of them right after the murder," Kendall said. "If he was innocent why would he have done that?"

"The only reason the police found that out was because your mother told me," Murphy said, "because you planted that seed in her mind."

"Sounds like something you'd do, Kendall," Heather said.

"You see, a month after your father's murder, the investigators were focused on another suspect and getting nowhere," Murphy said. "Woody was completely off our radar and you wanted to get rid of him."

"Why not just divorce him?" Tristan asked.

"Because Woody refused to leave," Heather said. "He flat out said he was comfortable where he was and if Kendall wanted to divorce him, she'd have to leave."

"But Woody was too smart for you. When he found out your father had been shot, he got rid of his guns—the two guns he had left. You'd hidden the gun you used to murder your father." Murphy asked her in a low voice, "Did Woody know it was you who killed him?"

"Woody was an idiot," Kendall said.

"He easily bought the lie you told him to make him run away," Murphy said. "I suspect you told him that the police were going to frame him for murder. You probably sent him to hide out in one of your drug dealers' safe houses."

"Then you called us to report that he'd run off," Boris said. "It was his gun. You stated that he had admitted to killing your father. The police were looking for him as a suspected killer."

"The ground work was laid," Murphy said. "What excuse did you use to lure him to your house?" He smirked. "As clever as you are, I'm sure it was a doozy."

A slim smile crossed her lips. "If I had set up Woody to kill him, and I'm not saying that I did, I would have lured him to the house with an excuse that he couldn't resist." She glanced at Jessica. "Like that your wife had passed his music on to Mac Faraday and he liked it enough to come out to my house to sign him to a summer concert deal at the Spencer Inn." She giggled. "Woody was such an idiot. If I had lured him to our house to kill him, he would have been so excited, that he'd never have notice the gun in my hand until I had put three bullets in him." A slim smile crossed her lips. "But that's not what happened. You can't prove I killed anyone."

"Actually, we can," Murphy said. "I'm sure forensics will pick up lead and gun powder on the running suit. And since the killer had the hoodie pulled up over her head, they'll find some of your hair, sweat, and other evidence to prove who was wearing it when your father was killed. And as for killing Woody, the angle of the shot to the ceiling is too steep to be a shot from across the room. Plus, the gunshot residue on Woody's hand indicates that someone placed the gun in his hand and pulled the trigger—after you killed him. Then, you placed the dishes in the sink and filled it with soapy water to stage the scene to look like you were washing dishes when he sneaked in to kill you." He chuckled. "Unfortunately for you, you thought you were so smart, that you missed one major thing. People put *dirty* dishes in the sink to wash."

"It was pretty clear to us that you had staged the scene when we saw that the dishwater and dishes were clean," J.J. said.

Heather scoffed. "Maybe if you washed a few dishes in your life you would have realized that!"

"Your mother said in her statement that you were the one who suggested that she take medication last night to help her sleep," Joshua said. "You wanted her properly drugged so she wouldn't be awake to see you murder your husband."

"Your father was only trying to help you," J.J. said.

"By making me miserable?" Kendall said. "Listen, addiction is only a problem if you see it as a problem. I'm happiest when I'm stoned. Booze and drugs are my best friends and Dad wanted to take them away from me." With one big gulp she drained the water bottle. Turning it over, she saw that it was empty. "Damn."

"He was our *father*," Heather sobbed while holding Cynthia in a hug.

"He told me that I had to choose between my friends and the family." Kendall shrugged. "So I did. He lost."

Boris took her by the arm. "Kendall Harris, you're under arrest for the murder of Commander Ross Caldwell and Woody Harris."

"And now you've lost," Murphy said.

EPILOGUE

"What are you so nervous about?" Joshua gave in to curiosity after three hours of watching J.J. shift back and forth in the passenger seat of the SUV.

"What makes you think I'm nervous?" His voice cracked. J.J. cleared his throat and swallowed.

"I hope you're not going through puberty again." With a shake of his head, Joshua gave up on the conversation and turned on the news.

J.J. hit the button to drop his seat into the reclining position and closed his eyes. Hopefully, he could catch up on the sleep that had been escaping him for the past two nights. Every time he closed his eyes, the conversation he had with Poppy two days before would echo throughout his mind:

"Did you get my message?"

Silence. That terminally long silence.

His heart catching in his throat, he croaked out, "Are you still there?"

"Yes, I got your message—all five of them," she said in a soft voice. "I'll see you when you get home, J.J."

With a heavy sigh, he draped his arm across his eyes in a vain effort to block out the memory. It was only due to pure exhaustion that he had managed to fall asleep. With a jolt, he woke when he felt the SUV make a sharp turn onto the lane leading up to the farm house.

"We're home." Joshua slapped his leg. "Wake up, sleepy head."

J.J. sat up and looked out his side window to see Captain Blackbeard running along the fence—racing the SUV up to the house. The stallion's black coat shone in the sun.

"There are our girls," Joshua said. "Perfect timing. It looks like they just got back from a trail ride."

On the other side of the barn yard, Poppy and Izzy were rubbing down their horses. Ollie was playing a game of tag with Charley. The huge white rooster appeared to be more serious about the game than the baby lamb. Izzy led her palomino Comanche into the barn.

Poppy cast a quick glance in their direction before packing up their brushes and other tackle supplies and putting them into the box on the bench.

Joshua parked the SUV in front of the house and climbed out.

J.J. felt a dark cloud of dread wash over him. His feet felt heavy as he climbed out of the SUV.

Carrying Ollie in her arms, Poppy was making her way toward him.

"Daddy!" Izzy ran across the barnyard and hugged Joshua. "Guess what! Comanche and I went jumping today! Poppy thinks—"

The rest of Izzy's words were jumbled in J.J.'s mind. All he was focused on was Poppy's expression as she moved toward him. It was impossible for him to read her face. Unable to decipher her feelings—he gave up to only admire her beauty—fresh—natural—glorious like the blossom petals raining around the farm.

His feet felt like they were encased in cement as he approached her. They met in the middle of the driveway—halfway to the barn.

"There's a case of beer cooling in the fridge," she said while stroking the top of Ollie's head. The baby appeared to have doubled in size while J.J. was gone.

He blurted out the words, "I'm sorry—"

"For what?"

"For what I said." He swallowed. "I was—I was drunk."

"Drunk?" She squinted at him. "J.J., I've never seen you drunk."

"It happens." He shoved his hands in his pockets. "Let's just forget everything I said." He kicked at a pebble on the ground.

"Even the part where you said that you'd blow your brains out if I didn't want to marry you and have your baby?"

"You said what?" Joshua interjected from where he was taking J.J.'s bags out of the SUV.

"When did you ask Poppy to marry you and have your baby?" Izzy asked J.J.

"Not just a baby," Poppy said with a sly grin. "He wants us to have a houseful of kids."

"When did this happen?" Joshua asked.

"He left me a voice mail." Poppy held up her hand with the fingers spread apart. "Actually, he left me five."

"Baaa," Ollie said as if to confirm that Poppy's statement was indeed true.

"You proposed *marriage* in a voice mail?" Joshua's eyes were wide.

Ollie uttered another "baaaa."

"It could have been worse," Izzy said. "He could have proposed with a text."

"I didn't even know you were dating," Joshua said.

"Will you two shut up?" J.J. pointed down the lane. "Go home!"

"But we want to know Poppy's answer." Turning to Poppy, Izzy bounced on her toes. A broad pleading grin filled her face. "Can I be a bridesmaid? Ollie can be the ring-bearer!" She gave the lamb a kiss on the nose.

"Get in the car, Izzy," Joshua said.

Muttering about how she was being sent home just when things were getting good, Izzy climbed into the SUV. J.J. stared down at his feet like a guilty child while Joshua turned the SUV around and drove off.

"Just forget I said anything," he told her in a soft voice. "I'd lost my head. Murphy had been kidnapped and hurt, and he and Jessica had a big fight right before he went missing. It got me thinking about you and how I felt—" He swallowed. "I'm really embarrassed, and would rather we just go back to how things have been."

Poppy frowned. "Does that mean you don't want the beer I bought for you?"

"No, you can leave the beer. It is light? Right?"

"Same type you always drink." She handed Ollie to him. "I also have a pot of vegetarian chili simmering on the stove and cornbread in the oven. I know we usually go out on Fridays, but I thought you'd like to spend the evening in."

"That's what I love about you, Poppy. You always know exactly what I want." His voice grew stronger. "We spend a lot of time together and enjoy each other's company. There's nothing wrong with that. Right?"

"If that's what you want." She picked up his overnight bag and slung the strap over her shoulder.

"That's what I want." He swatted Ollie's snout out of his ear.

"Okay."

"Okay."

Ollie agreed with a baaa.

J.J. set the lamb down and turned to pick up the other bag.

"You're right, J.J." Poppy said to his back.

He froze. Slowly, he turned around.

There she was, gazing up at him with those emerald green eyes. Her freckles glowed in the sun. A breeze caught her red hair to sweep it across her cheek. She brushed it back behind her ear. Then, she used her fingers as a comb to toss her long locks behind her shoulder. A sly grin crossed her face.

He felt his heart quicken.

Abruptly, Ollie took off after Charley. The two ran up the steps and around the corner of the wrap-around porch.

J.J. and Poppy were too focused on the wordless messages that could only be read in each other's eyes to notice the skirmish taking place behind them.

Poppy peered up at him through her long eyelashes. "Voice mail is the worst way to tell someone how much you love them for the first time. So much gets lost in the translation. You can't see the other person's expression. Their face. Feel the touch of their hands in yours."

She brushed her fingers across the back of his hand. He turned his hand over and she laced her fingers with his. She looked up into his face. "Look into their eyes to read what's between the lines." She stepped in closer. "The eyes say it all."

J.J. cleared his throat. "What are my eyes saying to you now?"

"They're saying this." She pressed her lips to his.

Wrapping her arms around his neck, she pressed against him. When she started to pull away, he pulled her back.

"Can you say that again?" he whispered. "I'm a slow reader."

"I love you, too, J.J." She kissed him softly before whispering into his ear. "Forever." She pressed her lips to his.

"Well then, we have a lot to talk about." He took her hand and led her up the porch.

"Let's start with you defining 'a bunch of kids.'"

He opened the door just in time for Charley and Ollie to dart inside.

ℰℐ ℰℐ ℰℐ

"Do you smell something burning?" Jessica lifted her head and sniffed around the kitchen.

"Only the sweet scent of your hair." Murphy rose up from where he had his face buried in her hair to breathe into her ear. "It's making me horny."

"You've been horny all afternoon."

"That's a good sign." He kissed her bare shoulder. "It means I'm getting better. Of course, now I can only see one of you." He flashed his wide smile at her. "But one of you is all I need."

"You're all I need, too." She caressed his face and kissed him.

As much as she was enjoying the adventure of an impromptu afternoon delight on the kitchen floor, Jessica was worried about the growing odor of burnt tomatoes, spinach, and noodles. She pushed Murphy aside, sat up, and sniffed. "What is—my lasagna!"

Desperate to save their dinner, she scrambled across the floor. She pulled herself to her feet by grabbing drawer handles and yanked open the oven door. Smoke billowed out of the confines of the oven.

"Oh, no!" She grabbed the oven mitts and, careful to not allow any of her naked body to touch the hot oven, pulled the blackened lasagna out.

Spencer trotted in, took one whiff of the smoke, and turned around to return to where she had been sleeping on the sofa.

"How did you do that?" Murphy waved a dishtowel to fan away the smoke.

"I had set the temperature for four-fifty instead of three-fifty." Jessica slammed the oven door shut. With a groan, she looked down at the lasagna and wondered if there was any hope in saving it. "I wanted to surprise you with a vegan lasagna like the one we made in Natalie's class. Look at it. It's burnt to a crisp."

"Yes, it is," Murphy said.

She threw down the oven mitts in a sign of defeat. "Inedible and ruined."

Murphy wrapped his arms around her waist and lifted her off her feet. "Inedible lasagna served with a double helping of 'what not'." He kissed her. "Just the way I like it."

"Yum." She kissed him behind the ear. "Sounds perfect."

"But first," he whispered in her ear, "how about some pre-dinner 'what not'?"

The End

ATTENTION BOOK CLUB-BERS!

Want to add some excitement to your next book club meeting? Are you curious about this mystery author's theme regarding the dark side of perfection? Do you wonder where she picks up her inspiration for such interesting characters? What does she have planned next for J.J. and Poppy? Well, now is your chance to ask this international best-selling mystery writer, in person, you and your book club.

That's right. Lauren Carr is available to personally meet with your book club to discuss *Murder by Perfection* or any of her best-selling mystery novels. Discussion questions can be found and downloaded directly from the book pages on her website.

Don't worry if your club is meeting on the other side of the continent. Lauren can pop in to answer your questions via webcam. But, if your club is close enough, Lauren would love to personally meet with your group. Who know! She may even bring her muse Sterling along!

To invite Lauren Carr to your next book club meeting, visit www.mysterylady.net and fill out a request form with your club's details.

ABOUT THE AUTHOR

Lauren Carr

Lauren Carr is the international best-selling author of the Thorny Rose, Lovers in Crime, Mac Faraday, and Chris Matheson Cold Case Mysteries—over twenty titles across four fast-paced mystery series filled with twists and turns!

Book reviewers and readers alike rave about how Lauren Carr seamlessly crosses genres to include mystery, suspense, crime fiction, police procedurals, romance, and humor.

Lauren is a popular speaker who has made appearances at schools, youth groups, and on author panels at conventions. She lives with her husband and two German Shepherds, including the real Sterling, on a mountain in Harpers Ferry, WV.

Visit Lauren Carr's website at www.mysterylady.net to learn more about Lauren and her upcoming mysteries.

CHECK OUT
LAUREN CARR'S MYSTERIES!

All of Lauren Carr's books are stand alone. However for those readers wanting to start at the beginning, here is the list of Lauren Carr's mysteries. The number next to the book title is the actual order in which the book was released.

Joshua Thornton Mysteries

Fans of the *Lovers in Crime Mysteries* may wish to read these two books which feature Joshua Thornton years before meeting Detective Cameron Gates. Also in these mysteries, readers will meet Joshua Thornton's five children before they had flown the nest.

1) A Small Case of Murder
2) A Reunion to Die For

Mac Faraday Mysteries

3) It's Murder, My Son
4) Old Loves Die Hard
5) Shades of Murder
    *(introduces the Lovers in Crime: Joshua Thornton
    & Cameron Gates)*
7) Blast from the Past
8) The Murders at Astaire Castle
9) The Lady Who Cried Murder
    *(The Lovers in Crime make a guest appearance
    in this Mac Faraday Mystery)*
10) Twelve to Murder
12) A Wedding and a Killing
13) Three Days to Forever

15) Open Season for Murder
!6) Cancelled Vows
17) Candidate for Murder
  (featuring Thorny Rose Mystery detectives
   Murphy Thornton & Jessica Faraday)
23) Crimes Past (Coming Fall 2018)

Lovers in Crime Mysteries

6) Dead on Ice
11) Real Murder
18) Killer in the Band

Thorny Rose Mysteries

14) Kill and Run
  (featuring the Lovers in Crime in
   Lauren Carr's latest series)
19) A Fine Year for Murder
22) Murder by Perfection

Chris Matheson Cold Case Mysteries
21) ICE

A Lauren Carr Novel

20) Twofer Murder

CRIMES PAST
A Mac Faraday Mystery

It's a bittersweet reunion for Mac Faraday when members of his former homicide squad arrive at the Spencer Inn. While it is sweet to attend the wedding of a late colleague's daughter, it is a bitter reminder that the mother of the bride had been the victim of a double homicide.

The brutal slaying weighing heavy on his mind, Mac is anxious to explore every avenue for a break in the cold case—even a suggestion from disgraced former detective Louis Gannon that one of their former friends is the killer.

When the investigator is brutally slain, Mac Faraday rips open the cold case with a ruthless determination to reveal which of his friends is a cold-blooded murderer.

Coming Fall 2018!

Pre-Order Your Copy Today!

Made in the
USA
Lexington, KY

54453373R10177